The Library of Literature

UNDER THE
GENERAL EDITORSHIP OF
JOHN HENRY RALEIGH
AND IAN WATT

———

MELVILLE'S WORKS
UNDER THE
GENERAL EDITORSHIP OF
CHARLES FEIDELSON, JR.
EDWIN S. FUSSELL
JOHN HENRY RALEIGH

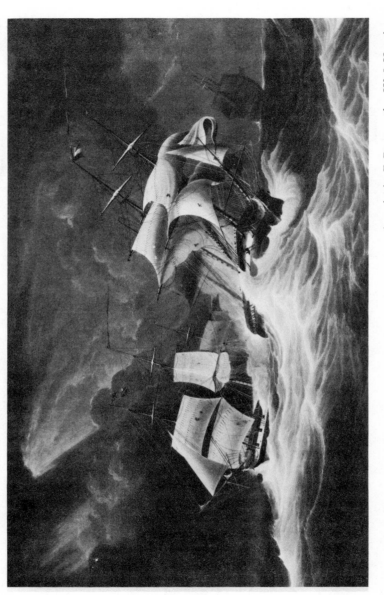

H.M.S. *Indefatigable* engages the French ship *Droits-de-L'Homme* in 1797, "the year of this narrative."

Aquatint by E. Duncan after W. J. Huggins. National Maritime Museum, London

Herman Melville

BILLY BUDD
SAILOR
An Inside Narrative

———

EDITED, WITH AN INTRODUCTION
AND ANNOTATION, BY
MILTON R. STERN

Bobbs-Merrill Educational Publishing
Indianapolis

The Bobbs-Merrill Company, Inc.
4300 West 62nd Street
Indianapolis, Indiana 46268

First Edition
Third Printing—1978

The editorial work for this volume was completed in 1971. Unanticipated delays
in production and in copyright agreements account for the discrepancy between
date of publication and dating of the Introduction.

The most solid scholarship ground for *Billy Budd* has been worked by Harrison
Hayford and Merton M. Sealts, Jr., who have blazed a coherent trail through the
swampy state of the manuscript. All subsequent editions will owe and should
acknowledge a deep and lasting debt to them, and all editions using their transcription of the manuscript ("The Genetic Text") as a point of departure will be
more or less valuable according to the ways in which they agree or disagree with
Hayford's and Sealts's conclusions in their version of "The Reading Text."

Material taken from *Billy Budd, Sailor: An Inside Narrative* by Herman Melville,
edited from the manuscript with introduction and notes by Harrison Hayford
and Merton M. Sealts, Jr., (copyright © 1962 by The University of Chicago)
are used with permission.

Library of Congress Cataloging in Publication Data

Melville, Herman, 1819–1891.
  Billy Budd, sailor.

  (The Library of literature series)
  Bibliography: p.
  1. Melville, Herman, 1819–1891. Billy Budd.
I. Stern, Milton R., ed. II. Title.
PS2384.B5 1974   813'.3   73–8967
ISBN 0–672–51466–4
ISBN 0–672–61040–X (pbk.)

Contents

Illustrations

Introduction

BILLY BUDD is an unfinished work. It has been presented in several versions by various editors and is the most vexing textual problem in all of Melville scholarship. The reader should be aware of the variations he will encounter from edition to edition. Because of the nature of the problem, no explanation of the choices made in a complete and careful text can be offered briefly and simply. Such explanations are likely to be tedious to the reader who wishes to read an introduction to *Billy Budd* but who does not wish to be encumbered with the burden of scholarship. Therefore, I have removed the discussion of this text to the back of the book, where it appears as Appendices One and Two. All readers are urged to consult that discussion, for it explains the nature of this edition and in presenting a history of the text offers materials that are important for interpretation; but it is tucked away where it will be easily available for those who are interested and where it will be unobtrusive for those who are not.

The Development of Billy Budd

By the time Melville was forty-seven, it was clear to him that he could not earn a living as a writer. He sought and received an appointment through the Treasury Department as a deputy-inspector in the customhouse, and he began his government employment at the very end of 1866. For almost the next two decades as he worked at his job, Melville wrote when and as he could, building up a file of materials, mostly poetry. As he grew older, his work at the customhouse became more arduous, and constantly he yearned for time for all the writing he wanted to do; yet his financial necessities made it impossible for him to retire. But beginning in 1884, the Melvilles began to receive payments from a legacy that had come to Herman's wife, Elizabeth, and on December 31, 1885, Melville handed in his resignation. By the tenth of January 1886, he had completed his last day of over nineteen years of work for the government, and he retired to devote himself to his books and his writing. Elizabeth rejoiced that he had a desk full of unfinished work to keep him busy.

The work he took up was the writing and arranging of poems, which were generally recollections of time past. After his retirement, Melville, in a quiet "grass-growing" mood of soul, began to live more and more in the past, began to dwell more and more on thoughts of death. The poems were reminiscent and nostalgic. Each lament of *ubi sunt* and *où sont les neiges* was associated with a dislike of change—an old man's quiet conservatism. One of the first poems he turned to was a ballad about a sailor who had been involved in a mutiny plot, had been apprehended, tried, and sentenced to hang. As Billy, the sailor, lay in irons before the hanging, his mind wandered over the past, recollecting good times and good shipmates. Melville was to call it "Billy in the Darbies," and he wrote a brief prose headnote for it to explain Billy's situation to the reader. The inclusion of a prose headnote was a practice he followed for several of his poems. One such poem, "John Marr," recounts in the headnote the old sailor's loneliness as he lives by himself, friendlessly, on the landlocked prairie, hungering for former chums of seafaring days. The verse is a sustained cry of nostalgic yearning. In 1888 Melville collected many such poems and prose-verse pieces into a gathering that he published as *John Marr and Other Sailors*. He continued to work on the prose section of "Billy in the Darbies" as Billy's situation intrigued him increasingly, and by the time he published *John Marr*, "Billy in the Darbies" had been separated from the other poems and the prose section had grown to one hundred and fifty pages of manuscript.

Melville had readied the *John Marr* volume for the printer in the spring, and in June, while revising the story of Billy, he read an article called "The Mutiny on the Somers," by Lieutenant H.

D. Smith, in the *American Magazine*. In 1842, three sailors on the U.S. brig *Somers*, Acting-Midshipman Philip Spencer (who was the son of the Secretary of War), Boatswain's Mate Samuel Cromwell, and Seaman Elisha Small, were suspected of plotting mutiny. The Captain, Alexander Slidell Mackenzie, summoned his officers not to convene a court, but to ask their advice. Without trial, without even being arraigned and so without the opportunity to defend themselves or even to ask questions, the three men were judged guilty and Mackenzie had them hanged. One of the men, Elisha Small, a great favorite with the crew and one whom many felt to be innocent, is reputed to have faced the flag and said, as he was about to be run up, "God bless that flag!" (See note 6 for leaf 281, p. 109.) The article brought to the forefront of Melville's mind an event he had never really forgotten, for the matter of the *Somers* had been in a peculiarly intimate way a family concern for many years.

The affair became a *cause célèbre*, as one might imagine (the fact that an article was written about it in a popular magazine as late as 1888, forty-six years after the event, is an indication of the stir it caused), and from the very first it made a deep and lasting impression on Melville. When Melville was a boy, his favorite hero had been his older cousin, Guert Gansevoort, who was the First Lieutenant aboard the *Somers*. As one of the officers advising Captain Mackenzie, Cousin Guert was deeply implicated in an act which brought down scorn, outrage, and hatred upon his head. Although Mackenzie and his officers were cleared by a formal naval board of inquiry, and although Melville's family all felt that Cousin Guert was innocent in the eyes of God and had courageously done what he had had to do as much as he loathed the necessity, nevertheless in the eyes of the world and of the sailors of the fleet, Cousin Guert was a fallen man. As the family understood the story within its own councils, Guert's "inside narrative" disclosed a situation of extreme urgency (even though it was peacetime) from which dire consequences would have followed if a total example had not been made of the three men. Guert himself, however, would make no public statements about the affair—he became the model for Melville's "Tom Tight," a

seaman who knew how to keep his lips tightly shut about a mutiny case aboard ship.

But the commentators who have identified the *Somers* case as
the chief source of *Billy Budd* are not quite correct: Melville had
completed over 100 pages of the tale before the *American Magazine* article appeared and, in any case, the true source was the
ballad he had written at the time he was preparing similar poems
for the *John Marr* volume—a ballad which had none of the focus
that either the *Somers* case or *Billy Budd* had. However, it is
very likely that the appearance of the article caused a change of
focus in Melville's view of the story he was writing, for by late
fall he began to emphasize new material in the tale. In the words
of Melville's biographer, Leon Howard, "the inside story and
the historical record were at odds in their implications concerning the puzzling actions of Lieutenant Gansevoort and presumably those of Captain Mackenzie, and Melville's interest was
diverted . . . to the problem of reconciling the conflicting implications. How could a man in a judicial position be held morally
free from guilt while condemning to death another human being
who was known to be morally innocent of wrongdoing?"[1] The
change in emphasis resulted in the development of the character
of the commander of the warship on which Billy was hanged, and
until Melville died it remained the aspect of the narrative on
which the author expended his energy and attention in developing the story.

The title phrase, "An inside narrative," probably does not have
as devious and arcane a meaning as some commentators have
given it (see especially William Braswell, "Melville's *Billy Budd*
as 'An Inside Narrative' " and Simon Lesser, *Fiction and the Unconscious*), nor is it necessarily an "insider's" justification of
Lieutenant Gansevoort's role in the *Somers* affair. (The view of
Billy Budd as an "inside" justification of the *Somers* incident was
first proposed by Charles Anderson in "The Genesis of *Billy
Budd*.") On leaf 49 of the manuscript, Melville asserts that the

---

[1] *Herman Melville*, p. 325. Full reference information about all works
cited is given in the bibliography at the end of this introduction.

narrative is concerned with "the inner life of one particular ship and the career of an individual sailor." Melville was telling his readers that his narrative was not giving them the kind of account one finds in official versions of events (leaves 340–344), but the darker, less explicable and more confusingly mysterious and *real*—the inside—view of history and human behavior in "what befell" Billy "in the year of the Great Mutiny." (For this view of the meaning of "An inside narrative" in the title, see Sidney Kaplan, "Explication" and the illuminating discussion in the Hayford and Sealts edition of *Billy Budd* [hereafter referred to as *H&S*], pp. 27–33 and pp. 134–135.) What had begun as a ballad and had then been expanded into a prose work introducing John Claggart and the conflict between an angelic foretopman and a demonic master-at-arms finally centered on Captain Vere and the nature of his responsibility in a world where the conflict of the "inside narrative" became a frightening metaphor for human existence in the world at large. It is on the character and function of Captain Vere, consequently, that critical attention has necessarily concentrated.

The Critical Question

As the bibliography appended to this introduction indicates, criticism of *Billy Budd* is quite extensive. When Raymond Weaver first published the tale in 1924, he had no idea that it was to become one of the most important works—perhaps second only to *Moby-Dick*—among all of Melville's writings in the attention it drew. In the whelming crosscurrents of critical disagreements, the same themes have remained perennially intriguing: good versus evil; innocence versus experience; idealism versus expediency; morality versus necessity; the reality of history; and, most of all, the problems of guilt, power, and responsibility. If guilt, power, and responsibility remain constant in their fascination for modern readers, what have changed are the perspectives from which those themes in *Billy Budd* are viewed.

Before World War II, most critics felt that *Billy Budd* was Melville's statement of acquiescence, of Christian resignation and peace, of quietly coming to terms with both necessity and God. Earlier readers generally missed what has since come to be very noticeable to more recent critics: the anger in Melville's view of the materials of his story—he is not at all peacefully resigned to the state of the world. Leading and influential examples of pre-World War II criticism are John Middleton Murray's article, "Herman Melville's Silence" (1924), and E. L. Grant Watson's essay, "Melville's Testament of Acceptance" (1933). The continuing influence of these readings is evident in post-World War II studies like Ronald Mason's little book, *The Spirit above the Dust: A Study of Herman Melville* (1951). But even in the 1920's and 1930's criticism split on Captain Vere, that fictional rock of a character. Some critics had early suspected what the revisions of the manuscript clearly indicate—that Vere had come to be the central figure in Melville's consciousness by the time the story was developed to the point it had reached when Melville died.

Centering on Vere, post-World War II commentators found that Melville was not accepting anything in peace but was lashing out furiously at the implications of his materials. Some critics found Melville to be bitter about the limitations of unaided innocence; some found him to be bitter about historical necessity. In the fifties, the prevailing mode was one in which Melville was read as ironic, especially in his presentation of Captain Vere. The earliest statement of the ironist school was Joseph Schiffman's article, "Melville's Final Stage, Irony: A Reexamination of *Billy Budd* Criticism" (1950). Most of the ironist readings were attacks on Captain Vere as establishmentarian tyrant, but some recognized that Melville was giving considerable force in the story to Vere's position if he was condemning it. Three of the most representative of these readings of the fifties are Karl E. Zink's essay, "Herman Melville and the Forms—Irony and Social Criticism in 'Billy Budd'" (1952); Wendell Glick's article, "Expediency and Absolute Morality in *Billy Budd*" (1953); and Richard Harter Fogle's commentary, "*Billy Budd*—Acceptance or Irony" (1958). The considerable similarities and differences among Zink, Glick, and Fogle illuminate the variety of responses to Vere that are generated by the questions raised by ironist read-ings. During the decade a few critiques disagreed with both the anti-Vere readings and the "testament of acceptance" school and argued that although Melville was indeed bitterly angry about the implications within his materials, nevertheless he was sympathetic to Vere in the role the Captain had to play. An example of this temporarily minority view can be found in my chapter on *Billy Budd* in *The Fine Hammered Steel of Herman Melville* (1957) or in my introduction to *Typee and Billy Budd* (1958).

Without question, the role of Captain Vere is the central factor determining the responses of readers. If he is seen sympathetically, the tale is read one way. If he is seen as totalitarian oppressor, the tale is read quite another way. The changes from pre- to post-World War II criticism involve a fascinating account of the changes in Departments of English in the United States following the war. In brief, World War II and the G.I. Bill that followed it marked a decisive change in American universities both in the kinds of people who inhabited higher educational institutions and in the kinds of methods and questions that were employed in literary studies, but an account of these changes cannot be de-tailed here. Furthermore, the intellectual atmosphere that was part of the general cultural motion toward radical change in the late fifties and the sixties made anti-establishmentarian attitudes inevitable, and they were reflected in Melville criticism as well as in all intellectual salients of national culture. Cultural change, academic change, and the history of Melville's reputation ran parallel courses, for it was in the 1950's that the rediscovery of Mel-ville, begun in the 1920's, swelling in the 1930's, cresting in the 1940's but delayed by the war, reached a consolidated peak of strength from which it has never subsided, and it was inevitable that aspects of national intellectual motion should be revealed in the Melville criticism that appeared in increasing quantities from American academies. The relationship of Melville criticism to two decades of American cultural history is too large a subject for treat-ment here, but it must be noted as an important reality in the assess-ment of readings of Captain Vere. Indeed, all meaningful treatment of Vere seems to involve one kind of political reality or another. Among the political guides useful in an introductory essay is an examination of the work from which *Billy Budd* arose.

The Politics of Melville's Poetry

As I have indicated earlier, *Billy Budd* arose from the poetry that Melville was working on during his last, retrospective years. The short novel began as one of many poems whose burden was the recollection of friends and times past. Among the many attitudes that can be isolated in the poems, of which "Billy in the Darbies" was one, two major recurrences are a sorrow—indeed, a resentment—occasioned by change, and a nostalgic joy in the celebration of the common sailor as a carefree child who gallantly does his duty. The first attitude is central in the psychology of conservatism—an insistence upon the past for the establishment of values by which the present may be guided. It is an insistence upon history, law, and precedent. But the second attitude, nostalgic joy in recalling the carefree sailor, also enters into Melville's political stance, as we shall see, and it is best to discuss the two attitudes one at a time.

Melville's attitude toward the past and change was not something that came to him in his last years only, for his Civil War poems return again and again to the themes of law versus anarchy, of order versus rebellion, and of art versus chaos. Even this last theme is one in which art becomes a metaphor for the ordered control of human affairs (Captain Vere's "forms, measured forms"), synonymous with law. The creation of measured forms became for Melville the highest expression of the human spirit in its struggle with the overwhelming, dark forces of an incomprehensible universe both inside and outside man—the unconquerable, double vastness he indicated in *Moby-Dick* and *Pierre*. There was something protoexistentialist about Melville, as about so many preexistentialist writers who wrestled with similar problems. He seemed to see the universe as enormously beyond a single unifying shape, meaning, or purpose, at least for the uses of human comprehension. Whatever ordered meaning, whatever formal shape, whatever moral purpose man saw in his existence, man put there. Man's fate, man's identity become what men make of themselves, and the making of man is in the terrible struggle of that weak, limited, mortal, animal creature to create out of raw existence the meaningful forms that are expressions of his own spirit. Everyone identifies the white whale by what he sees therein, and in so doing identifies himself. It is as though finite man were literally carving out of infinite, protean, and unconquerable force the forms of his own aspirations, knowing that the moment his back is turned the shapes will shift and melt back into their uncatchable, indifferent ur-being—but knowing too that his own glory and being come out of that necessary, endless struggle. The myth of Sisyphus has been made too much of in our day to need more words here. Suffice it to say that the idea of man's forging his human identity in the incessant necessity of interminably repeated struggle with the possibilities of experience—Sisyphus pushing that rock uphill—appealed strongly to Melville. In all his work, especially *Moby-Dick* (the endlessness of labor) and *Pierre* (the myth of Enceladus) Melville honored the attempt and the grimness of the terrible struggle: bear thee grimly, human heroes! Much more important (though only temporary) than the absolute and eternal meaning— or meaninglessness—of the universe are the meanings man tries to impose for his own time in order to become a being, an essence, and not merely a lump of existence. Therefore, knowing that although no matter what man does, no matter how he tries to harness the oceanic meanings of infinity and eternity, "the great shroud of the sea" will roll on "as it rolled five thousand years ago," still Ishmael-Melville exults reverently in the Sisyphus-Bulkington who returns continually to his intrepid, doomed, glorious, triumphant struggle with the eternal and endlessly deep waters of the indefinite universe. In his valiant mortality, his triumphant defeat, is the mark of form imposed by man on the face of existence: "But as in landlessness alone resides the highest truth, shoreless, indefinite as God—so, better is it to perish in that howling infinite, than be ingloriously dashed upon the lee, even if that were safety! For worm-like, then, oh! who would craven crawl to land! Terrors of the terrible; is all this agony so vain? Take heart, take heart, O Bulkington! Bear thee grimly, demigod! Up from the spray of thy ocean-perishing—straight up, leaps thy apotheosis!"

Melville preferred heroes. A worm exists, a cow exists, a rock, a tree exist. But they are not heroes. Men may be merely animated chunks of meat and never think to wrestle with chaos. But nothing ventured, nothing become. It is in the terrible agony, so vain and so necessary, that the artist, the former, the shaper, the maker, the orderer transforms his own small and personal mortality into a demigod apotheosis that is the glory of the entire race. Melville's poems are constant testimonials to the crucial importance of art as order. His Civil War poems constantly place the rebellion in the role, consequently, of the forces of chaos and anarchic change and the Union in the role of preserver, conserver, orderer. The temperamental antipathy to change, the nostalgia, in the late poems is prefigured in the metaphysics of Melville's political allegiances in the Civil War poems. Ironically, he opposed the South because of a conservative temperament. This is not to say that he did not care about slavery, human rights, and brotherhood—the driving democracy of Melville's mind was very much alive to moral ideologies involved in the war. What I am saying is that philosophically and temperamentally the mind behind *Moby-Dick* had shifted some of its priorities of belief and that Melville's political allegiance to the Union was essentially conservative. His support of formal order and art in his support of the Union is expressed in many of the war poems, most explicitly in "Dupont's Round Fight," a celebration of the victory of Commodore Samuel Dupont over the Confederate forts at Port Royal, South Carolina. Dupont's ships steamed around in a circle, first destroying the forts on one side of the sound and then on the other.

> In time and measure perfect moves
> All Art whose aim is sure;
> Evolving rhymes and stars divine
> Have rules, and they endure.

Nor less the Fleet that warred for Right,
And, warring so, prevailed,
In geometric beauty curved,
And in an orbit sailed.

The rebel at Port Royal felt
The Unity overawe,
And rued the spell. A type was here,
And victory of LAW.

The overtones of the war in heaven leave no doubts as to who is in the Royal right. As I will try to indicate, Melville recreated that "type" again in Captain Vere in different and more complex and more agonized circumstances.

The essentially conservative nature of Melville's poetry generally has been ignored. First of all, the man who wrote the books preceding the Civil War poems certainly did not appear to be primarily conservative. *Omoo* is, in part, an attack on established and institutionalized Christianity and evangelism. *White-Jacket* is a rebellious exposé of the mistreatment of sailors in the naval service of the United States government. *Redburn* is a continuing cry against the established forces of power, wealth, and privilege. An iconoclastically democratic spirit is everywhere seen in *Moby-Dick*. Yet, as Melville completed his "prose years" (*Typee*, 1846; *Omoo*, 1847; *Mardi*, 1849; *Redburn*, 1849; *White-Jacket*, 1850; *Moby-Dick*, 1851; *Pierre*, 1852; *Israel Potter*, 1855 [serialized in 1854]; *The Piazza Tales*, 1856 [which were tales and sketches he published in periodicals, 1853–1856]; and *The Confidence-Man*, 1857), his rebellious attitudes diminished—although his anger didn't—and his doubts about human progress and the nobility of the common man had increased considerably. The light in his books became dimmer as his view of man's fate became darker. One need only compare the atmosphere of light-drenched *Typee* and *Omoo* with the murky darkness of *The Confidence-Man*. As his writings indicate, Melville was not a simple man, and he held within him the germs of many mutually opposing attitudes. Within *Typee*, for instance, there is an undercurrent of the need to repudiate the idea of Eden regained in order to settle for the historical actualities, ugly though they may be, of one's own time. Melville's insistence on historical necessity and his sense of human limitation grew to both their greatest conflict and their greatest unity with his sense of the nobility of the common, savage man in the glories of *Moby-Dick*. But somewhere in the gathering darkness of *Pierre* (that book moves from light to dark within itself as the corpus of prose moves from light to dark with the jump from *Typee* and *Omoo* to *The Confidence-Man*) the tension of that magnificent balance was lost—which, I think, is what most centrally accounts for the semi-hysteria and decline in taut power in that book—and Melville's sense of human limitation began to grow. It became triumphant in the pitch blackness with which *The Confidence-Man* ends.

A sense of history and of historical necessity is not the sole property of the conservative. Far from it. However, I do suggest that when this sense is coupled with an insistence on human limitation and the consequent need for control and for guidance from the experience of the past—an insistence on law and precedence, together with a suspicion of change—that it becomes the philosophical and psychological center of conservatism. Nor is it inconsistent to identify a man as at once conservative and proto-existentialist. It is true that existentialism, with its view that man may achieve any possible change and identity through the intense exercise of his will and choice, is generally allied with radical and revolutionary postures. However, its view of the endlessness of repeated, Sisyphean effort may also serve conservative conclusions, and great men like Melville tend to expose the tyranny of labels in any case. Before they become too tyrannical here, my use of them should be clarified.

Contemporary American literary criticisms have evolved a tradition of attention to structure, image, symbol, myth, archetype, and critical method; they rarely see literature as political statement and have no language which allows commentators to talk easily about politics in literature. It has often been noted that *Billy Budd* is concerned with political choices, but few commentators have seen the true focus, the major dimension of the tale:

in essence it is a political fiction. The simple truth often has been lost in understandable fascination with the metaphysics of good and evil in the tale and with religious symbolism. When I say that *Billy Budd* is political fiction, I do not refer to novels about politics in the sense in which we usually use that word—novels, say, like Allen Drury's *Advise and Consent* or Edwin O'Connor's *The Last Hurrah*. The common usage connotes the intrigues of public political personalities jockeying for position: political parties, ethnic groups, pressure groups, rallies, town committees, state committees, bosses, delegate votes, and intra-party electioneering.

But fictions about the *trappings* of human politics are not necessarily political novels any more than political novels need have the trappings of politics as their subject matter. What I intend by "political" fiction is something more constant in human affairs than the particular topical matters of parties, politicians, and issues, something broader than the history of political forces or the temporal movements in struggles for power. I will go so far as to say that in its deepest concerns almost all serious literature is political. "Politics" has often been defined as "the art of the possible." But it does not take much reflection to realize that this "definition" is a bit too broad, a bit too smooth, a bit too easy—it can apply to anything and to nothing. Politics cannot be summed up so quickly. "The art of the possible" becomes a euphemistic way of recapitulating the necessities of compromise, the give and take that politicians enter into as they maneuver to discover workable expedients in the exercise of power. But the phrase only defines the kinds of actions they take. It does not define their politics. "The art of the possible" refers to the acts of manipulation, but it does not explain anything about the visions that impel the manipulation, and it is in the visions that people's politics are defined. Everyone is constantly engaged in manipulating people and events in all kinds of situations and at all kinds of levels: everyone alive is engaged in "the art of the possible." But when we think of politics as the government of human affairs, we really are thinking of something deeper than the ambitions and manipulations of politicians. We are thinking about *phi-*

losophies enacted in the state. After all, liberal, conservative, reactionary, and radical politicians engage in "the art of the possible," yet their politics remain very different from one another's. When we talk about people's politics, we really talk about their ways of seeing the meanings of human experience. We are really talking about deep attitudes and visions, often unspoken and even unformulated, concerning the nature of human possibility and, therefore, the nature and possibility and desirability of liberation and, therefore again, the nature and function of the state, the very concept of government. It is the underlying visions that I refer to when I say that *Billy Budd* is a political fiction and when I refer to politics as universal in human affairs. And even though obviously I cannot undertake here a definition of political philosophies, there are some useful general observations to be utilized within the context I suggest.

When divisions and subdivisions of social and political theory are categorized, they seem to indicate always two major and opposed definitions—consciously or unconsciously assumed—of the human being and human potential. In topical terms one may classify these tendencies as the "left" and the "right." But these terms, like "conservative" and "radical," like "revolutionary" or "reactionary," become necessarily less useful as they must be redefined in terms of particular people and particular issues at particular times. Perhaps the most useful terms have been supplied by a "conservative"—to use the traditional term for the moment—T. E. Hulme. In his famous and influential essay, "Romanticism and Classicism," Hulme defines the romantic impulse as a belief in inexhaustible human potential and, therefore, in individual liberty and in endless and perfectibilitarian change. He defines the classicist impulse as a belief in the limited nature of human potential and the fallen nature of man and, therefore, in control and decorum and in the illusory quality of change and perfectibility. It seems to me that when all is said and done these opposing tendencies define the continuing dialectic between left and right, between radical and conservative, and inform the topical allegiances of particular people in particular issues at particular times most deeply, beneath the considerable and vastly important particularities of selfish and private involvements.

Both positions surround profound truths, or at least profound recognitions of some of the most central meanings of human experience and necessity. The need for aspiration beyond the values and expediencies of the moment, the need to break old bonds and chart new possibilities, the hopeful sense of progressively new identity (particularly held by the young)—in short, the existential sense of the libertarian possibility of freeing man into a new essence—these become the center of one set of ageless human realities and needs. On the other hand, the recognition that history sees "revolution" become the same old struggle all over again (*"plus ça change plus c'est la même chose"*), that the limited human animal is capable of and constantly expresses the most fallen and depraved behavior and therefore is in constant need of control and enforced rules of some kind or other if any kind of sane society is to be possible—in short the sense of limitation, precedence, and law—these become the center of another set of ageless human realities and needs. In the most extreme, visible, and oversimplified opposition of these views, the conflict between the two has been historically one of anarchy on the one hand and the police state on the other.

In *Billy Budd*, Melville, in the classicism of his old age, directly confronts the opposition of revolution and order. He creates in Billy an unwitting type of all the possibilities of human goodness. The imagery creating his physical and moral natures and the imagery creating his death scene recall prelapsarian Adam and even Christ. He is associated with grace, redemption, resurrection, and almost unlimited perfection. Almost. He is, withal, mortal (his stutter is the sign of his limitations) and he is susceptible to that other creation of Melville, Claggart, a type of the hideousness of the human beast, the endless "mystery of iniquity." The imagery creating Claggart's physical and moral natures and the imagery creating his death scene recall fallen man and even Satan. He is associated with mortal sin, pride, hell and damnation. Animal imagery is applied to both Billy and Claggart, but the animals are as different as the St. Bernard and the serpent. Close scrutiny of incidents and imagery will reveal that Melville draws on the literary conventions of the fair character and the dark character to create two opposing categories. Within the literary traditions Melville draws on, the good and fair man is also the creature of spontaneous instincts and generous heart, as Billy is; he is the noble savage, the natural and innocent animal, the sunny creature of magnificent and warm body, the unspoiled Adam ("Angles" look like "angels") who is first toward heaven (the foretop), the redeeming Prince of Peace ("my Peacemaker"); he is the representative of the Sermon on the Mount. The dark man is "citified man" ("Cain's city"), the man of strong and devious intellect, of sallow, pale complexion and high forehead, an underworld creature (the bowels of the ship), the vengeful creature of "ire, envy, and despair," the fallen man, the Prince of Lies (his death is the judgment on Ananias); he is the representative of the Articles of War. Associated with Billy is an English identity; associated with Claggart is the faint hint of French origins (ironically reversed in the "official" version of the affair on the *Bellipotent*).

Between these two views of human identity, between Christ and Satan, if you will, Melville places Captain Vere, a governor who must impose his power on society on the basis of which type most closely characterizes the actual world he governs. Both types, both Billy and Claggart, die. But both are deathless. As the spar that Billy hung from is hunted by the crew as though a piece of it were a piece of the true cross, and as the last line of "Billy in the Darbies" tells you that the voice is still living in the depths of the sea, and as Billy in death mysteriously was not subject to the spasms of ordinary mortals, so too everything Claggart represents is continued by the erroneous version of the affair given in the naval chronicle's "News from the Mediterranean." Claggart's underworld in a man-of-war continues, the world of the gun continues, the history of depravity continues. Both human aspiration to heavenly goodness and human degradation in bestial history continue as opposing sets of yearnings and necessities, both of which lay heavy claim on the human spirit.

Ideally, a choice between the two would be easy. But Melville does not allow for such a simple choice between Christ and Satan. He makes history an amalgam of man's devilish nature and man's yearning for heaven. In a world of mixed necessities and mixed desires, how do you govern the ship? What is operative? What is not? The French Revolution, a monstrous and threatful presence like Camoens' Spirit of the Cape, becomes Melville's major metaphor for the mixed and bitter facts of history. It is a revolution that perhaps has effected good all along the lines for Europeans and yet it also results in a continuation of all the wrongs created by the upstart kings. England is the "sole free conservative Power," and yet it engages in impressment practices that reflect the brutality of war as much as does the Revolution. Welkin-eyed Baby is "homeward bound" on the "Rights of Man" on the "Narrow Seas." But always this heavenly babe, whose mother was eminently favored by "Love and the Graces" and whose father only "God knows, Sir," is nipped in the budd and never does go home through the straight and narrow gate. Mortal man, grave-ling, captains a ship of only temporary peace from which the peacemaking "jewel" of the crew is taken by the ship of war, eventually to be framed and crucified. The ship of the State is not a peace-ship but is a "fighting peace-maker."

The loyalties of the crew of the state's ship are torn between the laws of command and the promptings of the human heart. Summing up the agony of the crew and the officers in deeper feeling than anyone else's, the captain, who is responsible for the safety of the ship in which everyone sails, must activate his vision of man within the "art of the possible." In his speech to the court martial, Vere, whose very name suggests "truth," makes it clear that he recognizes the categories in which Billy and Claggart each belong and that he recognizes the anguish with which heaven must be postponed as an operative principle within the hellish immediacies of history. Yet what he knows—

he is a student of history and biography and an honest man of independent mind—is lost in his death. Just as Nelson's dying injunction was overruled by a less experienced officer, so Vere's dying knowledge is reversed in the "official" version of the affair in the naval chronicle. Always new Veres must go through the same crucifixions all over again. There is no end to the identity of Vere as there is no end to the identities of Billy and Claggart. All are mortal and all must die, and in the endlessness of their deaths and the continuation of their identities is the deathlessness of mortal necessity that is prefigured in the myth of Sisyphus. No generation can ever really give its experience to another; no final plateau is reached on the ultimate heights in which the human race can say, "There! we've made it! We have accomplished heaven!" The world is never Billy Budd's. Yet man keeps trying and the Veres keep struggling in agony, so the world is never wholly Claggart's, either. But our human experience will always be marked by struggle, and the devil's calling card will announce forever that our purest ideals in all their beauty will always go a-stuttering.

Is history, after all, an endless repetition of man's crucifixions of his loveliest hopes? Will the helplessness of innocence and unaided goodness condemn us always to the paradox of using the gun to put an end to the use of the gun? Has there already been a second coming and a third and a fourth and will there be an infinite series of them? Is there ever an escape from history, or must the wise and tortured ruler ever have to try to adjust Christ and Satan to human actualities within history rather than beyond it? In the complex and profound problems and contradictions and counter-contradictions that spin off these central questions, Melville created a most deeply political novel and expressed his conservative point of view.

When I identify Melville as a conservative in his classicism, I do not mean that automatically all leftists are romanticists and that all rightists are classicists. When we consider the particularities of people, issues, and times, history presents us with endless examples of betrayals of self-labelled positions and with exotic hybrids, from the "revolutionary" commissar who is an extreme exponent of repressive law and order to the "ultra-conservative" who seems to believe in the unlimited possibilities of the unusual, determined, and elite individual. Moreover, people are conservative in some issues, radical in others, and Melville was no exception. Generally, however, by the time Melville entered his "poetry years" (*Battle-Pieces*, 1866; *Clarel*, 1876; *John Marr and Other Sailors*, 1888; *Timoleon*, 1891—poems from the "Burgundy Club" group and from his projected volume, *Weeds and Wildings*, were given occasional publication after his death), the classicism implicit in "Dupont's Round Fight" predominated and was to do so all through the "poetry years," including the years of *Billy Budd*, to the end of Melville's life.

Another war poem, "The House-Top," helps to illustrate the distance between the politics of his poetry and the politics of his earlier prose.[2] When Melville considered the tension between invested power and the masses, between men as corporate and men as individuals at variance with the state, he championed the common man and democracy rather than kings and robes in his earlier prose. He emphasized the individual, the honest primitive,

---

[2] After I had completed the text and the introduction, I compiled the bibliography. One title in an annual bibliography caught my eye as possible corroboration of my idea about the poetry: Jane Donahue's essay, "Melville's Classicism: Law and Order in His Poetry" (1969). When I read the piece, I discovered that the idea, the language, and the conclusion were astonishingly close to my introduction—Miss Donahue even singles out "Dupont's Round Fight" and "The House-Top" as central poems in the revelation of Melville's classicism. There are a few differences between us: like many critics of *Billy Budd*, Miss Donahue is somewhat victimized by two decades (in American criticism that's enough time to create a tradition!) of articles about Vere as villain, so that she does not quite see the implications of her article for *Billy Budd:* she remains content to characterize Melville's treatment of Vere as "ambiguous." However, Miss Donahue's emphasis is not upon *Billy Budd* but upon the poetry, and I am delighted to find in her statement about the poetry the rare joy of complete agreement with a colleague. Although I had not read Miss Donahue's essay before I completed this volume, I am happy to acknowledge her commentary as first in time and idea. The reader is urged to consult "Melville's Classicism" for a more detailed substantiation of the point I make about the political orientation of the materials out of which *Billy Budd* grew.

and the worker rather than the requirements of power. Perhaps
his most famous statement of his romanticist point of view is in
the exalted prose of the familiar passages from the first "Knights
and Squires" chapter (XXVI) in *Moby-Dick:*

Men may seem detestable as joint stock-companies and nations;
knaves, fools, and murderers there may be; men may have mean and
meagre faces; but man, in the ideal, is so noble and so sparkling, such
a grand and glowing creature, that over any ignominious blemish in
him all his fellows should run to throw their costliest robes. That
immaculate manliness we feel within ourselves, so far within us, that
it remains intact though all the outer character seem gone; bleeds
with keenest anguish at the undraped spectacle of a valor-ruined man.
Nor can piety itself, at such a shameful sight, completely stifle her
upbraidings against the permitting stars. But this august dignity I
treat of, is not the dignity of kings and robes, but that abounding
dignity which has no robed investiture. Thou shalt see it shining in
the arm that wields a pick or drives a spike; that democratic dignity
which, on all hands, radiates without end from God; Himself! The
great God absolute! The centre and circumference of all democracy!
His omnipresence, our divine equality!

If, then, to meanest mariners, and renegades and castaways, I shall
hereafter ascribe high qualities, though dark; weave round them tragic
graces; if even the most mournful, perchance the most abased, among
them all, shall at times lift himself to the exalted mounts; if I shall
touch that workman's arm with some ethereal light; if I shall spread
a rainbow over his disastrous set of sun; then against all mortal
critics bear me out in it, thou just Spirit of Equality, which hast
spread one royal mantle of humanity over all my kind! Bear me out
in it, thou great democratic God! who didst not refuse to the swart
convict, Bunyan, the pale, poetic pearl; Thou who didst clothe with
doubly hammered leaves of finest gold, the stumped and paupered
arm of Cervantes; Thou who didst pick up Andrew Jackson from
the pebbles; who didst hurl him upon a war-horse; who didst
thunder him higher than a throne! Thou who, in all Thy mighty,
earthly marchings, ever cullest Thy selectest champions from the
kingly commons; bear me out in it, O God!

Yet, in "The House-Top," when Melville considers the opposition of the common masses to the state—the specific subject is

the New York draft riots of July 1863—his attitudes have changed considerably. Here the sound of the "commons" is "the Atheist roar of riot" and the lighting spread over this "most mournful" and "abased" group of "mariners, and renegades and castaways" is "red Arson." The self-expression of the masses in this poem becomes a dreadful recidivism, and the police power of the state, imposing law and order on the crowd, becomes necessary Draconian wisdom. Just as "Dupont's Round Fight" has little to do with topical particularities of person, issue, or times but has everything to with Melville's classicist view of rebellion, so "The House-Top" does not center on the political particulars of the draft riots. They were indeed terrible. Anti-draft mobs burned buildings indiscriminately and lynched all the Negroes they could lay their hands on. But like *Billy Budd*, which really gives almost no particulars of political history and offers very few specifics of Anglo-French antagonisms and concentrates instead on the deepest political *view* of those antagonisms, "The House-Top" does not concentrate on specific events of the riots but on the essentially classicist point of view from which those riots are seen. *Billy Budd, like the poetry it grew out of, does not offer a dramatization of political events but of a political perspective.* Melville is concerned less with the specifics of power manipulation than with his vision of limited human possibility. If in *Moby-Dick* the crew is a visible metaphor for both nobility and debasement, in *Billy Budd* the crew has become an indistinct background, a threatful presence that is a metaphor for potential chaos, like the mobs in Shakespeare's plays. In "The House-Top" what is clear is a dominant distrust of men, a sense of the limitations of fallen man, and a consequent need for formal imposition of law and order:

> No sleep. The sultriness pervades the air
> And binds the brain—a dense oppression, such
> As tawny tigers feel in matted shades,
> Vexing their blood and making apt for ravage.
> Beneath the stars the roofy desert spreads
> Vacant as Libya. All is hushed near by.
> Yet fitfully from far breaks a mixed surf

Of muffled sound, the Atheist roar of riot.
Yonder, where parching Sirius set in drought,
Balefully glares red Arson—there—and there.
The Town is taken by its rats—ship-rats
And rats of the wharves. All civil charms
And priestly spells which late held hearts in awe—
Fear-bound, subjected to a better sway
Than sway of self; these like a dream dissolve,
And man rebounds whole aeons back in nature.
Hail to the low dull rumble, dull and dead,
And ponderous drag that jars the wall,
Wise Draco comes, deep in the midnight roll
Of black artillery; he comes, though late;
In code corroborating Calvin's creed
And cynic tyrannies of honest kings;
He comes, nor parlies; and the Town, redeemed,
Gives thanks devout; nor, being thankful, heeds
The grimy slur on the Republic's faith implied,
Which holds that Man is naturally good,
And—more—is Nature's Roman, never to be scourged.

The angry, sarcastic bitterness of this poem and its explicit contrasts to "Knights and Squires" make the point quite clear. And when one turns to *Billy Budd* itself, it is significant to note that when Melville presents the common sailor, the knights and squires of *Moby-Dick* are gone. The closest one comes to a visible crewmember is the portrait of the Dansker. What had been the magnanimous veteran sailor, who was strength, generosity, and the glory of the democratic ideal in the earlier prose, is now a tight old veteran who knows the score and will not stick his neck out. Although there is a shadowy crew around Billy, a sense of masses of sailors, the Handsome Sailor stands alone. There are "Squeaks" and other bought traitors, faceless and all but nameless companions, but there is no Queequeg who will dive down to the head of the whale to save a friend. The crew, the mass, is not a force from which salvation might come, in which romantically seen glory exists, but is a force from which sullen confusion and violent mutiny threaten to erupt at every moment.

And when we turn to the noble sailor in the late poems—to that other attitude of Melville, his joy in the common sailor as a carefree and courageously daring child who obediently does his duty—we again come up against a view in which the romanticist or revolutionary sense of man is gone. Melville's joy in the common sailor was evident from the very beginning. He expressed delight at the feats and childlikeness of his sea-chums and handsome sailors. But there is a considerable difference between the celebration of the sailor in the "prose years" and in the "poetry years." There are many ways to sum up that difference and perhaps this is as good as any: early in the "prose years," in *White-Jacket*, the hero witnesses a flogging and, struck with the horror of it, determines that if ever he is carried to the gratings he will rush the captain and take him overboard in a rebellious act of suicide and murder. Late in the "poetry years," in *Billy Budd*, the hero witnesses a flogging and, struck with the horror of it, determines to be so good that he shall never give occasion to be carried to the gratings.

There are, as *Moby-Dick* so richly indicates, populist overtones as well as potentially conservative ones in the early prose celebration of the sailor. There are no populist overtones in the later poems or in *Billy Budd*. The nostalgic poetry of *John Marr* celebrates the common sailor *not* as a romanticist's political entity but as an apolitical child of danger who is too innocent, loyal, and obedient a rakehell to have any inclination toward rebellious political thought or action. The glamorously daring but fatalistic sailor has been politically castrated. Like the conception of the "darky" in Shirley Temple movies, the good sailor is the child who lives cheerfully, zestfully, and essentially mindlessly and gratefully under the care and control of the master. The good sailor may be associated with high-spirited glee and larking sport, with danger and daring, but never with any threat to law, order, and established power. It is this aspect of Melville's nostalgic late poems that tends to make some of them merely sentimental—the good times and good chums they yearn for are sometimes too simple to be fitting objects for such yearning, undeniably felt though it be. What Billy longs for in the darbies, for instance, is a bit of biscuit and a bit of grog as he remembers his friends. John Marr, remembering back to other times, recollects the good friends as those who acquiesce, not those who rebel, those cheerful children of the waves who simply take what befalls them with fatalistic gallantry:

> Once, for all the darkling sea,
> You your voices raised how clearly,
> Striking in when tempest sung;
> Hoisting up the storm-sail cheerly,
> *Life is storm—let storm!* you rung.
> Taking things as fated merely,
> Child-like though the world ye spanned;
> Nor holding unto life too dearly,
> Ye who held your lives in hand—
> Skimmers, who on oceans four
> Petrels were, and larks ashore.

The handsome sailor is the quintessence of all that is best and that is so nostalgically longed for. And when he is celebrated, as in the poem "Jack Roy" ("King" Jack, a memory of Jack Chase, the handsome sailor Melville had known aboard the frigate *United States*), the magnanimously carefree, uncaring, ever-young man emerges once more as the eternal child obedient to his patriotic duty:

> But thou, manly king o' the old *Splendid's* crew,
> The ribbons o' thy hat still a-fluttering, should fly—
> A challenge, and forever, nor the bravery should rue.
> Only in a tussle for the starry flag high,
> When 't is piety to do, and privilege to die,
> Then, only then, would heaven think to lop
> Such a cedar as the captain o' the *Splendid's* main-top:
> A belted sea-gentleman; a gallant, off-hand
> Mercutio indifferent in life's gay command.
> Magnanimous in humor; when the splintering shot fell,
> "Tooth-picks a-plenty, lads; thank 'em with a shell"
>
> . . . .
>
> Never relishing the knave, though allowing for the menial,
> Nor overmuch the king, Jack, nor prodigally genial.

Ashore on liberty, he flashed in escapade,
Vaulting over life in its levelness of grade,
Like the dolphin off Africa in rainbow a-sweeping—
Arch irridescent shot from seas languid sleeping.
Larking with thy life, if a joy but a toy,
Heroic in thy levity wert thou, Jack Roy.

The late poems make clear the origins of the characteristics that "belted Billy," that man-child, displays in his role of the handsome sailor. Also, it is not insignificant that the sea-poet recalled to Melville's mind as he developed the prose story of *Billy Budd* out of his "John Marr" kind of poems was Charles Dibdin (see note 4 for leaf 53, below, p. 22), whose patriotic sea songs were supposed to express the sentiments of His Majesty's navy's sailors. In Dibdin's songs the sailors are men of submission to authority, men of patriotic loyalty, men of childlike and courageous acceptance of their lot. When, in a reference reminiscent of "The House-Top," Melville in *Billy Budd* recalls the Great Mutiny as "the transmuting . . . of founded law and freedom defined into the enemy's red meteor of unbridled and unbounded revolt," he evokes Dibdin as "no mean auxiliary to the English Government at that European conjuncture," whose strains celebrate "among other things, the patriotic devotion of the British tar:

'And as for my life, 'tis the King's!' "

"The English Government at that European conjuncture" Melville defines as "a Power then all but the sole free conservative one of the Old World." It is a matter of stretching the tone considerably to insist that all these statements are ironically intended by Melville. One may stretch as one will, but when one considers the materials out of which *Billy Budd* grew, such stretching becomes less supportable.

Finally, the two attitudes I have been discussing merge into one in Melville's sense of a bleak present. Melville's celebration of the child of the sea is intimately connected in his nostalgia to his increasing dislike of change. The Jack Roys of the old wooden navies led a colorful life, "vaulting over life in its levelness of grade." With the departure of the sailor's old times, glee and vividness in life also departed. Melville's poems, both of the Civil War and of the later, "John Marr," variety, are consistently marked by an appraisal of the present as dull, mechanical, and monotonous, especially when held side by side with the old days of wooden-sided ships. The old man's certitude that life was better in the good old days (when the old man was a young man) psychologically intensified what had long been Melville's classicism. As he increasingly praised law, order, and measured form, and as he increasingly came to distrust change and assumptions of limitless human freedom and perfectibility, he reminisced more and more about the life and times of the Dibdin-sailor and saw the present as a gray, utilitarian, depersonalized era. In the prose headnote to "John Marr" the old sailor comes to realize what the difference is between his past and the present lives of the staid and practical working people among whom he now dwells: something had gone out of life and "that something was geniality, the flower of life springing from some sense of joy in it, more or less." In his earlier poem on the *Temeraire*, "that storied ship of the old English fleet," as he called it, Melville looked back to the glory of old ships in old sea-fights. His thoughts were those that might have been "suggested to an Englishman of the old order by the fight of the Monitor and Merrimac," and the distinction between the iron-clad, steam-powered present and the golden, oaken-hearted past is made clear:

> O, Titan Temeraire,
>   Your stern-lights fade away;
> Your bulwarks to the years must yield,
>   And heart-of-oak decay.
> A pigmy steam-tug tows you,
>   Gigantic, to the shore—
> Dismantled of your guns and spars,
>   And sweeping wings of war.
> The rivets clinch the iron-clads,
>   Men learn a deadlier lore;
> But Fame has nailed your battle-flags—
>   Your ghost it sails before:

> O, the navies old and oaken,
> O, the Temeraire no more!

As for the iron-clad present itself, "A Utilitarian View of the
Monitor's Fight" leaves no question about the evaluation made
by nostalgia:

> Hail to victory without the gaud
>   Of glory; zeal that needs no fans
> Of banners; plain mechanic power
> Plied cogently in War now placed—
>   Where War belongs—
>   Among the trades and artisans.
> . . . .
> War yet shall be, and to the end;
>   But war-paint shows the streaks of weather;
> War yet shall be, but warriors
> Are now but operatives; War's made
>   Less grand than Peace,
>   And a singe runs through lace and feather.

In *Billy Budd* itself the tone is unmistakable in the comparison
of Present and Past.

But as ashore knightly valor, though shorn of its blazonry, did not
cease with the knights, neither on the seas [did it cease], though
nowadays in encounters there a certain kind of displayed gallantry be
fallen out of date as hardly applicable under changed circumstances . . .

Nevertheless, to anybody who can hold the Present at its worth
without being inappreciative of the Past, it may be forgiven, if to
such a one the solitary old hulk at Portsmouth, Nelson's *Victory*,
seems to float there, not alone as the decaying monument of a fame
incorruptible, but also as a poetic reproach, softened by its picturesqueness, to the *Monitors* and yet mightier hulls of the European
ironclads. And this not altogether because such craft are unsightly,
unavoidably lacking the symmetry and grand lines of the old battle-
ships, but equally for other reasons.

But if times have changed, not so the fallen nature of man.
"War shall yet be, and to the end." The present is less grand
than the past, but sisyphean history never changes. This paradox,

formed at the juncture of temperamental and political conservatism, remains constant in the poems. The changelessness of
history and the human heart are perhaps most explicitly expressed in "The Conflict of Convictions," another Civil War
poem about the state of the nation:

> Age after age shall be
> As age after age has been,
> (From man's changeless heart their way they win);
> And death be busy with all who strive—
> Death, with silent negative.

> YEA AND NAY—
> EACH HATH HIS SAY;
> BUT GOD HE KEEPS THE MIDDLE WAY.
> NONE WAS BY
> WHEN HE SPREAD THE SKY;
> WISDOM IS VAIN, AND PROPHESY.

In sum, the classicism of Melville's outlook at the time he
wrote *Billy Budd*, a general conservatism made unmistakable in
all the poetry which was the genesis of the narrative, makes it
clear that if one is to take into account the mind of the writer
when evaluating the written product, the conservative tone of the
tale is to be taken not ironically but at face value. Seen from the
perspective of Melville's classicism, Captain Vere becomes a
sympathetic character.

In addition to evidence in the poetic genesis of *Billy Budd*,
there is evidence in the manuscript to indicate that Melville deliberately created Vere as a sympathetic character. Melville's
mind did not take a sudden and inexplicable jump away from the
long nurtured attitudes and ideas he was developing in the poems,
but rather it worked out an expression of those feelings as he
expanded his story. As the genetic text indicates, the largest
phase of the development of the narrative was that in which
Captain Vere was created (see Appendix One). Hayford and
Sealts, editors of the genetic text, have this to say about the revisions:

It seems fair to say that were it not for the effect of Melville's late pencil revisions . . . the critical controversy . . . over the story's tone in relation to Vere and his actions would scarcely have arisen. Even those interpreters who disapprove Vere's course could not well question the author's evident design . . . to establish that course in terms of "existing conditions in the navy." The cumulative effect—whatever the intention—of his subsequent deletions and insertions, however, was to throw into doubt not only the rightness of Vere's decision and the soundness of his mind but also the narrator's own position concerning him. As the revised sequence now stands, it is no longer as narrator but in terms of the surgeon's reflections that Melville introduces the reaction to Vere and his plan to place Billy on trial. He leaves the narrator pointedly noncommittal, telling the reader in so many words that he must decide for himself concerning the captain's state of mind. Yet in the unmodified paragraphs that Melville allowed to stand immediately after the surgeon's reflections, the narrator presents Vere's position in a sympathetic tone (*H&S*, p. 34).

In short, it is only in the interview between the captain and the surgeon that *revisions* create problems of interpretation. (I emphasize revisions because, unlike Hayford and Sealts, I think that the ironist critic can find many passages—Vere's speech to the court, for instance—to bend to his purpose quite regardless of anything in the manuscript.) The manuscript leaves in question are 229 through 237, including superseded leaves 229a, b, and c, but excluding the disputed leaves 229d, e, and f, which are discussed in Appendix One. The question of just exactly what Melville did in those leaves may lead to a conclusion somewhat different from that of Hayford and Sealts: the revisions do not bring Vere's "rightness" or "soundness of mind" into question, but they *endorse* Vere's behavior—they provide exactly the human anguish necessary to keep Vere from being a cold machine.

An examination of the leaves indicates that Melville's revisions stemmed from four concerns: (1) presenting the fact that the incident could not have occurred at a worse time (leaves 229b, 229c); (2) presenting the fact that Vere tried to prevent the very trouble that now existed, because he was acutely aware of the pressing and delicate nature of the moment (leaf 229c); (3) presenting the fact Vere was deeply and personally disturbed by the incident (leaves 229b, 231, 232, 234, 235, 236, 237); and (4) presenting Vere's realization that he very quickly must think out a decisive course of action in order to keep the trouble from enveloping the entire ship (leaves 229b, 233). As the quantity of leaves dedicated to particular purposes indicates, Melville's chief concern was with presenting Vere's emotional involvement in the affair. All four concerns were incorporated into the "finished" product, so that the substantive evidence of the superseded leaves (229a, b, and c) remains as usable evidence of Melville's intent. Concerns (1) and (2) occasion no real critical difficulty. The key critical questions become, what was Melville accomplishing by introducing Vere's momentary and anguished loss of emotional balance, and what was Melville accomplishing by indicating that Vere's decision to hold a drumhead court was unusual?

Once an examination of the revisions allows one to isolate these questions, two further considerations are raised. One is that the revisions reduce the surgeon from an observer in whom one is inclined to believe to an observer whose imaginative paucity and cold sobriety could not comprehend the nature of Vere's distraught condition. Questions of Vere's balance raised in *his* mind are stronger comments on his own narrow and shallow perception than on Vere's sanity. The other consideration is that it would be odd indeed for a man to spend five years and 351 leaves developing the problems he saw from the perspective that controlled his writing and his view of life during those years and long before, and then suddenly and inexplicably to reverse those years and that view and all the rest of the manuscript in just twelve of those leaves. But we are asked to assume just that if we are to believe that those leaves suddenly call Vere into question, especially if we see that were it not for the revisions "the critical controversy . . . over the story's tone in relation to Vere and his actions would scarcely have arisen," and especially if we see that "in the unmodified paragraphs that Melville allowed to stand immediately after the surgeon's reflections, the narrator presents Vere's position in a sympathetic tone." One need not go into

principles of critical theory to recognize that the question underlying the two key questions I have isolated is, how does Vere's
emotional involvement and how does his calling of a drumhead
court work to intensify Melville's total intention for Vere?
The answer, it seems to me, is particularly obvious in the case
of Vere's emotional involvement. Up to this point in the tale,
Melville has presented Vere as an unemotional, rational, perfectly
controlled and unpretentious commander. What Melville's revisions do is to add a very necessary new dimension to Vere's
dispassionate fairness—his underlying humanity and feeling beneath the King's uniform and brass buttons. Without this dimension, Vere's speech to the court would be no less correct, but
would be much less humanly pressing. There is a clear and easy
test: read the passages presenting Vere and delete the scenes of
his momentary loss of equilibrium. The Vere that emerges is a
very different and much smaller man than the Vere that exists
with the addition of the leaves I have cited. Obviously what
Melville felt he had to do was to indicate that Vere did not
address the court as he did simply out of a dutiful mind, an un-
touched heart, and no sense of involvement. Whether Vere was
politically "right" or "wrong," his speech to the court would
have been too easy were he uninvolved personally; it would have
been something less than admirable, regardless of the reader's
logical agreements or disagreements with the argument. Melville had to indicate in an "inside narrative" that Vere said what
he had to *despite* an aching heart and *at the expense of* an agonized mind and deep emotional involvement—a heavy expense.
The question here is not, what would have made Vere technically, legally correct or incorrect or even ethically logical or
illogical? but, what would have made Vere admirable, sympathetic, human, regardless of one's own political allegiance? Melville made it clear in the revisions that he wanted the sympathetic
human dimension in Vere's personality, and he referred to this
dimension three times after it was added in the leaves enumerated.
    First he suggested Vere's expression of his elemental self in
the closet interview with Billy. The private and emotional expression of their common humanity, their common victimization

by the necessities of human affairs, is different—as Vere had openly announced it to be in his court-martial speech—from the expression of the law that preserves the forms, measured forms. Second, Melville views Vere through the eyes of the First Lieutenant as Vere emerges from the closet interview. The "agony of the strong" in Vere's face indicates that what Melville "conjectures" as taking place between Billy and Vere did "in fact" take place: "two of great Nature's nobler order embrace[d]." Third, as Vere lay dying, his last words were, "Billy Budd, Billy Budd," and not in "the accents of remorse." Remorse would indicate that Vere had done wrong, and Melville denies any such imputation by deliberately denying remorse. Of course, one can read this as a subtly ironic statement that Vere was stubbornly inhuman or morally blind to the very end, but one can insist on this only by distorting the tone of the passages in which Vere's death is recounted and—more important—only by distorting precisely that emotional involvement and humanity that the leaves in question give to Vere. What Melville accomplished by introducing Vere's temporary loss of official balance was the highlighting of a relationship made explicit by Melville himself, a relationship that has an intricate and illuminating coherence within the political exploration of the story as a whole: Vere, who "was old enough to have been Billy's father," may "have caught Billy to his heart even as Abraham may have caught young Isaac on the brink of offering him up in obedience to the exacting behest." Melville's insistence on Vere's spontaneous feelings is an expression of the romantic element within Melville's classicism. It is as though Melville were saying that without a leavening energy of romantic vision and radical yearning, classical control becomes a merely repressive conservatism. Without loving comprehension of what man *might* be, the application of power according to passing exigencies becomes a merely sterile preservation of the status quo. Readers who see Vere only as a representative of the latter miss the historical and personal *awareness* that Melville gives him. They miss the measure with which he loves Billy and calls for him with his last breath. They miss the fact that unlike most of his fellow officers, who oppose the Revolution because it threat-

ens their privileges and prerogatives, Vere opposes it because in
his estimation it is mistaken in its assumptions and consequently
threatens "the lasting peace and welfare of mankind." I submit
that a consistently coherent reading of the tale, especially as
prompted by Melville's revisions in the Vere-Surgeon scene, must
see that what Melville intended was the portrayal of just such
agony as the strong Abraham would have felt in surrendering
all his deepest individual human feelings—and they were very
much *there*—to the greater necessities of a larger demand, a
higher morality. The difference between the Bible story and
Billy Budd is that the role of God has been taken by historical,
social necessity, but the problem is the same. To dismiss Vere as
villain because of his obedience to the law is the same as saying
that Abraham or Job were villains: it would be too simplistic a
dismissal of the problem posed in the Abraham-Isaac or Job story
—and Melville is known to have thought that those stories, particularly the story of Job, were fraught with the deepest, lasting
human significance. To dismiss Vere as villain in the context of
the very analogy that Melville deliberately draws attention to is
to demand that every single statement of sympathy for Vere, for
Vere's command, for command generally, for England, is to be
inverted and made to mean the opposite of what it says.

In the context of what is said right side up, Melville offers constant opposition, tempered with some real reservations, to the
French Directory and constant approbation, tempered with real
reservations about impressment practices, of the navy of Nelson
and England that Vere represents. A scrutiny of the delicate
and detailed parallels between Nelson and Vere make the intentional sympathy even more evident. Once more I insist that *Billy
Budd* is a politically conservative tale made complex by all the
bitterness Melville feels about fallen man, the doom of prelapsarian Billy, and historical necessity. Vere's anguish is Melville's.
Neither takes delight in his classicist position or in the causes of it.

In the related question, that of Vere's summoning the drum-
head court, it should be clear by now that Vere's decision to
hold the court is also consonant with Melville's attempt to enlarge the dimensions of Vere's character and to enlist a compli-

cated sympathy for him. Put most simply, the revisions point at
Vere's refusal to procrastinate or pass the buck when faced with
immediate and pressing necessity. It was only three days to the
Admiral and Vere could have turned the entire matter over to
him when the ship rejoined the fleet, but Vere well knew that it
might be only three minutes to a life-and-death engagement with
the French. He knew that the crew would expect a death sentence for the slaying of a superior officer. He knew that failure
to pronounce such sentence would be interpreted by the crew
as weakness. He knew that such an interpretation at that precise
historical moment would result in mutiny. And he knew that
under the circumstances the *Bellipotent*—ship, crew, and officers
—could not survive both mutiny and the French. Vere's speech
to the court makes clear the superior order of his realizations. He
is superior to the cold and unimaginative surgeon, certainly, and
he is superior to his officers, who did not see the pressing im-
mediacy of the case, or who, at least, were reluctant to see it.
The decision to hold the court was Melville's way of indicating
that Vere would meet his responsibilities no matter how repug-
nant and agonizing. His decision is consonant with all the sympathetic references throughout the tale—both indirectly in relation
to Vere and directly in relation to Nelson—to the awful responsibilities of the sleepless man on the bridge while the passengers
are snug in the cabin. The moral utilitarians of war might report
what should have been done, after the fact and after the obscuring smoke of battle has cleared, but "the *might-have-been* is but
boggy ground to build on." Simply, Vere refused to evade his
responsibility to confront what *is* "at that European conjuncture."

Melville's Politics and the Reader

So many analyses of *Billy Budd* have been written that any
interested reader can find quite as many discoveries and interpretations of images, symbols, and events as he wishes. I have no
desire to subject the reader to yet one more explication here. I
am satisfied to suggest only the political nature of the tale and to

open discussion into the key critical question of Captain Vere's role. I have tried to indicate how that crucial problem is greatly illuminated by the poetic genesis and by the manuscript of *Billy Budd*. Yet one vital question about *Billy Budd* criticism remains: if, as I claim, the story itself presents Vere sympathetically even if one is unfamiliar with the "poetry years" and with the genetic text, why then have so many critics found the tale to be an ironic condemnation of Vere and the power establishment?

Partly the answer lies in Melville's religious iconoclasm. Almost all readers have noted that in matters of religious institutions and religious belief, Melville, though recoiling from atheism, was continuingly, deeply, deviously, eloquently iconoclastic. He wrote "wicked books" which, telling the truth as he saw it, left him feeling "spotless as the lamb." In fact, one critic, Lawrance Thompson, has seen in all of Melville's work what amounts to a coded message that, when deciphered, is a diatribe against God. Thompson's study is an almost violent overstatement of the case, but there is a real element of truth in his book. And once a critical perception discerns a major and lasting dissenting and iconoclastic bent in a writer, it is difficult to see his work as conservative even though classicist elements are also discernible in the same body of work. Melville was both radical and conservative: in matters of religious belief, although he was strongly attracted to the idea of original sin as a profound metaphor for the reality of human existence, he remained to the end crusty, defiant, and humorously iconoclastic about religious orthodoxy. In matters of political philosophy that very same sense of original sin fed his classicism—a sense that had long been developing in Melville's writing and that has been common to most American conservative theoreticians from John Adams and Alexander Hamilton to the present day. Although one can point out, and rightly, the differences between the egalitarian romanticism in *Moby-Dick* and the strong classicism in the poetry, it is important to note that the classicist impulse had always been present in Melville's vision, side by side with the earlier romantic lyricism, and had often found expression as it had in Melville's celebration of Hawthorne's saying "No! in thunder" to the optimistic American theories of human perfectibility.

There is also a more immediate, if more temporary, answer to the question about divergent readings of Vere, and it is what I alluded to earlier as the changing nature of university scholars and critics following World War II. As I have indicated, the post-war academic generation tended to be more radical in politics and in literature than its pre-war predecessors; also, it tended to favor the New Criticism, which made it possible to find irony and unreliable narrators everywhere in fiction. As part of their intellectual times and generation, the younger critics broke from the emphasis on *Billy Budd* as a testament of Christian resignation and orthodox values.

I hope that no reader will understand my simple point too totally: I would not be surprised if some of the ironist readings came from people who were older or who were conservative. I am not advancing a formula whereby you can make an instant and summary and reliable judgment about a man's birthdate, politics, religious beliefs, and circumstances on the basis of his article about *Billy Budd*. Nor do I mean that critical opinions are merely the servants or children of political ideologies. I do mean, as I have said earlier, that when American academic criticism evaluates critical modes, it almost never takes into account the political dimensions of those modes. I do mean that there are subtle, complex, and often unnoticed connections between politics, critical conclusions, and even the kinds of critical questions that become dominant. Critics unconsciously will be directed temperamentally toward certain works and writers to find importance and values according to the internal hive of ideologies, allegiances, and associations that impel them toward the particular works in the first place. Critics are directed toward those writers they like who are contemporaneously considered worthwhile. To put the matter most crudely, a critic will not be disposed to find that a writer he admires, from whom he extracts priorities of value he considers meaningful, is in the political "enemy's" camp.

It is foolish to think that only classicist critics of *Billy Budd* are reliable. It is foolish to think that romanticist critics deliberately and knowingly distort Melville. I am simply saying what is obvious: as times change, new eras always find different values in the literature that manages to last into the new times.

In the decade following the critical readings of the 1950's *Billy Budd* emerged into an era in which the Vietnam War topicalized and debased the tensions between classicism and romanticism in the most polarized and extreme manifestations of what have become labeled the politics of "liberation" and the politics of "law and order." As a matter of intellectual adoption, anyone can choose either side, with all its gradations of sincere belief and grubby opportunism, as an abstract set of principles. As a matter of working temperament, however, romanticism tends to appeal more to the young, who look to a change in the condition of their world, and classicism to the old, who look to the protection and stability of order. One cannot say that most of the old tend to be classicists and most of the young tend to be romanticists, but one can say that most of the classicists tend to be older than most of the romanticists. "Over thirty" has become the mindless cry of division marking the borderline between the two. Perhaps one should say *vive la différence*. Probably there has never been a time without a "generation gap," but in the spiralling intensification with which history speeds up, never before the 1960's has the opposition been more absorbing. Significantly, like some of the commentators of the 1950's, young readers of the 1960's and early 1970's, especially college students, tend to find that Melville is not sympathetically presenting Vere. If they cannot succeed in that erroneous venture, they tend to reject *Billy Budd* and to find it, Vere, and Melville all hateful together. In the attempt to wrench or to dismiss *Billy Budd* the romanticist reader loses a fiction that most profoundly explores the very problem he finds most vital.

I find it curious to hear myself saying these things, for I entered graduate school and university English departments in the 1950's along with the rest of my post-World War II academic generation. I was trained in the New Criticism. I identify myself now as then as left of center. I came to Melville at the crest of his rediscovery, and I love his work. I find myself in sympathy with ironist readings although I disagree with them. I wish that Melville had developed an anti- or non-conservative orientation in the profundity of his ideas. To keep the record honest, that much, at least, should be said.

But no reader should despair that he does not find exactly and lastingly his own "definitive" Melville. It is true, of course, that in the impossibility of finding the perfect and lasting reading of *Billy Budd* we come again to Melville's classicist point that like Billy himself all readers live in an imperfect world and "in this particular" of our own critical stutters are "striking instances that the arch interferer, the envious marplot of Eden, still has more or less to do with every human consignment to this planet of earth. In every case, one way or another he is sure to slip in his little card, as much as to remind us—I too have a hand here." But in confronting our sisyphean limitations we come again to Melville's romanticist point that out of our struggles to understand our biases, new ideas and creativity arise. As our own human prejudices and changing times meet Melville's work, the ground for new dialogue, new life, is constantly prepared and enriched again. No final critical position is reached just as no final *Billy Budd* was ever written. As times and critics change, so will the uses of Melville, and that is exactly as it should be.

University of Connecticut, 1971

Chronology

1819   Herman Melville, third of eight children, born to Allan and Maria Gansevoort Melville on August 1 in New York City.

1830   Family moves to Albany, where Allan Melville sets up a fur business.

1832   Allan Melville dies, leaving family with great business debts. Melville clerks in a bank.

1835   Melville clerks in his brother Allan's store until the business fails, then teaches school near Pittsfield, Massachusetts.

1838   Family moves to Lansingburgh, New York, where Melville studies engineering in an unsuccessful attempt to get a job on the Erie Canal.

1839   Sails to Liverpool and back on the crew of the merchant ship *St. Lawrence*. Teaches school at Greenbush, New York.

1840   Visits his Uncle Thomas Melville in Galena, Illinois.

1841   Ships out in January on the whaler *Acushnet*, which stops at Rio de Janeiro, rounds Cape Horn, and cruises among the Galapagos Islands.

1842   Melville and a shipmate jump ship at Nuka Hiva in the Marquesas Islands, flee into the interior, and live with the notorious Typee tribe for a few weeks. Escapes and signs on the *Lucy Ann*, an Australian whaler. At Tahiti the crew rebels and is arrested by the British consul. Melville escapes to Eimo and ships out on the *Charles and Henry*, a Nantucket whaler.

1843 Does odd jobs in Honolulu. Enlists as ordinary seaman on
      the frigate *United States*, which visits the Marquesas,
      Tahiti, and various South American ports.

1844 Melville discharged in Boston; returns home to his family
      in Lansingburgh.

1845 Writes an account of his adventures in the Marquesas.

1846 This account, later known as *Typee*, published in London
      and New York.

1847 *Omoo*, an account of his adventures on the *Lucy Ann*, in
      Tahiti, and on Eimo. Marries Elizabeth Shaw, daughter of
      Chief Justice of Massachusetts, Lemuel Shaw. Settles in
      New York City.

1849 *Mardi*, an allegorical and philosophical romance. *Redburn*,
      based on his first voyage. Sails for England; visits the con-
      tinent. Son Malcolm born.

1850 *White-Jacket*, based on experiences on the *United States*.
      Moves to Pittsfield and forms friendship with Hawthorne.

1851 *Moby-Dick, or, The Whale*. Son Stanwix born.

1852 *Pierre, or, The Ambiguities*.

1853 Fire at Harper and Brothers destroys many unsold copies
      of his seven books. Begins publishing in the magazines.
      Daughter Elizabeth born.

1855 *Israel Potter* published in book form. Daughter Frances
      born.

1856 *The Piazza Tales*, a collection of his magazine stories. Fin-
      ishes *The Confidence-Man*. Sails for Europe and the Holy
      Land.

1857 *The Confidence-Man* published in New York and London.

1858–60 Public lecturing trips, mostly in the Middle West.

1860 Finishes a volume of poetry. Visits San Francisco on ship
      commanded by his brother Thomas.

1863 Settles in New York City.

1866 *Battle-Pieces*, a collection of Civil War poems. Becomes an inspector of customs in the port of New York, a position held until 1886.

1867 Eldest son Malcolm dies from self-inflicted pistol wound.

1869 Second son Stanwix goes to sea.

1876 *Clarel: A Poem and Pilgrimage in the Holy Land.*

1886 Stanwix dies in a San Francisco hospital.

1888 *John Marr and Other Sailors*, a collection of poems.

1891 *Timoleon*, a collection of poems. *Billy Budd* almost finished. Dies, September 28.

1924 *Billy Budd* published.

Bibliography

THE FOLLOWING ITEMS represent the spread and scope of scholarship on *Billy Budd* through 1971 even though the list is not complete. This bibliography concentrates on works in English, although it includes a few entries in other languages. Books and articles are not listed separately: all entries are listed alphabetically by author.

Abel, Darrell. "'Laurel Twined with Thorn': The Theme of Melville's *Timoleon*," *The Personalist*, XLI (1960), 330–340.

Anderson, Charles C. "The Genesis of *Billy Budd*," *American Literature*, XII (1940), 329–346.

Anderson, Quentin. "Second Trip to Byzantium," *Kenyon Review*, XI (1949), 516–520.

Arvin, Newton. *Herman Melville*. New York: William Sloane Associates, 1950; Viking Press, 1957.

_____. "A Note on the Background of *Billy Budd*," *American Literature*, XX (1948), 51–55.

Auden, W. H. *The Enchafèd Flood*. New York: Random House, 1950.

Baird, James. *Ishmael*. Baltimore: Johns Hopkins Press, 1956; New York: Harper & Brothers, 1960.

Baldini, Gabriele. *Melville o le Ambiguità*. Milan: Ricciardi Editore, 1952.

Barnet, Sylvan. "The Execution in *Billy Budd*," *American Literature*, XXXIII (1962), 517–519.

Barrett, Laurence. "The Differences in Melville's Poetry," *PMLA*, LXX (1955), 606–623.

Behl, C. R. W. "*Billy Budd* und *Benito Cereno*," *Die Literatur*, XL (1938), 691–692.

Bercovitch, Sacvan. "Melville's Search for National Identity: Son and Father in *Redburn*, *Pierre*, and *Billy Budd*," *College Language Association Journal*, X (1967), 217–228.

Bernstein, John. *Pacifism and Rebellion in the Writings of Herman Melville.* The Hague: Mouton, 1964.

Berthoff, Warner. *The Example of Melville.* Princeton: Princeton University Press, 1962.

————. " 'Certain Phenomenal Men': The Example of *Billy Budd,*" *ELH,* xxvii (1960), 334–351.

Berti, Luigi. *Boccaporto Secondo.* Florence: Parenti, 1944.

Bewley, Marius. "A Truce of God for Melville," *Sewanee Review,* lxi (1953), 682–700.

Blackmur, R. P., ed. *American Short Novels.* New York: Thomas Y. ✓ Crowell, 1960.

Bond, William H. "Melville and Two Years Before the Mast," *Harvard Library Bulletin,* vii (1953), 362–365.

Booth, Wayne C. *The Rhetoric of Fiction.* Chicago: University of Chicago Press, 1961.

Bowen, Merlin. *The Long Encounter: Self and Experience in the Writings of Herman Melville.* Chicago: University of Chicago Press, 1960, 1963.

Braswell, William. *Melville's Religious Thought: An Essay in Interpretation.* Durham: Duke University Press, 1943; New York: Pageant Books, 1959.

————. "Melville's *Billy Budd* as 'An Inside Narrative,' " *American Literature,* xxix (1957), 133–146.

Brodtkorb, Paul, Jr. "The Definitive *Billy Budd:* 'But Aren't It All Sham?' " *PMLA,* lxxxii (1967), 602–612.

Brown, John Mason. *As They Appear.* New York: McGraw-Hill, 1952.

Browne, Ray B. "*Billy Budd:* Gospel of Democracy," *Nineteenth Century Fiction,* xvii (1963), 321–337. Rejoinder by Bernard Suits, xviii (1963), 288–291.

Brumm, Ursula. "The Figure of Christ in American Literature," *Partisan Review,* xxiv (1957), 403–413.

Callan, Richard J. "The Burden of Innocence in Melville and Twain," *Renascence,* xvii (1965), 191–194.

Cameron, Kenneth W. "*Billy Budd* and 'An Execution at Sea,' " *Emerson Society Quarterly,* No. 2 (1956), pp. 13–15.

Campbell, Harry Modean. "The Hanging Scene in Melville's *Billy Budd, Foretopman,*" *Modern Language Notes,* lxvi (1951), 378–381.

_____. "The Hanging Scene in Melville's *Billy Budd:* A Reply to Mr. Giovannini," *Modern Language Notes*, LXX (1955), 497–500.

Canaday, Nicholas, Jr. *Melville and Authority.* University of Florida Monographs, Humanities Series, No. 28. Gainesville: University of Florida Press, 1968.

Carpenter, Frederick I. *American Literature and the Dream.* New York: Philosophical Library, 1955.

_____. "Melville: The World in a Man-of-War," *University of Kansas City Review*, XIX (1953), 257–264.

Casper, Leonard. "The Case against Captain Vere," *Perspective*, V (1952), 146–152.

Chandler, Alice. "Captain Vere and the 'Tragedies of the Palace,'" *Modern Fiction Studies*, XIII (1967), 259–261.

_____. "The Name Symbolism of Captain Vere," *Nineteenth Century Fiction*, XXII (1967), 86–89.

Chase, Richard. *Herman Melville: A Critical Study.* New York: Macmillan, 1949.

_____. *The American Novel and Its Tradition.* Garden City: Doubleday, 1957.

_____, ed. *Selected Tales and Poems by Herman Melville.* New York: Rinehart, 1950.

_____. "An Approach to Melville," *Partisan Review*, XIV (1947), 285–294.

_____. "Dissent on *Billy Budd,*" *Partisan Review*, XV (1948), 1212–1218.

Clive, Geoffrey. *The Romantic Enlightenment.* New York: Meridian Books, 1960.

_____. " 'Teleological Suspension of the Ethical' in Nineteenth-Century Literature," *Journal of Religion*, XXXIV (1954), 75–87.

Cowie, Alexander. *The Rise of the American Novel.* New York: American Book Co., 1948.

Coxe, Louis O., and Robert Chapman. *Billy Budd: A Play in Three Acts*, with foreword by Brooks Atkinson. Princeton: Princeton University Press, 1951.

Cramer, Maurice B. *"Billy Budd* and *Billy Budd,"* *Journal of General Education*, X (1957), 78–91.

Cunliffe, Marcus. *The Literature of the United States.* Harmondsworth, Middlesex: Penguin Books, 1954.

Doubleday, Neal F. "Jack Easy and Billy Budd," *English Language Notes*, II (1964), 39–42.

Duerksen, Roland A. "*Caleb Williams, Political Justice*, and *Billy Budd*," *American Literature*, XXXVIII (1966), 372–376.

————. "The Deep Quandary in *Billy Budd*," *New England Quarterly*, XLI (1968), 51–66.

Donahue, Jane. "Melville's Classicism: Law and Order in His Poetry," *Papers on Language and Literature*, V (1969), 63–72.

E————, T. T. "Melville's *Billy Budd*," *Explicator*, II (1943), Item 14.

Eckardt, Sister Mary Ellen. "An Interpretive Analysis of the Patterns of Imagery in *Moby-Dick* and *Billy Budd*," University of Notre Dame, *Dissertation Abstracts*, XXII (1962), 2134.

Eckner, Reider, ed. *Billy Budd*. Stockholm: Raben & Sjögren, 1955

Feidelson, Charles, Jr. *Symbolism and American Literature*. Chicago: University of Chicago Press, 1953.

Fiedler, Leslie A. *Love and Death in the American Novel*. New York: Criterion Books, 1960; rev. ed. New York: Stein and Day, 1966.

Fite, Olive L. "Billy Budd, Claggart, and Schopenhauer," *Nineteenth Century Fiction*, XXIII (1968), 336–343.

Fogle, Richard Harter. "*Billy Budd*—Acceptance or Irony," *Tulane Studies in English*, VIII (1958), 107–113.

————. "Melville and the Civil War," *Tulane Studies in English*, IX (1959), 61–89.

————. "*Billy Budd*: The Order of the Fall," *Nineteenth Century Fiction*, XV (1960), 189–205.

————. "The Themes of Melville's Later Poetry," *Tulane Studies in English*, XI (1961), 65–86.

Forster, E. M. *Aspects of the Novel*. New York: Harcourt, Brace, 1927, 1954.

————. "Letter," *The Griffin* [The Reader's Subscription, Inc.], I (1951), 4–6.

————, and Eric Crozier. Libretto for *Billy Budd: Opera in Four Acts*. London: Boosey and Hawkes, 1951.

Freeman, F. Barron, ed. *Melville's Billy Budd*. Cambridge, Mass.: Harvard University Press, 1948.

_____. "The Enigma of Melville's 'Daniel Orme,' " *American Literature*, xvi (1944), 208–211.

Freeman, John. *Herman Melville*. London and New York: Macmillan, 1926.

Freimarck, Vincent. "Mainmast as Crucifix in *Billy Budd*," *Modern Language Notes*, lxxii (1957), 496–497.

Gabriel, Ralph H. *The Course of American Democratic Thought*. New York: Ronald Press, 1940.

Gaskins, Avery F. "Symbolic Nature of Claggart's Name," *American Notes and Queries*, vi (1967), 56.

Geismar, Maxwell, ed. *Billy Budd* and *Typee*. New York: Washington Square Press, 1962.

Gettmann, Royal, and Bruce Harkness. *Teacher's Manual* for *A Book of Stories*. New York: Rinehart, 1955.

Giovannini, G. "The Hanging Scene in Melville's *Billy Budd*," *Modern Language Notes*, lxx (1955), 491–497.

Glick, Wendell. "Expediency and Absolute Morality in *Billy Budd*," *PMLA*, lxviii (1953), 103–110.

Goforth, David S. "Melville's Shorter Poems: The Substance and the Significance," Indiana University, *Dissertation Abstracts*, xxix (1969), 3097A.

Goldsmith, Arnold L. "The 'Discovery Scene' in *Billy Budd*," *Modern Drama*, iii (1961), 339–342.

Gollin, Richard and Rita. "Justice in an Earlier Treatment of the *Billy Budd* Theme," *American Literature*, xxviii (1957), 513–515.

Graves, Robert D. "Polarity in the Shorter Fiction of Herman Melville," Duke University, *Dissertation Abstracts*, xxvii (1966), 1821A–1822A.

Gross, John J. "Melville, Dostoevsky, and the People," *Pacific Spectator*, x (1956), 160–170.

Gross, Theodore. "Herman Melville: The Nature of Authority," *Colorado Quarterly*, xvi (1968), 397–412.

Hall, Joan Joffe. "The Historical Chapters in *Billy Budd*," *University Review*, xxx (1963), 35–40.

Hayford, Harrison, ed. *The Somers Mutiny Affair*. Englewood Cliffs, N.J.: Prentice-Hall, 1959.

_____, and Merton Sealts, Jr., eds. *Billy Budd, Sailor*. Chicago: University of Chicago Press, 1962.

————. "The Sailor Poet of *White-Jacket*," *Boston Public Library Quarterly*, III (1951), 226–227.

Head, Brian F. "Camões and Melville," *Revista Camoniana*, I (1964), 36–77.

Hillway, Tyrus. "Melville's *Billy Budd*," *Explicator*, IV (1945), Item 12.

————. "Billy Budd: Melville's Human Sacrifice," *Pacific Spectator*, VI (1952), 342–347.

Hitt, Ralph E. "Melville's Poems of Civil War Controversy," *Studies in the Literary Imagination*, II (1969), 57–68.

Howard, Leon. *Herman Melville: A Biography*. Berkeley and Los Angeles: University of California Press, 1951, 1958.

————. *Literature and the American Tradition*. Garden City: Doubleday and Company, 1960.

Humphreys, A. R. *Herman Melville*. Edinburgh: Oliver and Boyd, 1962; New York: Grove Press, 1962.

Ives, C. B. "*Billy Budd* and the Articles of War," *American Literature*, XXXIV (1962), 31–39.

Itofuji, Hiromi. "Another Aspect of *Billy Budd*," *Kyushu American Literature*, X (1957), 29–40.

Josephson, Matthew. "The Transfiguration of Herman Melville," *Outlook*, CL (1928), 809–811, 832, 836.

Kaplan, Sidney. "Explication," *Melville Society Newsletter*, XIII, No. 2 (1957), 3.

Kazin, Alfred. "Ishmael in His Academic Heaven," *New Yorker*, XXIV (February 12, 1949), 84, 87, 88–89.

Kilbourne, W. G., Jr. "Montaigne and Captain Vere," *American Literature*, XXXIII (1962), 514–517.

Kimball, William J. "Charles Sumner's Contribution to Chapter XVIII of *Billy Budd*," *South Atlantic Bulletin*, XXXII, iv (1967), 13–14.

Knox, G. A. "Communication and Communion in Melville," *Renascence*, IX (1956), 26–31.

Krieger, Murray. *The Tragic Vision*. New York: Holt, Rinehart & Winston, 1960.

Lang, Hans-Joachim. "Melvilles 'Billy Budd' und seine Quellen: Eine Nachlese," *Festschrift für Walther Fischer*. Heidelberg: Carl Winter, 1959.

Ledbetter, Kenneth. "The Ambiguity of *Billy Budd*," *Texas Studies in Language and Literature*, iv (1962), 130–134.

Lemon, Lee T. "*Billy Budd:* The Plot against the Story," *Studies in Short Fiction*, ii (1964), 32–43.

Lesser, Simon. *Fiction and the Unconscious*. Boston: Beacon Press, 1957.

Levin, Harry. *The Power of Blackness*. New York: Alfred A. Knopf, 1958; Vintage Books, 1960.

Lewis, R. W. B. *The American Adam*. Chicago: University of Chicago Press, 1955.

Leyda, Jay. *The Melville Log*, 2 vols. New York: Harcourt, Brace, 1951.

————, ed. *The Portable Melville*. New York; Viking Press, 1952.

Leyris, Pierre, ed. *Billy Budd*. Neuchatel and Paris: Attinger, 1935; Paris: Gallimard, 1937.

Lindeman, Jack. "Herman Melville's Civil War," *Modern Age*, ix (1965), 387–398.

————. "Herman Melville's Reconstruction," *Modern Age*, x (1966), 168–172.

London, Philip W. "The Military Necessity: *Billy Budd* and Vigny," *Comparative Literature*, xiv (1962), 174–186.

McCarthy, Paul. "Character and Structure in *Billy Budd*," *Discourse*, ix (1966), 201–217.

McElderry, B. R., Jr. "Three Earlier Treatments of the *Billy Budd* Theme," *American Literature*, xxvii (1955), 251–257.

McNamara, Anne. "Melville's *Billy Budd*," *Explicator*, xxi (1962), Item 11.

McQuitty, Robert A. "A Rhetorical Approach to Melville's 'Bartleby,' 'Benito Cereno,' and *Billy Budd*," Syracuse University, *Dissertation Abstracts*, xxix (1969), 4010A–4011A.

Mary Ellen, Sister. "Parallels in Contrast: A Study of Melville's Imagery in *Moby Dick* and *Billy Budd*," *Studies in Short Fiction*, ii (1965), 284–290.

Martin, Lawrence H., Jr. "Melville and Christianity: The Late Poems," *Massachusetts Studies in English*, ii (1969), 11–18.

Mason, Ronald. *The Spirit above the Dust: A Study of Herman Melville*. London: John Lehmann, 1951.

Matthiessen, F. O. *American Renaissance*. New York: Oxford University Press, 1941.

Mayoux, Jean Jacques. *Melville*. Trans. John Ashbery. New York: Grove Press, 1960.

Meldrum, Barbara. "Melville on War," *Research Studies*, xxxvII (1969), 130–138.

Miller, James E., Jr. *"Billy Budd:* The Catastrophe of Innocence," *Modern Language Notes*, LXXIII (1958), 168–176.

————. "Melville's Search for Form," *Bucknell Review*, VIII (1959), 260–276.

Millgate, Michael. "Melville and Marvell: A Note on *Billy Budd,*" *English Studies*, XLIX (1968), 47–50.

Mitchell, Charles. "Melville and the Spurious Truth of Legalism," *Centennial Review*, XII (1968), 110–126.

Montale, Eugenio, trans. *La Storia di Billy Budd.* Milan: Bompiani, 1942.

————. "An Introduction to *Billy Budd* (1942)," *Sewanee Review*, LXVIII (1960), 419–422.

Mumford, Lewis. *Herman Melville.* New York; Harcourt, Brace, 1929.

Murry, John Middleton. *John Clare and Other Studies.* London: Peter Neville, 1950.

————. "Herman Melville's Silence," *Times Literary Supplement*, No. 1173 (July 10, 1924), p. 433.

————. "Quo Warranto?" *Adelphi*, II (August, 1924), 194.

Nathanson, Leonard. "Melville's *Billy Budd*, Chapter I," *Explicator*, XXII (1964), Item 75.

Noone, John B., Jr. *"Billy Budd:* Two Concepts of Nature," *American Literature*, XXIX (1957), 249–262.

Okamoto, Hidoo. "Billy Budd, Foretopman as Melville's Testament of Acceptance," *Studies in English Literature* [English Literary Society of Japan], XXV, No. 2 (1959), 225–243.

Olson, Charles. *Call Me Ishmael.* New York: Reynal & Hitchcock, 1947; Grove Press, 1958.

————. "David Young, David Old," *Western Review*, XIV (1949), 63–66.

Palmer, R. R. "Herman Melville et la Révolution Française," *Annales Historiques de la Révolution Française*, XXVI (1954), 254–256.

Parker, Herschel. "Melville and Politics: A Scrutiny of the Political Milieux of Herman Melville's Life and Works," Northwestern University, *Dissertation Abstracts*, xxiv (1964), 5390–5391.

Paul, Sherman. "Melville's 'The Town-Ho's Story,'" *American Literature*, xxi (1949), 212–221.

Pearson, Norman Holmes. "Billy Budd: 'The King's Yarn,'" *American Quarterly*, iii (1951), 99–114.

Perry, Robert L. "*Billy Budd:* Melville's *Paradise Lost*," *Midwest Quarterly*, x (1969), 173–185.

Phelps, Leland R. "The Reaction to *Benito Cereno* and *Billy Budd* in Germany," *Symposium*, xiii (1959), 294–299.

Plomer, William, ed. *Billy Budd, Foretopman*. London: John Lehmann, 1946.

Pommer, Henry F. *Milton and Melville*. Pittsburgh: University of Pittsburgh Press, 1950.

Quasimodo, Salvatore. *Billy Budd: Un Atto di H. Melville*. Milan: Edizioni Suvini Zerboni, 1949.

————. "Oratorio per Billy Budd," *Inventario*, ii (1949), 109–121, 155.

Rathbun, John W. "*Billy Budd* and the Limits of Perception," *Nineteenth Century Fiction*, xx (1965), 19–34.

Reich, Charles A. "The Tragedy of Justice in *Billy Budd*," *Yale Review*, lvi (1967), 368–389.

Renvoisé, Jean-Paul. "*Billy Budd:* Opéra de Benjamin Britten," *Etudes Anglaises*, xviii (1965), 367–382.

Robillard, Douglas. "Theme and Structure in Melville's *John Marr and Other Sailors*," *English Language Notes*, vi (1969), 187–192.

Rogers, Robert. "The 'Ineludible Gripe' of Billy Budd," *Literature and Psychology*, xiv (1964), 9–22.

Rosenberry, Edward H. "The Problem of *Billy Budd*," *PMLA*, lxxx (1965), 489–498.

Roudiez, Leon S. "Strangers in Melville and Camus," *French Review*, xxxi (1958), 217–226.

Sale, Arthur. "Captain Vere's Reasons," *Cambridge Journal*, v (1951), 3–18.

Schiffman, Joseph. "Melville's Final Stage, Irony: A Reexamination of *Billy Budd* Criticism," *American Literature*, xxii (1950), 128–136.

Schneider, Herbert W. *A History of American Philosophy*. New York: Columbia University Press, 1946.

Schroth, Evelyn. "Melville's Judgment on Captain Vere," *Midwest Quarterly*, x (1969), 189–200.

Sedgwick, William Ellery. *Herman Melville: The Tragedy of Mind.* Cambridge, Mass.: Harvard University Press, 1944.

Seelye, John D. *Melville: The Ironic Diagram.* Evanston, Illinois: Northwestern University Press, 1970.

Shattuck, Roger. "Two Inside Narratives: *Billy Budd* and *L'Étranger*," *Texas Studies in Literature and Language*, iv (1962), 314–320.

Shaw, Richard O. "The Civil War Poems of Herman Melville," *Lincoln Herald*, lxviii (1962), 44–49.

Sherwood, John C. "Vere as Collingwood: A Key to *Billy Budd*," *American Literature*, xxxv (1964), 476–484.

Short, Raymond W., ed. *Four Great American Novels.* New York: Henry Holt, 1946.

————. "Melville as Symbolist," *University of Kansas City Review*, xv (1948), 38–46.

Shulman, Robert. "Montaigne and the Techniques of Tragedy of Melville's *Billy Budd*," *Comparative Literature*, xvi (1964), 322–330.

Simon, Jean. *Herman Melville, marin, métaphysicien et poète.* Paris: Boiven, 1939.

Snyder, Oliver. "A Note on 'Billy Budd,' " *Accent*, xi (1951), 58–60.

Spangler, Eugene R. "Harvest in a Barren Field: A Countercomment," *Western Review*, xiv (1950), 305–307.

Stafford, William T., ed. *Melville's Billy Budd and the Critics.* San Francisco: Wadsworth, 1961, 1968.

————. "The New *Billy Budd* and the Novelistic Fallacy: An Essay-Review," *Modern Fiction Studies*, viii (1962), 306–311.

Stallman, Robert W., and R. E. Watters, eds. *The Creative Reader.* New York: Ronald Press, 1954.

Stein, William Bysshe. "The Motif of the Wise Old Man in *Billy Budd*," *Western Humanities Review*, xiv (1960), 99–101.

————. " 'Billy Budd': The Nightmare of History," *Criticism*, iii (1961), 237–250.

Stern, Milton R. *The Fine Hammered Steel of Herman Melville.* Urbana: University of Illinois Press, 1957.

————, ed. *Typee and Billy Budd.* New York: E. P. Dutton, 1958.

————. "Melville's Tragic Imagination: The Hero Without a Home," in *Patterns of Commitment in American Literature.* Ed. M. La France. Toronto: University of Toronto Press, 1967.

Stewart, Randall. *American Literature and Christian Doctrine.* Baton Rouge: Louisiana State University Press, 1958.

————. "The Vision of Evil in Hawthorne and Melville," in *The Tragic Vision and the Christian Faith.* Ed. N. A. Scott, Jr. New York: Association Press, 1957.

————. "Moral Crisis as Structural Principle in Fiction," *Christian Scholar,* XLII (1959), 284–289.

Stone, Geoffrey. *Melville.* New York: Sheed and Ward, 1949.

————. "Herman Melville: Loyalty to the Heart," in *American Classics Reconsidered.* Ed. Harold C. Gardiner, S. J. New York: Charles Scribner's Sons, 1958.

Sühnel, Rudolf. "Melvilles *Billy Budd,*" *Sprache und Literatur Englands und Amerikas,* III. Tübingen: Niemeyer, 1959.

Sundermann, K. H. *Herman Melvilles Gedankengut.* Berlin: Collignon, 1937.

Sutton, Walter. "Melville and the Great God Budd," *Prairie Schooner,* XXXIV (1960), 128–133.

Thompson, Lawrance. *Melville's Quarrel with God.* Princeton: Princeton University Press, 1952.

Thorp, Willard, ed. *Herman Melville: Representative Selections.* New York: American Book Co., 1938.

————, ed. *Billy Budd and Other Tales.* New York: New American Library, 1961.

————. "Herman Melville," in *Literary History of the United States.* Ed. Robert E. Spiller *et al.* 3 vols. New York: Macmillan, 1948.

Tilton, Eleanor M. "Melville's 'Rammon': A Text and Commentary," *Harvard Library Bulletin,* XIII (1959), 50–91.

Tindall, William York. "The Ceremony of Innocence," in *Great Moral Dilemmas in Literature, Past and Present.* Ed. R. M. MacIver. New York: Harper and Brothers, 1956.

Van Doren, Carl, ed. *"Billy Budd," "Benito Cereno" and "The Enchanted Isles."* New York: Readers Club, 1942.

Vincent, Howard P., ed. *Twentieth Century Interpretations of Billy Budd.* Englewood Cliffs, N.J.: Prentice-Hall, 1971.

Wagner, Vern. "Billy Budd as Moby Dick: An Alternate Reading," in *Studies in Honor of John Wilcox.* Ed. A. D. Wallace and W. O. Ross. Detroit: Wayne State University Press, 1958.

Warner, Rex, ed. *Billy Budd and Other Stories*. London: John Lehmann, 1951.

Watson, E. L. Grant. "Melville's Testament of Acceptance," *New England Quarterly*, vi (1933), 319–327.

Watters, R. E. "Melville's Metaphysics of Evil," *University of Toronto Quarterly*, ix (1940), 170–182.

——————. "Melville's 'Isolatoes,'" *PMLA*, lx (1945), 1138–1148.

——————. "Melville's 'Sociality,'" *American Literature*, xvii (1945), 33–49.

Weaver, Raymond. *Herman Melville: Mariner and Mystic*. New York: George H. Doran, 1921; Pageant Books, 1960; Cooper Square, 1961.

——————, ed. *The Shorter Novels of Herman Melville*. New York: Horace Liveright, 1928.

Weir, Charles, Jr. "Malice Reconciled: A Note on Melville's *Billy Budd*," *University of Toronto Quarterly*, xiii (1944), 276–285.

West, Ray B., Jr. "The Unity of 'Billy Budd,'" *Hudson Review*, v (1952), 120–128.

——————. "Primitivism in Melville," *Prairie Schooner*, xxx (1956), 369–385.

White, Eric Walter. "Billy Budd," *Adelphi*, xxviii (1952), 492–498.

Willett, Ralph W. "Nelson and Vere: Hero and Victim in *Billy Budd, Sailor*," *PMLA*, lxxxii (1967), 370–376.

Wilson, G. R., Jr. "*Billy Budd* and Melville's Use of Dramatic Technique," *Studies in Short Fiction*, iv (1967), 105–111.

Winters, Yvor. *Maule's Curse*. Norfolk: New Directions, 1938.

——————. *In Defense of Reason*. New York: Swallow Press & William Morrow, 1947.

Wirzberger, Karl-Heinz. *Vortoppmann Billy Budd und andere Erzählungen*. Leipzig: Dieterich, 1956.

Withim, Phil. "*Billy Budd*: Testament of Resistance," *Modern Language Quarterly*, xx (1959), 115–127.

Wright, Nathalia. *Melville's Use of the Bible*. Durham: Duke University Press, 1949.

——————. "Biblical Allusion in Melville's Prose," *American Literature*, xii (1940), 185–199.

Zink, Karl E. "Herman Melville and the Forms—Irony and Social Criticism in 'Billy Budd,'" *Accent*, xii (1952), 131–139.

A Note to the Reader

THE DISCUSSION of the text presented in this edition is given in Appendix One. A reading of the discussion will make clear why it is important for an interested scholar to be able to refer to the leaf numbers of the *Billy Budd* manuscript. Therefore, footnotes in this edition refer both to page and leaf numbers, when necessary, when citing references to the text. Leaves are indicated by the number in the margin of the text; the first word of that leaf is preceded by the symbol, °, in the text. The numbering in the margins and in the "List of Textual Changes" (Appendix Two) are the same as in the Hayford and Sealts edition of the genetic text in *Billy Budd, Sailor* (see bibliography), where each leaf can be found transcribed in full.

BILLY BUDD
Sailor

An Inside Narrative[1]

[1] See Appendix One, pp. 156–159.

1 °Dedicated to
Jack Chase
Englishman
Wherever that great heart may now be
Here on earth or harbored in Paradise
Captain of the Main-Top
in the year 1843
in the U. S. Frigate
United States[2]

[2] Homeward bound from his whaling voyage, Melville served with Jack Chase aboard the U. S. Navy frigate, the *United States*. Chase impressed himself indelibly on Melville's mind. He was the handsome sailor of Melville's early book, *White-Jacket* (1850), and remained in Melville's imagination through the last thing Melville ever wrote. Chase had served aboard the frigate *Macedonian* in the British navy. E. Curtis Hine, a shipmate of Melville and Chase on the *United States* in 1843–1844, published a short tale called *Orlando Melville or the Victims of the Press-Gang* (Boston, 1848), in which the master-at-arms—called "Jimmy Leggs," a nautical nickname which was standard naval usage—brings false charges against the friends of the hero, a British handsome sailor. The master-at-arms is frustrated by a naval encounter in which the *Macedonian* is defeated by the *United States*. As Hayford and Sealts suggest in presenting this material, Melville in later life was reminiscing about his own past as a sailor and about the sailormen he had known, and recorded his reminiscences in his poems, particularly *John Marr and Other Sailors*. Jack Chase was an older man, and, as handsome sailor, was the model for the first version of *Billy Budd*, which began as a ballad about an older tar about to be executed for mutiny. Though Billy became younger and was changed in crucial ways as Melville revised the tale that he developed out of the ballad (which was later placed at the end of the narrative), Jack Chase, the original model, was still in Melville's mind within the imaginative amalgam of memories, and is a fitting subject for the dedication of the "inside narrative." (See Harrison Hayford, "The Sailor Poet of *White-Jacket*," *Boston Public Library Quarterly*, III [1951], 226–227, and the discussion in *H&S*, pp. 31–33.)

[1]

°IN THE TIME before steamships, or then more frequently than 2
now, a stroller along the docks of any considerable sea-port
would occasionally have his attention arrested by a group of
bronzed mariners, man-of-war's men or merchant-sailors in holi-
day attire ashore on liberty. In certain instances they would
flank, or, like a body-guard quite surround some superior figure
of their own class, °moving along with them like Aldebaran³   3
among the lesser lights of his constellation. That signal object
was the "Handsome Sailor" of the less prosaic time alike of the
military and merchant navies. With no perceptible trace of the
vainglorious about him, rather with the off-hand unaffectedness
of natural regality, he seemed to accept the spontaneous homage
of his shipmates.

   A somewhat remarkable instance recurs to me. In Liverpool,
now half a century ago, I saw under the shadow of the great
dingy street-wall of Prince's Dock °(an obstruction long since   4
removed) a common sailor, so intensely black that he must needs
have been a native African of the unadulterate blood of Ham.⁴
A symmetric figure much above the average height. The two
ends of a gay silk handkerchief thrown loose about the neck

   ³ Aldebaran is the brightest star in the constellation Taurus. It is the eye
of the bull. With Aldebaran, Melville introduces the animal imagery that
characterizes the strength, force, innocence, and grace of the handsome
sailor, continuing in the introductory paragraphs with references to the
Assyrian sacred bull (leaf 6), Alexander on Bucephalus, and the horns of
Taurus (leaf 8), and throughout the tale with various images including the
St. Bernard dog.

   ⁴ "And Noah begat three sons, Shem, Ham, and Japheth" (Gen. 6:10).
Because Ham looked upon his drunken father's nakedness, he was cursed.
"A servant of servants he shall be unto his brethren" (Gen. 9:18–27).
Europeans justified enslavement of blacks by referring to the Bible story
and identifying Ham as the father of the Negro race.

danced upon the displayed ebony of his chest; in his ears were big
hoops of gold, and a Scotch Highland bonnet with a tartan band
set off his shapely head. It was a hot noon in July; and his face,
5 lustrous with perspiration, beamed with barbaric good humor. °In
jovial sallies right and left, his white teeth flashing into view, he
rollicked along, the centre of a company of his shipmates. These
were made up of such an assortment of tribes and complexions as
would have well fitted them to be marched up by Anacharsis
Cloots before the bar of the first French Assembly as Representa-
tives of the Human Race.[5] At each spontaneous tribute rendered
by the wayfarers to this black pagod of a fellow—the tribute of
a pause and stare, and less frequently an exclamation—the motley
6 retinue showed that they took that °sort of pride in the evoker of
it which the Assyrian priests doubtless showed for their grand
sculptured Bull when the faithful prostrated themselves.
7   °To return. If in some cases a bit of a nautical Murat[6] in setting
forth his person ashore, the handsome sailor of the period in question evinced nothing of the dandified Billy-be-Damn, an amusing
character all but extinct now, but occasionally to be encountered,
and in a form yet more amusing than the original, at the tiller of
the boats on the tempestuous Erie Canal or, more likely, vapor-
8 ing in the groggeries along the tow-path. °Invariably a proficient in his perilous calling, he was also more or less of a mighty
boxer or wrestler. It was strength and beauty. Tales of his prow-
ess were recited. Ashore he was the champion; afloat the spokes-

---

[5] Baron de Cloots (Jean Baptiste du Val-de-Grâce, 1755–1794) was a
Prussian educated in France and steeped in the rebellious thought of the
Enlightenment. On June 19, 1790, he dressed followers from the Paris slums
in the costumes of various nations, and identifying himself as the voice of
all men, presented them before the bar of the National Assembly, asking
for (and getting) the right to confederate the entire human race into one
vast and democratic whole. He renounced his title, hating distinctions of
rank among men. "My heart is French and my soul is sansculotte," he once
said. During the Terror he was guillotined. Cloots (spelled Clootz in
Moby-Dick) was a lasting type of democracy in Melville's imagination,
his deputation being used to characterize the oneness of all men in the
voyage of the *Pequod* in *Moby-Dick* and the *Fidèle* in *The Confidence-Man*.

[6] Joachim Murat (1771–1815) was a vain and dashing follower of Napoleon, who made him King of Naples in 1808. Murat was known for his
romantic verve, displayed, among other ways, in dazzling uniforms and
dress.

man; on every suitable occasion always foremost. Close-reefing topsails in a gale, there he was, astride the weather yard-arm-end, foot in the Flemish horse as "stirrup," both hands tugging at the "earring" as at a bridle, in very much the attitude of young Alexander curbing the fiery Bucephalus.[7] A superb figure, tossed up as by the horns of Taurus against the thunderous °sky, cheerily hallooing to the strenuous file along the spar.   9

The moral nature was seldom out of keeping with the physical make. Indeed, except as toned by the former, the comeliness and power, always attractive in masculine conjunction, hardly could have drawn the sort of honest homage the Handsome Sailor in some examples received from his less gifted associates.

°Such a cynosure, at least in aspect, and something such too in   10 nature, though with important variations made apparent as the story proceeds, was welkin-eyed Billy Budd, or Baby Budd, as more familiarly under circumstances hereafter to be given he at last came to be called, aged twenty-one, a foretopman of the British fleet toward the close of the last decade of the eighteenth century. It was not very long prior to the time of the narration that follows that he had entered the King's Service, having been impressed on the Narrow Seas[8] °from a homeward-bound En-   11 glish merchantman into a seventy-four outward-bound, H.M.S. *Bellipotent;* which ship, as was not unusual in those hurried days, having been obliged to put to sea short of her proper complement of men. Plump upon Billy at first sight in the gangway the boarding officer, Lieutenant Ratcliffe, pounced, even before the merchantman's crew was formally mustered on the quarter-deck for

---

[7] A great and fierce horse that only Alexander could ride. The sailors' tasks are explained in *Standard Seamanship for the Merchant Service,* by Felix Riessenberg (2nd ed., New York, 1936), cited in *H&S,* p. 137.

[8] The seas immediately around England, including the English Channel. Melville had long been aware of the practices of British press-gangs, noting in both *Israel Potter* and in *White-Jacket* that impressment often deprived a man of his liberties at the very doorway of home, a home which was supposed to be a bastion of freedom. Placing the impressment in the Narrow Seas further complicates the political and historical issues that are important in an evaluation of the narrative's events, and helps create the implicit conclusion of the story, a conclusion which envisions in no place and at no time a clear and lasting triumph of human desires for goodness or even a clear definition of what is desired.

his deliberate inspection. And him only he elected. For whether
it was because the other men when ranged before him showed
12 to °ill advantage after Billy, or whether he had some scruples in
view of the merchantman being rather short-handed, however it
might be, the officer contented himself with his first spontaneous
choice. To the surprise of the ship's company, though much to
the Lieutenant's satisfaction, Billy made no demur. But, indeed,
any demur would have been as idle as the protest of a goldfinch
popped into a cage.

13   °Noting this uncomplaining acquiescence, all but cheerful one
might say, the shipmaster turned a surprised glance of silent reproach at the sailor. The shipmaster was one of those worthy
mortals found in every vocation, even the humbler ones—the sort
of person whom everybody agrees in calling "a respectable man."
And—nor so strange to report as it may appear to be—though a
ploughman of the troubled waters, life-long contending with the
14 intractable elements, there was nothing this honest soul °at heart
loved better than simple peace and quiet. For the rest, he was
fifty or thereabouts, a little inclined to corpulence, a prepossess-
ing face, unwhiskered, and of an agreeable color—a rather full
face, humanely intelligent in expression. On a fair day with a fair
wind and all going well, a certain musical chime in his voice
seemed to be the veritable unobstructed outcome of the inner-
most man. He had much prudence, much conscientiousness, and
there were occasions when these virtues were the cause of over-
15 much disquietude in him. °On a passage, so long as his craft was
in any proximity to land, no sleep for Captain Graveling.[9] He

---

[9] Captain Graveling is a typical Melvillean portrait of the ordinary john
doe grave-ling who, though no candidate for deathlessness, does the necessary daily work of the world and is one, thereby, with all mortal men. One
should note that Melville indicates that Mr. John Citizen is at once victimized and protected by the forces of the state. The common man wants
above all only to be left alone and to enjoy his pipe after his dinner, but
the impingement of history is inescapable in Graveling's life and destroys
his short-lived peace. Melville's attitude toward this nonheroic common
man is a mixture of amusement and sympathy, condescension and respect.
The amusement and condescension are submerged in the earlier books, like
Moby-Dick, where the workaday laborer assumes heroic proportions and
supplies the world's needs.

took to heart those serious responsibilities not so heavily borne by
some shipmasters.

Now while Billy Budd was down in the forecastle getting his
kit together, the *Bellipotent*'s Lieutenant, burly and bluff, nowise
disconcerted by Captain Graveling's omitting to proffer the customary hospitalities on an occasion so unwelcome to him, an
omission simply caused by preoccupation of thought, unceremo-
niously invited himself into the cabin, and also to a flask from the
spirit-locker, °a receptacle which his experienced eye instantly   16
discovered. In fact he was one of those sea-dogs in whom all the
hardship and peril of naval life in the great prolonged wars of his
time never impaired the natural instinct for sensuous enjoyment.
His duty he always faithfully did; but duty is sometimes a dry
obligation, and he was for irrigating its aridity, whensoever possible, with a fertilizing decoction of strong waters. For the cabin's
proprietor there was nothing left but to play the part of the
enforced host with whatever grace and alacrity were practicable.
°As necessary adjuncts to the flask, he silently placed tumbler and   17
water-jug before the irrepressible guest. But excusing himself
from partaking just then, he dismally watched the unembarrassed
officer deliberately diluting his grog a little, then tossing it off in
three swallows, pushing the empty tumbler away, yet not so far as
to be beyond easy reach, at the same time settling himself in his seat
and smacking his lips with high satisfaction, looking straight at
the host.

These proceedings over, the Master broke the silence; °and   18
there lurked a rueful reproach in the tone of his voice; "Lieutenant, you are going to take my best man from me, the jewel
of 'em."

"Yes, I know" rejoined the other, immediately drawing back
the tumbler °preliminary to a replenishing; "Yes, I know. Sorry."   19

"Beg pardon, but you don't understand, Lieutenant. See here
now. Before I shipped that young fellow, my forecastle was a
rat-pit of quarrels. It was black times, I tell you, aboard the
'*Rights*' here. I was worried to that degree my pipe had no com-
fort for me. But Billy came; and it was like a Catholic priest
striking peace in an Irish shindy. Not that he preached to them

or said or did anything in particular; but a virtue went out of
him, sugaring the sour ones. They took to him like hornets to
20 treacle; all but the buffer[10] °of the gang, the big shaggy chap
with the fire-red whiskers. He indeed out of envy, perhaps, of the
newcomer, and thinking such a 'sweet and pleasant fellow,' as he
mockingly designated him to the others, could hardly have the
spirit of a game-cock, must needs bestir himself in trying to get
21 up an ugly row with him. °Billy forebore with him and reasoned
with him in a pleasant way—he is something like myself, Lieutenant, to whom aught like a quarrel is hateful—but nothing served.
So, in the second dog-watch one day the Red Whiskers in presence of the others, under pretence of showing Billy just whence
a sirloin steak was cut—for the fellow had once been a butcher—
insultingly gave him a dig under the ribs. Quick as lightning Billy
let fly his arm. I dare say he never meant to do quite as much as
he did, but anyhow he gave the burly fool a terrible drubbing.
22 °It took about half a minute, I should think. And, lord bless you,
the lubber was astonished at the celerity. And will you believe it,
Lieutenant, the Red Whiskers now really loves Billy—loves him,
or is the biggest hypocrite that ever I heard of. But they all love
23 him. °Some of 'em do his washing, darn his old trousers for him;
the carpenter is at odd times making a pretty little chest of draw-
ers for him. Anybody will do anything for Billy Budd; and it's
the happy family here. But now, Lieutenant, if that young fellow
goes—I know how it will be aboard the '*Rights*.' Not again very
soon shall I, coming up from dinner, lean over the capstan smoking a quiet pipe—no, not very soon again, I think. Ay, Lieutenant,
you are going to take away the jewel of 'em; you are going to
take away my peacemaker!" And with that the good soul had
really some ado in checking a rising sob.
24   °"Well," said the Lieutenant who had listened with amused
interest to all this, and now was waxing merry with his tipple;
"Well, blessed are the peacemakers, especially the fighting peacemakers! And such are the seventy-four beauties some of which

---

[10] Usually printed as "bluffer" prior to *H&S*. A "buffer" is a bully, a fighter,
a gangleader.

you see poking their noses out of the port-holes of yonder war-
ship lying-to for me,"[11] pointing through the cabin window at
the *Bellipotent*. "But courage! don't look so downhearted, man.
Why, I pledge you in advance the royal approbation. Rest as-
sured that His Majesty will be delighted °to know that in a time   25
when his hard tack is not sought for by sailors with such avidity
as should be; a time also when some shipmasters privily resent the
borrowing from them a tar or two for the service; His Majesty,
I say, will be delighted to learn that *one* shipmaster at least cheerfully surrenders to the King the flower of his flock, a sailor who
with equal loyalty makes no dissent.—But where's my beauty?
Ah," looking through the cabin's open door, °"here he comes;   26
and, by Jove—lugging along his chest—Apollo with his port-
manteau!—My man," stepping out to him, "you can't take that
big box aboard a warship. The boxes there are mostly shot-boxes.
Put your duds in a bag, lad. Boot and saddle for the cavalryman,
bag and hammock for the man-of-war's man."

The transfer from chest to bag was made. And, after seeing
his man into the cutter and then following him down, the Lieutenant °pushed off from the *Rights-of-Man*. That was the merchant-   27
ship's name; though by her master and crew abbreviated in sailor
fashion into "*The Rights*." The hard-headed Dundee owner was

---

[11] Identification of the *Bellipotent* as a "74" meant that it was a ship-of-
the-line most likely to see action. The heavy battleships went into action
in a straight line of battle in order to avoid confusion during the obscuring
smoke of conflict; consequently they became known as "ships-of-the-line"
or "line-of-battle" ships, eventually shortened to "battle-ships." Only ships-
of-the-line were heavy enough to absorb and deal out the punishment of
fleet-to-fleet confrontation; the frigates and other lighter ships of rates
below ships-of-the-line were used as cruisers and destroyers are today, as
scouts and maritime fleet protectors—"the eyes and ears of the fleet"—
rather than as line-of-battle ships. A few huge ships, generally flagships,
had three decks with 100 guns, but the "100's" were too ponderous for
good maneuverability during battle. There were some 84 and 90 gun ships,
also with three gun decks, but they were rare and were also too heavy for
really maneuverable use. The workhorse line-of-battle ship most employed,
therefore, was the "74," with two gun decks, and it saw the most action.
The nature of the ship should be kept in mind when one considers Captain
Vere's sense of time, place, and urgency—especially on detached service—
in the affair of "one William Budd, foretopman."

a staunch admirer of Thomas Paine, whose book in rejoinder to Burke's arraignment of the French Revolution had then been published for some time and had gone everywhere. In christening his vessel after the title of Paine's volume, the man of Dundee was something like his contemporary shipowner, Stephen Girard of Philadelphia, whose sympathies, alike with his native land and its liberal philosophers, he evinced by naming his ships after Voltaire, Diderot, and so forth.[12]

28   °But now, when the boat swept under the merchant-man's stern, and officer and oarsmen were noting—some bitterly and others with a grin—the name emblazoned there; just then it was that

29   °the new recruit jumped up from the bow where the coxswain had directed him to sit, and waving his hat to his silent shipmates sorrowfully looking over at him from the taffrail, bade the lads a genial good-bye. Then, making a salutation as to the ship herself, "And good-bye to you too, old *Rights-of-Man*."

"Down, Sir!" roared the Lieutenant, instantly assuming all the rigor of his rank, though with difficulty repressing a smile.

30   °To be sure, Billy's action was a terrible breach of naval decorum. But in that decorum he had never been instructed; in consideration of which the Lieutenant would hardly have been so energetic in reproof but for the concluding farewell to the ship. This he rather took as meant to convey a covert sally on the new

[12] The ships' names are signs for the problems raised by the narrative. Burke's *Reflections on the Revolution in France* (1790) was the most cogently argued conservative statement championing the necessity for governmental order. Paine's *Rights of Man* (1791), a compelling reply to the *Reflections*, was outlawed in England, but clandestinely outsold the *Reflections* by a considerable margin, capturing the revolutionary spirit of the times. The books represent opposing views of the possibilities of human nature, human society and its institutions, and human history—the essential oppositions of conservatism and radicalism. In general, in *Billy Budd*, with many modifications and exceptions, with anger and depression, Melville is making a tortured choice for conservatism. Stephen Girard (1750–1831), of radical persuasion, was born in Bordeaux, France, but settled in Philadelphia in 1769. He bought out the Bank of the United States, and his immense fortune was the major source of American finances during the War of 1812. Fiercely devoted to the principles of the Enlightenment, he applauded the teachings of the *philosophes* and was bitterly opposed to the British monarchy.

A British seventy-four of the late eighteenth and early nineteenth centuries.

recruit's part, a sly slur at impressment in general, and that of himself in especial. And yet, more likely, if satire it was in effect, it was hardly so by intention, for Billy, though happily endowed with the gayety of high health, youth, and a free heart, was yet by no means of a satirical turn. The will to it and the sinister dexterity were alike wanting. To deal in double meanings and insinuations of any sort was quite foreign to his nature.

31   °As to his enforced enlistment, that he seemed to take pretty much as he was wont to take any vicissitude of weather. Like the animals, though no philosopher, he was, without knowing it, practically a fatalist. And, it may be, that he rather liked this adventurous turn in his affairs, which promised an opening into novel scenes and martial excitements.

Aboard the *Bellipotent* our merchant-sailor was forthwith rated as an able-seaman and assigned to the starboard watch of the fore-
32   top.[13] °He was soon at home in the service, not at all disliked for his unpretentious good looks and a sort of genial happy-go-lucky air. No merrier man in his mess: in marked contrast to certain other individuals included like himself among the impressed portion of the ship's company; for these when not actively employed were sometimes, and more particularly in the last dog-watch when the drawing near of twilight induced revery, apt to fall into a saddish mood which in some partook of sullenness. But they were not so young as our foretopman, and no few of them
33   must °have known a hearth of some sort; others may have had wives and children left, too probably, in uncertain circumstances, and hardly any but must have had acknowledged kith and kin, while for Billy, as will shortly be seen, his entire family was practically invested in himself.

[13] Able seaman is the highest rating given a sailor. In his other fiction, Melville mentions the topmen as the best of the sailors, both in proficiency and personality, cheerfully performing their dangerous and acrobatic work in a light, clear, airy station high above the troubles of the ship-world below. As a foretopman, Billy is in a station that becomes a physical sign of his general opposition to Claggart, whose world is in the dark, closed air far below decks, in the thick of the intrigues of the ship.

"A group of bronzed mariners, man-of-war's men or merchant sailors" of the period.

[2]

34 °THOUGH OUR NEW-MADE foretopman was well received in the top and on the gun-decks, hardly here was he that cynosure he had previously been among those minor ship's companies of the merchant marine, with which companies only had he hitherto consorted.

He was young; and despite his all but fully developed frame, in aspect looked even younger than he really was, owing to a lingering adolescent expression in the as yet smooth face, all but
35 feminine in purity of natural complexion, °but where, thanks to his seagoing, the lily was quite suppressed and the rose had some ado visibly to flush through the tan.

To one essentially such a novice in the complexities of factitious life, the abrupt transition from his former and simpler sphere to the ampler and more knowing world of a great warship; this might well have abashed him had there been any conceit or vanity in his composition. Among her miscellaneous multitude, the *Belli-*
36 *potent* mustered °several individuals who, however inferior in grade, were of no common natural stamp, sailors more signally susceptive of that air which continuous martial discipline and repeated presence in battle can in some degree impart even to the average man. As the *handsome sailor*, Billy Budd's position aboard the seventy-four was something analogous to that of a rustic beauty transplanted from the provinces and brought into competition with the highborn dames of the court. °But this change
37 of circumstances he scarce noted. As little did he observe that something about him provoked an ambiguous smile in one or two harder faces among the blue-jackets. Nor less unaware was he of the peculiar favorable effect his person and demeanor had upon

14

the more intelligent gentlemen of the quarter-deck.[1] Nor could this well have been otherwise. °Cast in a mould peculiar to the finest physical examples of those Englishmen in whom the Saxon strain would seem not at all to partake of any Norman or other admixture, he showed in face that humane look of reposeful good nature which the Greek sculptor in some instances gave to his heroic strong man, Hercules. But this again was subtly modified by another and pervasive quality. The ear, small and shapely, the arch of the foot, the curve in mouth and nostril, even the indurated hand dyed to the orange-tawny of the toucan's bill, a hand telling alike of the halyards °and tar-bucket,[2] but, above all, something in the mobile expression, and every chance attitude and

38

39

---

[1] The quarterdeck was the exclusive preserve of the officers, and extended aft from the mainmast to the stern. It is not actually a physically distinct deck, but is an area of the maindeck, and, following the sea custom which allows that part of the deck to the men whose quarters or stations are above or below (see leaves 153 and 159), is allotted to the officers because their quarters are aft. The quarterdeck was reserved for ceremonial functions; the small deck raised above the quarterdeck at the stern, from which the captain surveyed the ship or addressed the crew when all hands were assembled, is the poop deck. Generally the inhabitants of the quarterdeck were of higher birth and station and education than the crew, and Melville's assumption is that such people would be more likely than the crew to appreciate Billy's unusual qualities.

[2] Seamen were often occupied in tarring the ship's ropes and canvas, and their hands became almost indelibly stained in the process. Here Melville reinforces the notion, already introduced in the fact of Billy's impressment, that there is no safe home or snug harbor one ever reaches, no unstained pink and white condition of innocence uncolored by contact with the necessities of the world. In emphasizing Billy's "Saxon" strain, and later the angelic qualities of his "Angle's" complexion and features (leaves 308–309), Melville uses a common convention of nineteenth-century fiction that appears in many of his other works. The blue-eyed blond-haired fair character was allied with truth, purity, nobility, and goodness; the dark character was allied with mystery, evil, passion, and, often, a high and brooding intellect. A conflict between the good heart and the driving mind is constant in this convention, and although Melville made it clear that he prefers the generous heart, it is dangerous to subject Melville's characters to the simple one-to-one equation that the convention became in the hands of lesser and formulaic writers. Melville sometimes inverts and always complicates the convention. It is noteworthy that here Melville points out that Billy's "indurated hand" is tar-dyed even at the point of emphasizing his "Saxon" qualities.

movement, something suggestive of a mother eminently favored by Love and the Graces; all this strangely indicated a lineage in direct contradiction to his lot. The mysteriousness here, became less mysterious through a matter of fact elicited when Billy, at the capstan, was being formally mustered into the service. Asked by the officer, a small, brisk little gentleman as it chanced, among other questions, his place of birth, he replied, "Please, Sir, I don't know."

"Don't know where you were born?—Who was your father?"

40   °"God knows, Sir."

Struck by the straightforward simplicity of these replies, the officer next asked, "Do you know anything about your beginning?"

"No, Sir. But I have heard that I was found in a pretty silk-lined basket hanging one morning from the knocker of a good man's door in Bristol."

41   °"*Found*, say you? Well," throwing back his head and looking up and down the new recruit; "well, it turns out to have been a pretty good find. Hope they'll find some more like you, my man; the fleet sadly needs them."

Yes, Billy Budd was a foundling, a presumable by-blow, and, evidently, no ignoble one. Noble descent was as evident in him as in a blood horse.

For the rest, with little or no sharpness of faculty or any trace
42   of the wisdom of the serpent, nor yet °quite a dove, he possessed that kind and degree of intelligence going along with the unconventional rectitude of a sound human creature, one to whom not yet has been proffered the questionable apple of knowledge. He was illiterate; he could not read, but he could sing, and like the illiterate nightingale was sometimes the composer of his own song.

Of self-consciousness he seemed to have little or none, or about as much as we may reasonably impute to a dog of Saint Bernard's breed.

43   °Habitually living with the elements and knowing little more of the land than as a beach, or, rather, that portion of the terraqueous globe providentially set apart for dance-houses, doxies,

and tapsters, in short what sailors call a "fiddlers'-green," his simple nature remained unsophisticated by those moral obliquities which are not in every case incompatible with that manufacturable thing known as respectability.[3] But are sailors, frequenters of "fiddlers'-greens," without vices? No; but less often than with landsmen do their vices, so called, partake of crookedness of heart, seeming °less to proceed from viciousness than exuberance   44 of vitality after long constraint; frank manifestations in accordance with natural law. By his original constitution aided by the cooperating influences of his lot, Billy in many respects was little more than a sort of upright barbarian, much such perhaps as Adam presumably might have been ere the urbane Serpent wriggled himself into his company.

And here be it submitted that apparently going to corroborate the doctrine of man's fall, a doctrine now popularly ignored,[4] it is observable that where certain virtues pristine and unadulterate °peculiarly characterize anybody in the external uniform of civili-   45 zation, they will upon scrutiny seem not to be derived from custom or convention, but rather to be out of keeping with these, as if indeed exceptionally transmitted from a period prior to Cain's city and citified man.[5] The character marked by such qualities

---

[3] The origin of the term "fiddler's green" is obscure, but its meaning is clear. A center for cheap dancehalls, doxies (whores), and taverns, the fiddler's green is the red-light district of the waterfront.

[4] Though very far from the Dutch Reform orthodoxy of his mother's family, Melville retained always a sense of the Fall as a metaphor for the inescapable reality of the human condition. This sense is at the heart of what attracted him to Hawthorne's fiction as well as of the streak of conservatism that was always in his nature.

[5] As man fell from grace into the world east of Eden, so he fell from Edenic (pastoral) innocence into the murderous actuality of history, typified by the city in the Romantic conventions of the late eighteenth and the nineteenth centuries. The "city" as so used—and the usage extends, through the *Symbolistes*, into modern literature of the twentieth century— is the exact opposite of the City on the Hill, which was the Renaissance ideal of the City of God to be approximated as closely as possible in the true "plantation religious" of the true believer. After his act of murder, "Cain knew his wife and she conceived, and bare Enoch: and he builded a city, and called the name of the city after the name of his son, Enoch" (Gen.

has to an unvitiated taste an untampered-with flavor like that of berries, while the man thoroughly civilized, even in a fair specimen of the breed, has to the same moral palate a questionable smack as of a compounded wine. To any stray inheritor of these primitive qualities found, like Caspar Hauser,[6] wandering dazed in any Christian capital of our time, °the good-natured poet's famous invocation, near two thousand years ago, of the good rustic out of his latitude in the Rome of the Cesars, still appropriately holds:—

46

> "Honest and poor, faithful in word and thought,
> What hath thee, Fabian, to the city brought?"[7]

Though our Handsome Sailor had as much of masculine beauty as one can expect anywhere to see; nevertheless, like the beautiful

---

4:17). Melville portrays Billy as the opposite of "citified man" (as Claggart is its representative) by insisting on his primitive, barbarian, animal qualities of the prelapsarian Adam. However, as those readers who are familiar with Melville's first book, *Typee* (1846), will be aware, the "Edenic" innocence of the primitive, natural, animal state is by no means an untainted blessing or even man's highest state of being, but has its own various kinds of "tar" stains. It is interesting that one sign of the shortcomings of "Eden" in *Typee* is the failure of language—of almost any kind of communication or mind—and that in Melville's last book, forty-five years later, the essentially mindless young bud of a baby of an "upright barbarian," or "noble blood horse," or "dog of Saint Bernard's breed," or unselfconscious "young Adam before the Fall" has his stutter. The Edenic state as a metaphor for the human condition always turns out to be a beautiful but imperfect and inoperative dream in Melville's work, and always the Fall as metaphor turns out to be the inescapable reality within which men must actually live and with which they must wrestle. This idea is part of the burden of Captain Vere's address to the drumhead court.

6 Kasper Hauser was a mysterious German foundling whose case captured the Romantic imagination. Probably born in 1812, he was found wandering the streets of Nürnberg in 1826. He told a story of having been brought up in solitary confinement. He was thought to be of noble birth and became one of the most celebrated and controversial of the "feral" children, brought up in the wild without the taint of "citified man," and so dear to the "noble savage" beliefs of Romantic primitivism and educational theory. His short life ended in 1833.

7 Martial, *Epigrams*.

woman in one of Hawthorne's minor tales,[8] there was just one thing amiss in him. No visible blemish indeed, as with the lady; no, but an occasional liability to a vocal defect. Though in the hour °of elemental uproar or peril he was everything that a sailor should be, yet under sudden provocation of strong heart-feeling, his voice otherwise singularly musical, as if expressive of the harmony within, was apt to develop an organic hesitancy, in fact more or less of a stutter or even worse. °In this particular Billy was a striking instance that the arch interferer, the envious marplot of Eden, still has more or less to do with every human consignment to this planet of earth. In every case, one way or another he is sure to slip in his little card, as much as to remind us—I too have a hand here.

The avowal of such an imperfection in the Handsome Sailor should be evidence not alone that he is not presented as a conventional hero, but also that the story in which he is the main figure is no romance.

47

48

---

8 "The Birthmark" is a perfect analogy for Melville to make here. In Hawthorne's tale, Georgiana's cheek is marred by a tiny hand, indicating Nature's touch of mortal limitation upon what would otherwise be the perfect beauty of her face—as though to remind the beholder of the mortality and shortcomings attendant upon the natural condition short of Edenic grace, as though "the envious marplot of Eden" slipped in "his little card, as much as to remind us—I too have a hand here."

National Maritime Museum, London

Portsmouth Point in 1801, by T. Rowlandson. The scene is a representation of "what sailors called a 'fiddlers'-green.'"

[3]

°AT THE TIME of Billy Budd's arbitrary enlistment into the   49
Bellipotent that ship was on her way to join the Mediterranean
fleet. No long time elapsed before the junction was effected. As
one of that fleet the seventy-four participated in its movements,
though at times on account of her superior sailing qualities, in
the absence of frigates, dispatched on separate duty as a scout and
at times on less temporary service. But with all this the story has
little concernment, restricted as it is to the inner life of one particular ship and the career of an individual sailor.

°It was the summer of 1797. In the April of that year had oc-   50
curred the commotion at Spithead followed in May by a second
and yet more serious outbreak in the fleet at the Nore.[1] The latter
is known, and without exaggeration in the epithet, as the Great
Mutiny. It was indeed °a demonstration more menacing to En-   51
gland than the contemporary manifestoes and conquering and

---

[1] Beginning on April 15, 1797, the British sailors at Spithead, in the
English Channel, struck for higher pay. They won increased salaries, but
there remained deep and bitter feelings about the conditions—often unbe-
lievable to the modern reader—that remained for the common sailor in
the navy. On May 20 at the Nore, in the mouth of the Thames, the mutiny
reached its most serious proportions. The demands of the sailors at this
point became truly revolutionary, threatening the very structure of established authority and privilege. "Labor relations" had become radical action.
Depending upon one's political perspectives, the Mutiny at the Nore may
be seen either as a threat to civilization or as a blow for really new free-
doms. Melville obviously tends toward a conservative reading of the event.
What is important to an understanding of the narrative is the fact that
during the mid- and late summer of 1797, when the story takes place, there
were small "by-product" mutinies in the Mediterranean fleet, the fleet to
which the *Bellipotent* belongs. In historic fact there was great justification
for Captain Vere's fears of mutiny at any sign of vacillation or weakness
on the part of the officers, and Melville's use of the historical facts is another indication of his justification of Captain Vere.

proselyting armies of the French Directory.[2] To the British Empire the Nore Mutiny was what a strike in the fire-brigade would be to London threatened by general arson. In a crisis when the kingdom might well have anticipated the famous signal that some years later published along the naval line of battle what it was that upon occasion England expected of Englishmen;[3] *that* was 52 the time °when at the mast-heads of the three-deckers and seventy-fours moored in her own roadstead—a fleet, the right arm of a Power then all but the sole free conservative one of the Old World—the blue-jackets, to be numbered by thousands, ran up with huzzas the British colors with the union and cross wiped out; by that cancellation transmuting the flag of founded law and freedom defined, into the enemy's red meteor of unbridled and unbounded revolt. Reasonable discontent growing out of practical 53 grievances in the fleet had been ignited °into irrational combustion, as by live cinders blown across the Channel from France in flames.

The event converted into irony for a time those spirited strains of Dibdin—as a song-writer no mean auxiliary to the English government at that European conjuncture—strains celebrating, among other things, the patriotic devotion of the British tar:

"And as for my life, 'tis the King's!"[4]

[2] The constitution of the year III (following the French re-dating of the calendar from the year of the Revolution) went into effect in August 1795. The constitution provided for the branches of government, among which were an executive, called the Directory, made up of five members with staggered terms, one elected annually. After the suppression of the royalist revolution in Paris (the 13th Vendémiaire, October 5, 1795), Napoleon dissolved the Convention that gave the Republic the constitution of the year III, and from October 16 of 1795 until November 9–10, 1799 (the revolution of the 18th and 19th Brumaire, when Napoleon abolished the Directory), the government of France was known as the Directory.

[3] As the Battle of Trafalgar began, the signal flags of Nelson's flagship read, "England expects every man to do his duty." The battle took place off Cádiz, in the same locale as the events of *Billy Budd*, "some years later," on October 21, 1805.

[4] The patriotic sea songs of Charles Dibdin (1745–1814), a playwright, songwriter, and government pensioner, were filled with sentiments of unquestioning loyalty to authority, of carefree acceptance of one's lot, and of

Such an episode in the Island's grand naval story her naval
historians naturally abridge; one of them (William James) can-
didly acknowledging that fain would he pass it over did not "impartiality forbid fastidiousness." °And yet his mention is less a   54
narration than a reference, having to do hardly at all with details.
Nor are these readily to be found in the libraries. Like some other
events in every age befalling states everywhere, including America, the Great Mutiny was of such character that national pride
along with views of policy would fain shade it off into the historical
background. Such events can not be ignored, but there is a con-
siderate way of historically treating them. If a well-constituted
individual refrains from blazoning aught amiss or calamitous in
his family, a nation in the like circumstance may without reproach be equally discreet.[5]

°Though after parleyings between Government and the ring-   55
leaders, and concessions by the former as to some glaring abuses,
the first uprising—that at Spithead—with difficulty was put
down, or matters for the time pacified; yet at the Nore the unforeseen renewal of insurrection on a yet larger scale, °and em-   56
phasized in the conferences that ensued by demands deemed by
the authorities not only inadmissible but aggressively insolent, indicated—if the Red Flag did not sufficiently do so—what was the
spirit animating the men. Final suppression, however, there was;
but only made possible perhaps by the unswerving loyalty of the

---

submissive devotion to service. Again, Melville's approving attitude toward
the songs is indicative of the perspective from which he views the uses of
history: the sentiments of the songs were the exact opposite of those expressed at Spithead and the Nore.

[5] Melville had planned to present an instance of the kind of shameful
event that Americans kept hidden in their own military history, the Union
blockade of medical supplies for the South. Melville's note, circled, at the
bottom of leaf 54 reads: ✓

> Do we publish
> no medicines pass the lines
> &c

It is difficult to know whether Melville abandoned the idea but left the
notation on the page, or whether he planned an addition on this subject.
Presumably he would have included it had he lived to complete a final copy.

marine corps and a voluntary resumption of loyalty among influential sections of the crews.

    To some extent the Nore Mutiny may be regarded as analogous
57 to the °distempering irruption of contagious fever in a frame con-
stitutionally sound, and which anon throws it off.

    At all events, of these thousands of mutineers were some of
the tars who not so very long afterwards—whether wholly
prompted thereto by patriotism, or pugnacious instinct, or by
both—helped to win a coronet for Nelson at the Nile, and the
naval crown of crowns for him at Trafalgar.[6] To the mutineers,
those battles, and especially Trafalgar, were a plenary absolution
and a grand one. For all that goes to make up scenic naval display
and heroic magnificence in arms, those battles, especially Trafalgar, stand unmatched in human annals.

    [6] Nelson was crowned Baron Nelson of the Nile and given a pension of
$10,000 after his great victory over the French in the Bay of Aboukir on
August 1, 1798. His greatest victory, the "crown of crowns" won at Trafalgar on October 21, 1805, and historically much, much greater than a
baronial coronet, ended with his own death in battle. The edition of Robert
Southey's *Life of Nelson,* from which Melville drew much of his material
for *Billy Budd,* was published in New York in 1855.

[4]

°*Concerning "The greatest sailor since our world began."* [1]

IN THIS MATTER of writing, resolve as one may to keep to the main road, some by-paths have an enticement not readily to be withstood. I am going to err into such a by-path. If the reader will keep me company I shall be glad. At the least we can promise ourselves that pleasure which is wickedly said to be in sinning, for a literary sin the divergence will be.

Very likely it is no new remark that the inventions of our time have at last brought °about a change in sea-warfare in degree corresponding to the revolution in all warfare effected by the original introduction from China into Europe of gunpowder.[2] The first European fire-arm, a clumsy contrivance, was, as is well known, scouted by no few of the knights as a base implement,

---

[1] From "Ode on the Death of the Duke of Wellington," by Tennyson. See the statement for leaf 58 in the list of "Textural Changes," p. 165.

[2] Melville's sense of the change in the nature of naval warfare was historically accurate. For approximately three hundred years, from the mid-sixteenth to the mid-nineteenth century, the essential nature of warships and tactics remained unchanged. In the nineteenth century, the introduction of explosive shells, steam power, and ironclad ships changed navies and tactics almost entirely. In this "by-path" chapter, Melville recalls the earlier days of sail in order to emphasize the conditions which made individual courage more noticeable and more crucial than in the more impersonal modern navy. A good man or a bad man would have had much greater effect upon the ship as a whole, and the commander's bravery and determination were central in the close-up actualities and exigencies of navy life and battle. Furthermore, it was not unlikely that in the old navy a common seaman would be known to the ship's commander because individual qualities were more highly visible.

good enough peradventure for weavers too craven to stand up
crossing steel with steel in frank fight. But as ashore knightly
valor, though shorn of its blazonry, did not cease with the
60 knights, neither on the seas, °though nowadays in encounters
there a certain kind of displayed gallantry be fallen out of date
as hardly applicable under changed circumstances, did the nobler
qualities of such naval magnates as Don John of Austria, Doria,
Van Tromp, Jean Bart, the long line of British Admirals, and the
American Decaturs of 1812 become obsolete with their wooden
walls.[3]

61   °Nevertheless, to anybody who can hold the Present at its
worth without being inappreciative of the Past, it may be forgiven, if to such an one the solitary old hulk at Portsmouth,
Nelson's *Victory*, seems to float there, not alone as the decaying
monument of a fame incorruptible, but also as a poetic reproach,
softened by its picturesqueness, to the *Monitors* and yet mightier
hulls of the European ironclads. And this not altogether because
such craft are unsightly, unavoidably lacking the symmetry and
grand lines of the old battle-ships, but equally for other reasons.

[3] Don John of Austria (1547–1578), as commander of the Holy League,
ended the day of oar-power for warships at the Battle of Lepanto (1571).
Andrea Doria (1468–1560) was a Genoese naval mercenary who liberated
Genoa from the French, defeated the Turks in Greece, suppressed the
Barbary pirates, and organized the Genoese fleet. Maarten Harpertzoon
Tromp (1597–1653) led the Dutch fleets to victory over Spain in 1639. In
the wars with England he won control of the English Channel, but was
killed in battle during a Channel action. Jean Bart (1650–1702) broke the
blockade of Dunkerque maintained by the combined British and Dutch
fleets. He helped lead the French to victory over those fleets in 1693, his
ship, the *Glorieux*, alone accounting for six of the enemy. Stephen Decatur
(1752–1808) gained fame as a successful contender with British ships during
the Revolutionary War. His more famous son, Stephen (1779–1820), became known for his intense courage during terrible hand-to-hand fighting
in the Tripolitanian War, which he helped to win. He helped build and
later commanded the *United States*, mentioned in the dedication to *Billy
Budd*, during the capture of the British ship, *Macedonian* (see note 2, leaf 1,
above). He won further fame in the War of 1812 for heroic action against the
British, and was, of course, the only one of "the American Decaturs" Melville
referred to who saw action in that war. Decatur subdued the Algerine pirates,
and is famous for his saying, which is an American reflection of the songs of
Dibdin (see note 4, leaf 53, above): "My country—may she ever be right,
but, right or wrong, my country."

°There are some, perhaps, who while not altogether inacces-   62
sible to that poetic reproach just alluded to, may yet on behalf of
the new order, be disposed to parry it; and this to the extent of
iconoclasm, if need be. For example, prompted by the sight of the
star inserted in the *Victory*'s quarter-deck designating the spot
where the Great Sailor fell, these martial utilitarians may suggest
considerations implying that Nelson's ornate publication of his
person in battle was not only unnecessary, but not military, nay,
savored of foolhardiness and vanity. °They may add, too, that at   63
Trafalgar it was in effect nothing less than a challenge to death;
and death came; and that but for his bravado the victorious Admiral might possibly have survived the battle, and so, instead of
having his sagacious °dying injunctions overruled by his immedi-   64
ate successor in command, he himself when the contest was
decided might have brought his shattered fleet to anchor, a proceeding which might have averted the deplorable loss of life by
shipwreck in the elemental tempest that followed the martial one.

Well, should we set aside the more than disputable point
whether for various reasons it was possible to anchor the fleet,
then plausibly enough the Benthamites of war may urge the
above. °But the *might-have-been* is but boggy ground to build   65
on. And, certainly, in foresight as to the larger issue of an encounter, and anxious preparations for it—buoying the deadly
way and mapping it out, as at Copenhagen[4]—few commanders
have been so painstakingly circumspect as this same reckless de-
clarer of his person in fight.

Personal prudence even when dictated by quite other than
selfish considerations surely is no special virtue in a military man;
while an excessive love of glory, impassioning a less burning
impulse, the honest sense of duty, is the first. If the name *Wellington* is not so much of a trumpet to the blood as the simpler °name   66
Nelson, the reason for this may perhaps be inferred from the

[4] The Danes had removed all the markers from the intricate and dangerous Copenhagen waters. Through unremitting effort, Nelson took new
soundings and laid new buoys, and then carefully and successfully led his
fleet into the channel. Nelson annihilated the Danish fleet and shore
batteries in the Battle of Copenhagen, April 2, 1801.

above. Alfred in his funeral ode on the victor of Waterloo ven-
tures not to call him the greatest soldier of all time, though in
the same ode he invokes Nelson as "the greatest sailor since our
world began."

At Trafalgar Nelson on the brink of opening the fight sat
down and wrote his last brief will and testament. If under the
presentiment of the most magnificent of all victories to be
crowned by his own glorious death, a sort of priestly motive led
67 him to dress his °person in the jewelled vouchers of his own
shining deeds; if thus to have adorned himself for the altar and
the sacrifice were indeed vainglory, then affectation and fustian
is each more heroic line in the great epics and dramas, since in
such lines the poet but embodies in verse those exaltations of
sentiment that a nature like Nelson, the opportunity being given,
vitalizes into acts.

This famous portrait of Horatio Nelson by Lemuel Abbott was painted in 1797, the year in which *Billy Budd* is set. Nelson, then Rear Admiral of the blue, was recovering from the loss of his right arm, suffered at the battle of Santa Cruz. From his neck hangs a medal awarded for service at the battle of Cape St. Vincent, February 14, 1797. On his left breast he wears the star of the Order of the Bath, awarded by George III for the action at Santa Cruz.

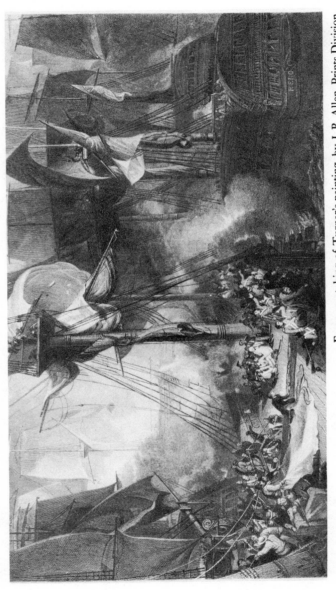

From an etching of Turner's painting by J. B. Allen. Prints Division,
The New York Public Library, Astor, Lenox and Tilden Foundations

The death of Nelson, by J. M. W. Turner. "Of these thousands of mutineers were some of the tars who . . . ;
helped to win a coronet for Nelson at the Nile, and the naval crown of crowns for him at Trafalgar."

[5]

°YES, THE OUTBREAK at the Nore was put down. But not   68
every grievance was redressed. If the contractors, for example,
were no longer permitted to ply some practices peculiar to their
tribe everywhere, such as providing shoddy cloth, rations not
sound, or false in the measure, not the less impressment, for one
thing, went on. By custom sanctioned for centuries, and judicially
maintained by a Lord Chancellor as late as Mansfield,[1] that mode
of manning the fleet, a mode now fallen into a sort of abeyance
but never formally renounced, it was not practicable to give up
in those years. °Its abrogation would have crippled the indispens-   69
able fleet, one wholly under canvas, no steam-power, its innumer-
able sails and thousands of cannon, everything in short, worked
by muscle alone; a fleet the more insatiate in demand for men,
because then multiplying its ships of all grades against con-
tingencies present and to come of the convulsed Continent.

°Discontent foreran the Two Mutinies, and more or less it   70
lurkingly survived them. Hence it was not unreasonable to apprehend some return of trouble sporadic or general. One instance
of such apprehensions: In the same year with this story, Nelson,
then Vice Admiral Sir Horatio,[2] being with the fleet off the
Spanish coast, was directed by the Admiral in command to shift

[1] William Murray, Earl of Mansfield (1705–1793), was England's chief
justice from 1756 to 1788. His official sanction of impressment was not historically distant from the time of *Billy Budd*'s events.

[2] Melville was in error here. Nelson was made Rear Admiral of the blue
early in 1797. He did not become Vice Admiral until January 1, 1801. It
is surprising that Melville made this mistake, for he followed his source,
Southey's *Life of Nelson*, so closely as to be plagiaristic in his language
when he explained Nelson's transfer from the *Captain* to the *Theseus*. See
H&S, note 70, pp. 151–152.

31

his pennant from the *Captain* to the *Theseus;* and for this reason:
71 that the latter ship having newly °arrived on the station from
home, where it had taken part in the Great Mutiny, danger was
72 apprehended from the temper of the men; and °it was thought
that an officer like Nelson was the one, not indeed to terrorize
the crew into base subjection, but to win them, by force of his
mere presence and heroic personality, back to an allegiance if not
as enthusiastic as his own, yet as true.

So it was that for a time, on more than one quarter-deck
anxiety did exist. At sea precautionary vigilance was strained
against relapse. At short notice an engagement might come on.
When it did, the lieutenants assigned to batteries felt it incumbent
on them, in some instances, to stand with drawn swords behind
the men working the guns.

[6]

°BUT ON BOARD the seventy-four in which Billy now swung   73
his hammock, very little in the manner of the men and nothing
obvious in the demeanor of the officers would have suggested to
an ordinary observer that the Great Mutiny was a recent event.
In their general bearing and conduct the commissioned officers of
a war-ship naturally take their tone from the commander, that is
if he have that ascendancy of character that ought to be his.

°Captain the Honorable Edward Fairfax Vere, to give his full   74
title, was a bachelor of forty or thereabouts, a sailor of distinction
even in a time prolific of renowned seamen. Though allied to the
higher nobility, his advancement had not been altogether owing
to influences connected with that circumstance. He had seen
much service, been in various engagements, always acquitting
himself as an officer mindful of the welfare of his men, but never
tolerating an infraction of discipline; thoroughly versed in the
science of his profession, and intrepid to the verge of temerity,
°though never injudiciously so. For his gallantry in the West   75
Indian waters as Flag-Lieutenant under Rodney in that Admiral's
crowning victory over De Grasse, he was made a Post-Captain.[1]

Ashore in the garb of a civilian, scarce anyone would have
taken him for a sailor, more especially that he never garnished
unprofessional talk with nautical terms, and grave in his bearing,
evinced little appreciation of mere humor. It was not out of keeping with these traits that °on a passage when nothing demanded   76

[1] Charles Anderson, in "The Genesis of *Billy Budd*," *American Literature*, XII (November 1940), 329–346, finds that in career and personality,
Sir William George Fairfax, a heroic participant in Baron Rodney's
victory over the French Admiral, De Grasse (Dominica, 1782), probably
provided Melville with a model for Captain the Honorable Edward Fairfax Vere.

his paramount action, he was the most undemonstrative of men. Any landsman observing this gentleman not conspicuous by his stature and wearing no pronounced insignia, emerging from his cabin to the open deck, and noting the silent deference of the officers retiring to leeward, might have taken him for the King's
77 °guest, a civilian aboard the King's-ship, some highly honorable discreet envoy on his way to an important post. But in fact this unobtrusiveness of demeanor may have proceeded from a certain unaffected modesty of manhood sometimes accompanying a resolute nature, a modesty evinced at all times not calling for pronounced action, and which shown in any rank of life suggests a
78 virtue aristocratic in kind. °As with some others engaged in various departments of the world's more heroic activities, Captain Vere though practical enough upon occasion would at times betray a certain dreaminess of mood. Standing alone on the weatherside of the quarter-deck, one hand holding by the rigging, he would absently gaze off at the blank sea. At the presentation to
79 him °then of some minor matter interrupting the current of his thoughts he would show more or less irascibility; but instantly he would control it.

In the navy he was popularly known by the appellation—Starry Vere. How such a designation happened to fall upon one who, whatever his sterling qualities, was without any brilliant ones was in this wise: A favorite kinsman, Lord Denton, a free-hearted fellow, had been the first to meet and congratulate him upon his return to England from his West Indian cruise; and but the day previous turning over a copy of Andrew Marvell's poems had lighted, not for the first time however, upon the lines entitled
80 *Appleton House*, the name of one of the seats of their °common ancestor, a hero in the German wars of the seventeenth century, in which poem occur the lines,

> "This 'tis to have been from the first
> In a domestic heaven nursed,
> Under the discipline severe
> Of Fairfax and the starry Vere."[2]

---

[2] The "starry Vere" referred to by Captain Vere's cousin is not a male ancestor as the context seems to imply, but is Anne Vere, who married Lord Fairfax in 1637 and became mistress of Appleton House.

And so, upon embracing his cousin fresh from Rodney's great victory wherein he had played so gallant a part, brimming over with just family pride in the sailor of their house, he exuberantly exclaimed, "Give ye joy, Ed; give ye joy, my starry Vere!" This got currency, and the novel prefix serving in familiar parlance readily to distinguish the *Bellipotent*'s Captain from another Vere his senior, a distant relative, an officer of like rank in the navy, it remained permanently attached to the surname.

J. A. Atkinson, *circ.* 1800
National Maritime Museum, London
A British naval captain of the late eighteenth century.

[7]

81 °IN VIEW of the part that the Commander of the *Bellipotent* plays in scenes shortly to follow, it may be well to fill out that sketch of him outlined in the previous chapter.

Aside from his qualities as a sea-officer Captain Vere was an exceptional character. Unlike no few of England's renowned sailors, long and arduous service with signal devotion to it had not resulted in absorbing and *salting* the entire man. He had a
82 marked leaning °toward everything intellectual. He loved books, never going to sea without a newly replenished library, compact but of the best. The isolated leisure, in some cases so wearisome, falling at intervals to commanders even during a war-cruise, never was tedious to Captain Vere. With nothing of that literary taste which less heeds the thing conveyed than the vehicle, his bias was towards those books to which every serious mind of superior order occupying any active post of authority in the world, naturally inclines: books treating of actual men and events no
83 matter of what era—history, biography and °unconventional writers like Montaigne, who, free from cant and convention, honestly and in the spirit of common sense philosophize upon realities.

In this line of reading he found confirmation of his own more reserved thoughts—confirmation which he had vainly sought in social converse, so that as touching most fundamental topics, there had got to be established in him some positive convictions, which he forefelt would abide in him essentially unmodified so long as his intelligent part remained unimpaired. In view of the troubled period in which his lot was cast this was well for him.
84 His settled convictions were as a dyke against °those invading waters of novel opinion, social, political and otherwise, which carried away as in a torrent no few minds in those days, minds by

36

nature not inferior to his own. While other members of that aristocracy to which by birth he belonged were incensed at the
innovators mainly because their theories were inimical to the
privileged classes, Captain Vere disinterestedly opposed them not
alone because they seemed to him insusceptible of embodiment
in lasting institutions, but at war with the peace of the world and
the true welfare of mankind.

°With minds less stored than his and less earnest, some officers   85
of his rank, with whom at times he would necessarily consort,
found him lacking in the companionable quality, a dry and book-
ish gentleman, as they deemed. Upon any chance withdrawal
from their company one would be °apt to say to another, some-   86
thing like this: "Vere is a noble fellow, Starry Vere. Spite the
gazettes, Sir Horatio," meaning him who became Lord Nelson, "is
at bottom scarce a better seaman or fighter. But between you and
me now, don't you think there is a queer streak of the pedantic
running through him? Yes, like the King's yarn in a coil of navy-
rope?"

Some apparent ground there was for this sort of confidential
criticism; since not only did the Captain's discourse never fall into
the jocosely familiar, but in illustrating of any point touching
the stirring personages °and events of the time he would be   87
apt to cite some historic character or incident of antiquity with
the same easy air that he would cite from the moderns.[1] He

[1] Melville's revisions here are instructive in an interpretation of Vere's
role and character. Originally Melville had written that Vere would be as
apt to cite from the ancients "as freely . . . ," cancelled that and wrote,
"quite as freely . . . ," and cancelled that. In a later revision he wrote that
Vere would cite from antiquity "with the same easy air that he would
cite from the moderns." He cancelled the words, "with the same easy,"
leaving an incoherent clause that read, "he would be as apt to cite from
some historic character or incident of antiquity air that he would cite from
the moderns." Hayford and Sealts simply rewrite the clause for Melville
thus: "he would be as apt to cite some historic character or incident of
antiquity as he would be to cite from the moderns." Perhaps Melville
intended the sentence to be free of any phrase qualifying Vere's citation
of the ancients, but one can never be sure: the fact that he cancelled only
the qualification after wrestling with it and leaving an incoherent sentence
might indicate that he intended to return with a modifier that would satisfy
him. This edition restores the last coherent version Melville had written

seemed unmindful of the circumstance that to his bluff company
such remote allusions, however pertinent they might really be,
were altogether alien to men whose reading was mainly confined
to the journals. But considerateness in such matters is not easy to
natures constituted like Captain Vere's. Their honesty prescribes
to them directness, sometimes far-reaching like that of a migratory
fowl that in its flight never heeds when it crosses a frontier.

---

before the revision created incoherence. (In the patch on which the
sentence is written in the manuscript, "with the same easy air" is the
original phrase. Thus restoring the last coherent version is in effect the
same as restoring the original, a practice followed in *H&S* for heavily revised passages. It is surprising that in this case Hayford and Sealts did not
follow their own principle.) The revisions are instructive because they show
that Melville did not want implications of "freeness" or "easiness" attached
to Vere's conversation. He did want Vere's strong historical knowledge
and his seriousness to remain as a characteristic of the man. Obviously he
wanted to indicate that Vere was an educated man who, with the freedom and ease of his sure knowledge and without pretension, could quote
from ancient authorities and from historical precedent and point out the
continuity of past and present. However, Melville evidently wanted a
word other than "free" or "easy" with which to convey Vere's air, for
"free" and "easy" work against the impression of thoughtfulness and careful intelligence with which Melville characterizes Vere. The restoration of
"easy" in this edition is based on a preference to use Melville's last cancellations rather than to invent new prose for Melville; furthermore, in the
context of the passage, Vere's sobriety is not marred by the use of "easy"
in the characterization. Regardless of editorial choice, however, the incomplete revisions suggest that as Melville reworked the manuscript he was
increasingly aware of presenting Vere as a sympathetic and reliable character.

National Maritime Museum, London

Lord George Graham, by William Hogarth. Unlike the unostentatious and "disinterested" Captain Vere, this typical British naval captain of the eighteenth century, pictured with his purser, chaplain, cook, black servant, and pets, represents the aristocracy to which almost all high-ranking naval officers belonged and which hated the French revolutionaries because "their theories were inimical to the privileged classes."

[8]

88 °THE LIEUTENANTS and other commissioned gentlemen forming Captain Vere's staff it is not necessary here to particularize, nor needs it to make any mention of any of the warrant-officers. But among the petty-officers was one who, having much to do with the story, may as well be forthwith introduced. His portrait I essay, but shall never hit it. This was John Claggart, the Master-at-arms. But that sea-title may to landsmen seem some-
89 what equivocal. Originally doubtless °that petty-officer's function was the instruction of the men in the use of arms, sword or cutlas. But very long ago, owing to the advance in gunnery making hand-to-hand encounters less frequent and giving to nitre and sulphur the preeminence over steel, that function ceased; the Master-at-arms of a great war-ship becoming a sort of Chief of Police, charged among other matters with the duty of preserving order on the populous lower gun-decks.
90   Claggart was a man about five and thirty, °somewhat spare and tall, yet of no ill figure upon the whole. His hand was too small and shapely to have been accustomed to hard toil. The face was a notable one; the features all except the chin cleanly cut as those on a Greek medallion; yet the chin, beardless as Tecumseh's,[1] had something of strange protuberant broadness in its make

---

[1] Tecumseh (1768–1813), a Shawnee chief, established Tippecanoe Village as a model for the Indian tribes he attempted to unite against the whites. He was defeated by William Henry Harrison, whose campaign cry in his contest for the Presidency was "Tippecanoe and Tyler [his running mate] too." Melville's reference here reflects Tecumseh's part in turning against the United States in the War of 1812 and allying himself with the British. In his use of Tecumseh in characterizing Claggart, Melville had the idea of treason in mind, although an objective historian would find it difficult to accuse Tecumseh of treason against what the Shawnee considered to be *his* own nation. In this sense Melville's use of Tecumseh be-

40

that recalled the prints of the Rev. Dr. Titus Oates, the historic deponent with the clerical drawl in the time of Charles II and the fraud of the alleged Popish Plot.[2] It served Claggart in his office that his eye could cast a tutoring glance. His brow was of the sort phrenologically associated with more than average intellect; silken jet curls partly °clustering over it, making a foil to the pallor below, a pallor tinged with a faint shade of amber akin to   91

---

comes most illuminating, for although it was part of the general image of the chieftain in contemporary popular culture, Melville was not the kind of man to acquiesce to such images in the face of the cultural relativism he had learned independently as a young man. But the fact that he uses Tecumseh as a sign of treason indicates the extent to which he abandoned his earlier rebellious attitudes in favor of conservatism. The narrative is filled with similar signals, announcing a general disposition in Melville's mind to defend the state's need for order and allegiance in the telling of this tale. Such signals do not necessarily confirm *Billy Budd* as Melville's "testament of acceptance," as earlier critics have had it. But they may be seen as at least an indication of the political crustiness of a man who, while still exalting the seaman's world of dangerous labor, did not thereby imply the ascendency of the proletariat or subscribe to the attitudes of implicit rebelliousness that Ishmael suggests, for instance, in the celebrations of proletarian democracy in *Moby-Dick*. Simply, it seems clear that as Melville became older he became more conservative politically.

[2] The association of treachery and perjury with Claggart is much more clear in the use of Oates than in the use of Tecumseh. Titus Oates (1649–1705) was a clergyman who was expelled from various schools and congregations, apparently learning early from his father, also a clergyman, how to ruin people's lives by smear and slander: while Titus was still a boy, the father-and-son team destroyed a schoolteacher by spreading unconfirmed tales about him. Oates became a Catholic in 1677 and used his knowledge of Catholicism to concoct the story of a "Popish Plot" against Charles II (he lost no time between conversion and reconversion in the opportunistic baiting of Catholics), a plot in which James, the Duke of York, and the Jesuits were to take over control of England, massacre Protestants, and burn the cities. The "revelation" of the "Plot" resulted in a witch-hunting hysteria that sent many people to their ruin or death and that procured for Oates a fat government pension. He was later exposed and imprisoned under James, and released under William and Mary. He became a Baptist preacher, but his congregation soon kicked him out. The introduction of Claggart *via* Oates foreshadows Claggart's plot. Moreover, the ironic complexities of the problem of revolution versus order, so central to *Billy Budd*, is suggested by Melville's use of the Master-at-arms, the man who is to preserve the order of the state by preserving order over the populace, as the very man associated with the plots and insurrections (Oates and Tecumseh) that are so feared at the historical moment of Spithead and the Nore.

the hue of time-tinted marbles of old. This complexion, singularly
contrasting with the red or deeply bronzed visages of the sailors,
and in part the result of his official seclusion from the sunlight,
though it was not exactly displeasing, nevertheless seemed to hint
of something defective or abnormal in the constitution and blood.
But his general aspect and manner were so suggestive of an education and career incongruous with his naval function that when
92   °not actively engaged in it he looked like a man of high quality,
social and moral, who for reasons of his own was keeping incog.
Nothing was known of his former life. It might be that he was
an Englishman; and yet there lurked a bit of accent in his speech
suggesting that possibly he was not such by birth, but through
93   naturalization in early childhood. °Among certain grizzled sea-
gossips of the gun-decks and forecastle went a rumor perdue that
the Master-at-arms was a *chevalier*[3] who had volunteered into the
King's navy by way of compounding for some mysterious swindle
whereof he had been arraigned at the King's Bench. The fact that
94   nobody could substantiate this °report was, of course, nothing
against its secret currency. Such a rumor once started on the
gun-decks in reference to almost anyone below the rank of a
commissioned officer would, during the period assigned to this
narrative, have seemed not altogether wanting in credibility to the
tarry old wiseacres of a man-of-war crew. And indeed a man of
Claggart's accomplishments, without prior nautical experience
entering the navy at mature life, as he did, and necessarily allotted
at the start to the lowest grade in it; a man too who never made
allusion to his previous life ashore; these were circumstances which
in the dearth of exact knowledge as to his true antecedents opened
to the invidious a vague field for unfavorable surmise.
95   °But the sailors' dog-watch[4] gossip concerning him derived a

---

[3] As used here, "chevalier" means not knight or gentleman, but picaro,
rogue, a soldier of fortune who opportunistically takes his advantages
wherever his wanderings carry him.
[4] The dogwatch is broken into two half-watches (4–6 and 6–8) in order
that there will be an odd number of watches—seven instead of the six into
which the twenty-four-hour day divides—thus rotating the crew so that the
same men do not stand the same watch each day. Crewmen stood one dog-

vague plausibility from the fact that now for some period the
British Navy could so little afford to be squeamish in the matter
of keeping up the muster-rolls, that not only were press-gangs
notoriously abroad both afloat and ashore, but there was little or
no secret about another matter, namely that the London police
were at liberty to capture °any able-bodied suspect, any ques-   96
tionable fellow at large and summarily ship him to the dock-yard
or fleet. Furthermore, even among voluntary enlistments there
were instances where the motive thereto partook neither of patriotic impulse nor yet of a random desire to experience a bit of sea-
life and martial adventure. Insolvent debtors of minor grade,
together with the promiscuous lame ducks of morality, found in
the Navy a convenient and secure refuge. Secure, because once
enlisted aboard a King's-Ship, they were as much in sanctuary as
the transgressor of the Middle Ages harboring himself under the
shadow of the altar. °Such sanctioned irregularities, which for   97
obvious reasons the Government would hardly think to parade at
the time and which consequently, and as affecting the least influential class of mankind, have all but dropped into oblivion, lend
color to something for the truth whereof I do not vouch, and
hence have some scruple in stating; something I remember having
seen in print though the book I can not recall; but the same thing
was personally communicated to me now more than forty years
ago by an old pensioner in a cocked hat with whom I had a most
interesting talk on the terrace at Greenwich, a Baltimore Negro,
a Trafalgar man. °It was to this effect: In the case of a warship   98
short of hands whose speedy sailing was imperative, the deficient
quota, in lack of any other way of making it good, would be eked
out by draughts culled direct from the jails. For reasons previously
suggested it would not perhaps be easy at the present day directly
to prove or disprove the allegation. But allowed as a verity, how
significant would it be of England's straits at the time confronted
by those wars which like a flight of harpies rose shrieking from

---

watch on and one off, the off dogwatch being devoted to visiting, prome-
nading on the gun decks, smoking in those parts of the gun decks "allotted
to the pipe" and gossiping (see leaves 113 and 164–165, below).

99 the din and dust of the fallen Bastille. °That era appears measurably clear to us who look back at it, and but read of it. But to the grandfathers of us graybeards, the more thoughtful of them, the genius of it presented an aspect like that of Camoen's Spirit of the Cape, an eclipsing menace mysterious and prodigious.[5] Not America was exempt from apprehension. At the height of Napoleon's unexampled conquests, there were Americans who had fought at Bunker Hill who looked forward to the possibility that the Atlantic might prove no barrier against the ultimate schemes of this French portentous upstart from the revolutionary chaos who seemed in act of fulfilling judgement prefigured in the Apocalypse.[6]

100   °But the less credence was to be given to the gun-deck talk touching Claggart, seeing that no man holding his office in a man-of-war can ever hope to be popular with the crew. Besides, in derogatory comments upon anyone against whom they have a grudge, or for any reason or no reason mislike, sailors are much like landsmen; they are apt to exaggerate or romance it.

        About as much was really known to the *Bellipotent*'s tars of the Master-at-arms' career before entering the service as an
101 astronomer knows °about a comet's travels prior to its first observable appearance in the sky. The verdict of the sea quidnuncs[7] has been cited only by way of showing what sort of moral impression the man made upon rude uncultivated natures whose con-

---

[5] Luis Vas de Camões (1524–1580) was Portugal's greatest poet. In his ten-canto epic poem, *Os Lusiadas* (the *Lusiads*), which celebrates the valorous feats of the Portuguese, a horrendous figure representing the hostile and terrifying forces of nature tries to swamp Vasco Da Gama's fleet on its historic voyage round the Cape of Good Hope.

[6] At the beginning of the Directory period (see note 2, leaf 51, above) there was a momentary lull in internal political conflicts in France, and the Directory employed the chance to send the French armies into enormous expeditions abroad. In contrast to the large armies of the north, which were experiencing mixed fortunes against Germany and Austria, Napoleon, in the south, began his crushing, brilliant, and unparalleled victories against the Italians and the Austrians. It seemed that nothing could stop him, and, for the time, nothing did. In 1797, the year of the narrative, Napoleon was at the height of his successes.

[7] quidnunc: literally, "what now?" A busybody, a gossip.

ceptions of human wickedness were necessarily of the narrowest, limited to ideas of vulgar rascality—a thief among the swinging hammocks during a night-watch, or the man-brokers and land-sharks of the seaports.

°It was no gossip, however, but fact, that though, as before   102
hinted, Claggart upon his entrance into the navy was, as a novice, assigned to the least honorable section of a man-of-war's crew, embracing the drudgery, he did not long remain there. The superior capacity he immediately evinced, his constitutional sobriety, an ingratiating deference to superiors, together with a peculiar ferreting genius manifested on a singular occasion, all this capped by a certain austere patriotism abruptly advanced him to the position of Master-at-arms.

°Of this maritime Chief of Police the ship's-corporals, so called,   103
were the immediate subordinates, and compliant ones; and this, as is to be noted in some business departments ashore, almost to a degree inconsistent with entire moral volition. His place put various converging wires of underground influence under the Chief's control, capable when astutely worked through his under-strappers of operating to the mysterious discomfort, if nothing worse, of any of the sea-commonalty.

A Hogarthian view of impressment. "Not only were press-gangs noto-riously abroad both afloat and ashore, but . . . the London police were at liberty to capture any able-bodied suspect . . . and summarily ship him to the dock-yard or fleet."

A naval recruiting poster of the late eighteenth century. The small print at the bottom reads: "For the Encouragement of DISCOVER-ING Seamen, that they may be impressed, a REWARD of TWO POUNDS will be given for Able, and THIRTY SHILLINGS for Ordinary Seamen. Success to His Majesty's NAVY! With Health and Limbs to the Jolly Tars of Old England." (facing page)

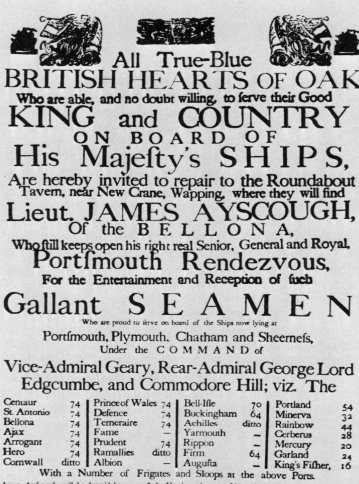

All True-Blue
BRITISH HEARTS OF OAK
Who are able, and no doubt willing, to ferve their Good
KING and COUNTRY
ON BOARD OF
His Majefty's SHIPS,
Are hereby invited to repair to the Roundabout
Tavern, near New Crane, Wapping, where they will find
Lieut. JAMES AYSCOUGH,
Of the BELLONA,
Who ftill keeps open his right real Senior, General and Royal,
Portfmouth Rendezvous,
For the Entertainment and Reception of fuch
Gallant SEAMEN
Who are proud to ferve on board of the Ships now lying at

Portfmouth, Plymouth, Chatham and Sheernefs,
Under the COMMAND of

Vice-Admiral Geary, Rear-Admiral George Lord Edgcumbe, and Commodore Hill; viz. The

Centaur	74	Prince of Wales	74	Bell-Ifle	70	Portland	54
St. Antonio	74	Defence	74	Buckingham	64	Minerva	32
Bellona	74	Temeraire	74	Achilles	ditto	Rainbow	44
Ajax	74	Fame	—	Yarmouth	—	Cerberus	28
Arrogant	74	Prudent	74	Rippon	—	Mercury	20
Hero	74	Ramallies	ditto	Firm	64	Garland	24
Cornwall	ditto	Albion	—	Augufta	—	King's Fifher,	16

With a Number of Frigates and Sloops at the above Ports.

Lieut. Ayfcough will be damn'd happy to fhake Hands with any of his old Ship-mates in particular, or their jolly Friends in general—Keep it up, my Boys!—Twenty may play as well as one.

Able Seamen will receive Three Pounds Bounty, and Ordinary Seamen Two Pounds, with Conduct-Money, and their Chefts, Bedding, &c. fent Carriage free.

N. B. For the Encouragement of DISCOVERING Seamen, that they may be impreffed, a REWARD of Two POUNDS will be given for Able, and THIRTY SHILLINGS for Ordinary Seamen.

Succefs to His Majefty's NAVY! With Health and Limbs to the Jolly Tars of Old England—JAMES AYSCOUGH
GOD SAVE THE KING.

Printed by R. HILTON, in WELLCLOSE-SQUARE

Department of Naval Recruiting,
Royal Navy, London

47

From an etching by George Cruikshank, 1825 National Maritime Museum, London
A flogging at the gangway. "The first formal punishment Billy had ever witnessed befell the day following his impressment."

[9]

°LIFE IN THE FORE-TOP WELL agreed with Billy Budd. 104
There, when not actually engaged on the yards yet higher aloft,
the topmen, who as such had been picked out for youth and ac-
tivity, constituted an aerial club lounging at ease against the
smaller stun'sails rolled up into cushions, spinning yarns like the
lazy gods, and frequently amused with what was going on in the
busy world of the decks below. No wonder then that a young
fellow of Billy's disposition was well content in such society.
Giving no cause of offence to anybody, he was always alert at a
call. °So in the merchant service it had been with him. But now 105
such a punctiliousness in duty was shown that his topmates would
sometimes good-naturedly laugh at him for it. This heightened
alacrity had its cause, namely, the impression made upon him by
the first formal gangway-punishment he had ever witnessed,
which befell the day following his impressment. It had been incurred by a little fellow, young, a novice, an afterguardsman absent from his assigned post when the ship was being put about; a
dereliction resulting in a rather serious hitch to that manœuvre,
one demanding instantaneous promptitude in letting go and making fast. °When Billy saw the culprit's naked back under the 106
scourge gridironed with red welts, and worse; when he marked
the dire expression on the liberated man's face as with his woolen
shirt flung over him by the executioner he rushed forward from
the spot to bury himself in the crowd, Billy was horrified. He
resolved that never through remissness would he make himself
liable to such a visitation or do or omit aught that might merit
even verbal reproof. What then was his surprise and concern
when ultimately he found himself getting into petty trouble occasionally about such matters as the stowage of his bag or some-

49

107 thing amiss in his hammock, matters under the police °oversight
of the ship's-corporals of the lower decks, and which brought
down on him a vague threat from one of them.
So heedful in all things as he was, how could this be? He could
not understand it, and it more than vexed him. When he spoke
to his young topmates about it they were either lightly incredu-
lous or found something comical in his unconcealed anxiety. "Is
it your bag, Billy?" said one. "Well, sew yourself up in it, bully
boy, and then you'll be sure to know if anybody meddles with it."
Now there was a veteran aboard who because his years began
108 to disqualify him for more active work °had been recently assigned duty as main-mast-man in his watch, looking to the gear
belayed at the rail roundabout that great spar near the deck. At
off-times the foretopman had picked up some acquaintance with
him, and now in his trouble it occurred to him that he might be
the sort of person to go to for wise counsel. He was an old Dansker long anglicized in the service, of few words, many wrinkles
and some honorable scars. His wizened face, time-tinted and
weather-stained to the complexion of an antique parchment, was
here and there peppered blue by the chance explosion of a gun-
cartridge in action.
109 °He was an *Agamemnon*-man; some two years prior to the time
of this story having served under Nelson, when but Sir Horatio,[1]
in that ship immortal in naval memory, and which dismantled and
in part broken up to her bare ribs is seen a grand skeleton in
Haden's etching.[2] As one of a boarding-party from the *Agamem-*

[1] Melville again errs about Nelson's rank. He intended to indicate that
Nelson was still only Sir Horatio, not yet Lord Nelson. However, it was
with the baronetcy that Nelson became Sir Horatio, and that was in 1798
(he became Lord Nelson when he was made viscount in 1801). Since Melville is referring to the year 1795 ("some two years prior to the time of
this story"), Nelson, still post-captain, was not yet "Sir." Hayford and Sealts
rewrite the sentence for Melville thus: "having served under Nelson when
still captain in that ship." But, as I have pointed out elsewhere, Melville
possibly was conscious of rank for its thematic uses in this narrative, and
rewriting Melville for the sake of literal correctness is undesirable. This
edition preserves what Melville actually wrote.

[2] Sir Francis Seymour Haden (1818–1910) was an etcher and a surgeon.
Some of his engravings were collected in *The Engraved Work of Sir*

non he had received a cut slantwise along one temple and cheek leaving a long pale scar like a streak of dawn's light falling athwart the dark visage. It was on account of that scar and the affair in which it was known that he had received it, as well as from his blue-peppered complexion, that the Dansker went among the *Bellipotent*'s crew by the name of "Board-her-in-the-smoke."

°Now the first time that his small weazel-eyes happened to light   110 on Billy Budd, a certain grim internal merriment set all his ancient wrinkles into antic play. Was it that his eccentric unsentimental old sapience, primitive in its kind, saw or thought it saw something which in contrast with the war-ship's environment looked oddly incongruous in the handsome sailor? But after slyly studying him at intervals, the old Merlin's equivocal merriment was modified; for now when the twain would meet, it would start in his face a quizzing sort of look, but it would be but momentary °and sometimes replaced by an expression of speculative query as   111 to what might eventually befall a nature like that, dropped into a world not without some man-traps and against whose subtleties simple courage lacking experience and address and without any touch of defensive ugliness, is of little avail; and where such innocence as man is capable of does yet in a moral emergency not always sharpen the faculties or enlighten the will.

However it was, the Dansker in his ascetic way rather took to Billy. Nor was this only because of a certain philosophic interest in such a character. There was another cause. °While the old   112 man's eccentricities, sometimes bordering on the ursine, repelled the juniors, Billy, undeterred thereby, revering him as a salt hero, would make advances, never passing the old *Agamemnon*-man without a salutation marked by that respect which is seldom lost on the aged however crabbed at times or whatever their station in life.

There was a vein of dry humor, or what not, in the mast-man; and, whether in freak of patriarchal irony touching Billy's youth

---

Francis Haden in 1910. One of his most famous etchings is "The Breaking up of the Agamemnon," which was first published in 1870 and was widely reprinted. See page 54.

and athletic frame, or for some other and more recondite reason, from the first in addressing him he always substituted Baby for Billy. The Dansker in fact being the originator of the name by which the foretopman eventually became known aboard ship.

113   °Well then, in his mysterious little difficulty going in quest of the wrinkled one, Billy found him off duty in a dog-watch ruminating by himself, seated on a shot-box of the upper gun-deck, now and then surveying with a somewhat cynical regard certain of the more swaggering promenaders there. Billy recounted his trouble, again wondering how it all happened. The salt seer attentively listened, accompanying the foretopman's recital with queer twitchings of his wrinkles and problematical little sparkles of his small ferret eyes. Making an end of his story, the foretopman asked, "And now, Dansker, do tell me what you think of it."

114   °The old man, shoving up the front of his tarpaulin[3] and deliberately rubbing the long slant scar at the point where it entered the thin hair, laconically said, "Baby Budd, *Jemmy Legs*"[4] (meaning the Master-at-arms) "is down on you."

"*Jemmy Legs!*" ejaculated Billy, his welkin eyes expanding; "what for? Why, he calls me *the sweet and pleasant young fellow*, they tell me."

"Does he so?" grinned the grizzled one; then said, "Ay, Baby lad, a sweet voice has *Jemmy Legs*."

115   °"No, not always. But to me he has. I seldom pass him but there comes a pleasant word."

"And that's because he's down upon you, Baby Budd."

Such reiteration along with the manner of it, incomprehensible to a novice, disturbed Billy almost as much as the mystery for which he had sought explanation. Something less unpleasingly oracular he tried to extract; but the old sea-Chiron, thinking per-

---

[3] A weatherproof hat.

[4] "Jemmy Legs" was a universal designation for the master-at-arms in both the British and American navies. The appellation was variously spelled "Jimmy Leggs," "Jemmy Leggs," and "Jimmy Legs," as well as "Jemmy Legs." Melville's emendations indicated his preference for "Jemmy Legs" in final revision, and this edition, like *H&S*, regularizes the spelling to Melville's latest intention.

haps that for the nonce he had °sufficiently instructed his young   116
Achilles,[5] pursed his lips, gathered all his wrinkles together and
would commit himself to nothing further.

Years, and those experiences which befall certain shrewder men
subordinated life-long to the will of superiors, all this had developed in the Dansker the pithy guarded cynicism that was his
leading characteristic.

[5] Phoenix and Chiron were the teachers of Achilles. Chiron, the Centaur,
was famed throughout Greece for his legendary wisdom, especially in the
arts of healing. He was supposed to have been the teacher of the father
of physicians, Aesculapius, and, together with Amphitryon, he educated
Hercules. Accidentally wounded by Hercules, he begged for death, and
the gods translated him into the heavens as the constellation Sagittarius.

The breaking up of the *Agamemnon*, by Sir Francis Seymour Haden.

54

[10]

THE NEXT DAY an incident served to confirm Billy Budd in his incredulity as to the Dansker's strange summing up of the case submitted. °The ship at noon, going large before the wind, was rolling on her course, and he below at dinner and engaged in some sportful talk with the members of his mess, chanced in a sudden lurch to spill the entire contents of his soup-pan upon the new scrubbed deck. Claggart, the Master-at-arms, official rattan in hand, happened to be passing along the battery in a bay of which the mess was lodged, and the greasy liquid streamed just across his path. Stepping over it, he was proceeding °on his way without comment, since the matter was nothing to take notice of under the circumstances, when he happened to observe who it was that had done the spilling. His countenance changed. °Pausing, he was about to ejaculate something hasty at the sailor, but checked himself, and pointing down to the streaming soup, playfully tapped him from behind with his rattan, saying in a low musical voice peculiar to him at times "Handsomely done, my lad! And handsome is as handsome did it too!" And with that passed on. Not noted by Billy, as not coming within his view, was the involuntary smile, or rather grimace, that accompanied Claggart's equivocal words. Aridly it drew down the thin corners of his shapely mouth. But everybody taking his remark as °meant for humorous, and at which therefore as coming from a superior they were bound to laugh, "with counterfeited glee"[1] acted ac-

117

118

119

120

[1] The phrase, "with counterfeited glee," is from Oliver Goldsmith's poem, "The Deserted Village" (1770). The passage, describing the relation between the village children and the teacher, indicates the relationship between the sailors and the Master-at-arms:

There, in his noisy mansion, skill'd to rule,
The Village master taught his little school;

cordingly; and Billy tickled, it may be, by the allusion to his being the handsome sailor, merrily joined in; then addressing his messmates exclaimed "There now, who says that Jemmy Legs is down on me!" "And who said he was, Beauty?" demanded one Donald with some surprise. Whereat the foretopman looked a little foolish, recalling that it was only one person, Board-her-in-the-smoke, who had suggested what to him was the smoky idea
121   that this °Master-at-arms was in any peculiar way hostile to him. Meantime that functionary, resuming his path, must have momentarily worn some expression less guarded than that of the bitter smile, and usurping the face from the heart, some distorting expression perhaps; for a drummer-boy heedlessly frolicking along from the opposite direction, and chancing to come into light collision with his person, was strangely disconcerted by his aspect. Nor was the impression lessened when the official, impulsively giving him a sharp cut with the rattan, vehemently exclaimed, "Look where you go!"

A man severe he was, and stern to view,
I knew him well, and every truant knew;
Well had the boding tremblers learned to trace
The day's disasters in his morning face;
Full well they laugh'd with counterfeited glee,
At all his jokes, for many a joke had he;
Full well the busy whisper circling round,
Convey'd the dismal tidings when he frowned (lines 195–205).

[11]

°WHAT WAS THE MATTER with the Master-at-arms? And,   122
be the matter what it might, how could it have direct relation to
Billy Budd with whom, prior to the affair of the spilled soup, he
had never come into any special contact official or otherwise?
What indeed could the trouble have to do with one so little inclined to give offence as the merchant-ship's *peacemaker*, even
him who in Claggart's own phrase was "the sweet and pleasant
young °fellow"? Yes, why should *Jemmy Legs*, to borrow the   123
Dansker's expression, be *down* on the Handsome Sailor? But, at
heart and not for nothing, as the late chance encounter may indicate to the discerning, down on him, secretly down on him, he
assuredly was.

Now to invent something touching the more private career of
Claggart, something involving Billy Budd, of which something the
latter should be wholly ignorant, some romantic incident implying °that Claggart's knowledge of the young blue-jacket began   124
at some period anterior to catching sight of him on board the
seventy-four—all this, not so difficult to do, might avail in a way
more or less interesting to account for whatever of enigma may
appear to lurk in the case. But in fact there was nothing of the
sort. And yet the cause, necessarily to be assumed as the sole
one assignable, is in its very realism as much charged with that
°prime element of Radcliffian romance, *the mysterious*, as any   125
that the ingenuity of the author of the *Mysteries of Udolpho*
could devise.[1] For what can more partake of the mysterious than

---

[1] Ann Ward Radcliffe (1764–1823) was a leading writer of gothic novels.
The Mysteries of Udolpho (1794), the best known and most popular of her
novels, was an intricate tale of mysteries both of circumstance and character, all ultimately explained as having natural causes.

an antipathy spontaneous and profound, such as is evoked in certain exceptional mortals by the mere aspect of some other mortal, however harmless he may be, if not called forth by this very harmlessness itself?

Now there can exist no irritating juxtaposition of dissimilar personalities comparable to that which is possible aboard a great war-ship fully manned and at sea. °There, every day among all ranks almost every man comes into more or less of contact with almost every other man. Wholly there to avoid even the sight of an aggravating object one must needs give it Jonah's toss[2] or jump overboard himself. Imagine how all this might eventually operate on some peculiar human creature the direct reverse of a saint?

But for the adequate comprehending of Claggart by a normal nature, these hints are insufficient. To pass from a normal nature to him one must cross "the deadly space between." And this is best done by indirection.

127   °Long ago an honest scholar, my senior, said to me in reference to one who like himself is now no more, a man so unimpeachably respectable that against him nothing was ever openly said though among the few something was whispered, "Yes, X—— is a nut not to be cracked by the tap of a lady's fan. You are aware that I am the adherent of no organized religion much less of any philosophy built into a system.[3] Well, for all that, I think that to try and get into X——, enter his labyrinth and get out again, without a clue derived from some source other than what is known as

126

[2] Fearing that Jonah had brought a storm upon them by fleeing the Lord, the sailors tossed Jonah overboard to end the tempest (Jon. 1:7–15).

[3] Within the framework of Melville's values and prejudices, this statement heightens rather than reduces the credibility of the "honest scholar." Throughout his writings Melville indicated his distrust of systematized philosophy. His depiction of clerics and clerical establishments—Reverend Falsgrave in *Pierre* and "The Two Temples" are the outstanding examples, as Father Mapple in *Moby-Dick* is the outstanding but problematical exception—indicates his lifelong suspicion of foolishness and hypocrisy in institutionalized religion. The types Melville honored most in his fiction as in life were those whose minds, like Captain Vere's, possessed "honesty" and "directness, sometimes far-reaching like that of a migratory fowl that in its flight never heeds when it crosses a frontier."

knowledge of the world—that were hardly possible, at least for me."

°"Why," said I, "X——, however singular a study to some, is   128
yet human, and knowledge of the world assuredly implies the
knowledge of human nature, and in most of its varieties."

"Yes, but a superficial knowledge of it, serving ordinary purposes. But for anything deeper, I am not certain whether to know
the world and to know human nature be not two distinct branches
of knowledge, which while they may coexist in the same heart,
yet either may exist with little or nothing of the other. Nay, in an
average man of the world, his constant rubbing with it blunts
°that finer spiritual insight indispensable to the understanding of   129
the essential in certain exceptional characters, whether evil ones
or good. In a matter of some importance I have seen a girl wind
an old lawyer about her little finger. Nor was it the dotage of
senile love. Nothing of the sort. But he knew law better than he
knew the girl's heart. Coke and Blackstone[4] hardly shed so much
light into obscure spiritual places as the Hebrew prophets. And
who were they? Mostly recluses."

At the time my inexperience was such that I did not quite see
the drift of all this. It may be that I see it now. And, indeed, if
that lexicon which °is based on Holy Writ[5] were any longer   130
popular, one might with less difficulty define and denominate
certain phenomenal men. As it is, one must turn to some authority
not liable to the charge of being tinctured with the Biblical element.

In a list of definitions included in the authentic translation of
Plato, a list attributed to him, occurs this: "Natural Depravity: a

---

[4] Sir Edward Coke (1552–1634) labored heroically in the cause of the
supremacy of the common law over royal authority. Sir William Blackstone (1723–1780) introduced at Oxford the teaching of constitutional law
in British universities. Coke and Blackstone are the great names in the
development of common and constitutional law.

[5] Melville was not referring to a particular work here, but to theological
language based upon the Bible. Here, presumably, the reference would be
particularly to the fall of man and generally to the history of evil recounted
in the Bible stories.

depravity according to nature." A definition which though savor-
131 ing of Calvinism, by no means involves °Calvin's dogma as to total
mankind.[6] Evidently its intent makes it applicable but to individuals. Not many are the examples of this depravity which the
gallows and jail supply. At any rate for notable instances, since
these have no vulgar alloy of the brute in them, but invariably are
dominated by intellectuality, one must go elsewhere. Civilization,
especially if of the austerer sort, is auspicious to it. It folds itself in
the mantle of respectability. It has its certain negative virtues serving as silent auxiliaries. It never allows wine to get within its guard.
132 °It is not going too far to say that it is without vices or small sins.
There is a phenomenal pride in it that excludes them. It is never
mercenary or avaricious. In short the depravity here meant par-
takes nothing of the sordid or sensual. It is serious, but free from
acerbity. Though no flatterer of mankind it never speaks ill of it.

But the thing which in eminent instances signalizes so exceptional a nature is this: though the man's even temper and discreet
bearing would seem to intimate a mind peculiarly subject to the
133 law °of reason, not the less in his heart he would seem to riot in
complete exemption from that law, having apparently little to do
with reason further than to employ it as an ambidexter implement
for effecting the irrational. That is to say: Toward the accom-
plishment of an aim which in wantonness of atrocity would seem
to partake of the insane, he will direct a cool judgement sagacious
and sound.
134   °These men are true madmen, and of the most dangerous sort,
for their lunacy is not continuous but occasional, evoked by some
special object; it is protectively secretive, which is as much as to
say it is self-contained, so that when moreover, most active, it is to
the average mind not distinguishable from sanity, and for the
reason above suggested, that whatever its aims may be—and the

---

[6] John Calvin (1509–1564) was one of the greatest leaders of Protestant-
ism. At the Synod of Dort (1618–1619), Calvin's teachings were affirmed
in a series of principles enunciated by the Synod. The dogma Melville
refers to here is that of total depravity, the belief that all men are born
totally depraved in their very natures as a consequence of Adam's Fall
from Grace.

aim is never declared—the method and the outward proceeding are always perfectly rational.

Now something such an one was Claggart, in whom was the mania of an evil nature, not engendered by vicious training or corrupting books or licentious living, but born with him and innate, in short "a depravity according to nature."

°Dark sayings are these, some will say. But why? Is it because 135 they somewhat savor of Holy Writ in its phrase "mysteries of iniquity"?[7] If they do, such savor was far enough from being intended, for little will it commend these pages to many a reader of to-day.

The point of the present story turning on the hidden nature of the Master-at-arms has necessitated this chapter. With an added hint or two in connection with the incident at the mess, the resumed narrative must be left to vindicate, as it may, its own credibility.

---

[7] "For the mystery of iniquity doth already work: only he who now letteth will let, until he be taken out of the way" (2 Thess. 2:7).

[12]

°Lawyers, Experts, Clergy[1]

BY THE WAY, can it[2] be the phenomenon, disowned or at least conceded, that in some criminal cases puzzles the courts? For this cause have our juries at times not only to endure the prolonged contentions of lawyers with their fees, but also the yet more perplexing strife of the medical experts with theirs?—But why leave it to them? why not subpoena as well the clerical profi-

cients? Their vocation °bringing them into peculiar contact with so many human beings, and sometimes in their least guarded hour, in interviews very much more confidential than those of physician and patient; this would seem to qualify them to know something about those intricacies involved in the question of moral responsibility; whether in a given case, say, the crime proceeded from mania in the brain or rabies of the heart. As to any differences among themselves these clerical proficients might develop on the stand, these would hardly be greater than the direct contradictions exchanged between the remunerated medical experts.

---

[1] See Appendix One, pp. 155–156, and the statement for leaf 135a in Appendix Two.

[2] "It" is the "mystery of iniquity" Melville sees as "natural depravity."

[13]

THAT CLAGGART'S FIGURE was not amiss, and his face, save the chin, well moulded, has already been said. Of these favorable points he seemed not insensible, for he was not only neat but careful in his dress. But the form of Billy Budd was heroic; and if his face was without the intellectual look of the pallid Claggart's, not the less was it lit, like his, from within, though from a different source. The bonfire in his heart made luminous the rosetan in his cheek.

°In view of the marked contrast between the persons of the 137 twain, it is more than probable that when the Master-at-arms in the scene last given applied to the sailor the proverb *Handsome is as handsome does;* he there let escape an ironic inkling, not caught by the young sailors who heard it, as to what it was that had first moved him against Billy, namely, his significant personal beauty.

Now envy and antipathy, passions irreconcilable in reason,

---

¹ "Thus while he [Satan in the 'borrow'd visage' of a 'stripling Cherub'] spake, each passion dimm'd his face,/Thrice chang'd with pale, ire, envy and despair,/Which marr'd his borrow'd visage, and betray'd/Him counterfeit, if any eye beheld" (*Paradise Lost*, IV, 114–117). Melville's reading, "pale ire, envy and despair," is highly understandable. However, in Milton's usage, "pale" has the force of a noun: while Satan spoke, his face dimmed with additional pallor three times under the impact of the three emotions, ire, envy and despair. *H&S* deletes the title in the interest of consistency: Melville did not regularly title the chapters. However, this kind of consistency should be subordinated to providing for the reader the fullest materials. The title is clearly indicated in the manuscript. In fact, Elizabeth Melville had pencilled in notations about the title, indicating that she questioned it, but had then erased the notations, indicating that the title was to stand. Furthermore, it is unfortunate to deprive the reader of an allusion to Satan in a chapter directly concerned with Claggart.

nevertheless in fact may spring conjoined like Chang and Eng[2] in one birth. Is Envy then such a monster? Well, though many an
138 °arraigned mortal has in hopes of mitigated penalty pleaded guilty to horrible actions, did ever anybody seriously confess to envy? Something there is in it universally felt to be more shameful than even felonious crime. And not only does everybody dis-
139 own it, °but the better sort are inclined to incredulity when it is in earnest imputed to an intelligent man. But since its lodgement is in the heart not the brain, no degree of intellect supplies a guarantee against it. But Claggart's was no vulgar form of the
140 passion. Nor, as directed toward Billy Budd °did it partake of that streak of apprehensive jealousy that marred Saul's visage perturbedly brooding on the comely young David.[3] Claggart's envy struck deeper. If askance he eyed the good looks, cheery health and frank enjoyment of young life in Billy Budd, it was because these went along with a nature that, as Claggart magnetically felt, had in its simplicity never willed malice or experienced the reactionary[4] bite of that serpent. To him, the spirit lodged within Billy, and looking out from his welkin eyes as from windows, that
141 ineffability it was which °made the dimple in his dyed cheek, suppled his joints, and dancing in his yellow curls made him preeminently the Handsome Sailor. One person excepted, the Master-at-arms was perhaps the only man in the ship intellectually capable of adequately appreciating the moral phenomenon pre-

[2] Chang and Eng were born in Bangesau, Siam, in 1811. They were the originals after whom the term "Siamese twins" was coined. They were exhibited in the United States, where they became citizens and resided until their death in 1874.

[3] Saul, who was subject to fits of "the evil spirit from God," heard David, son of Jesse, praised for his beauty and valor. Saul sent for David to be his armorbearer, but as time went on and David found favor in everyone's eyes (he was the Handsome Sailor of Saul's court), Saul became increasingly envious. On the day that David slew Goliath, the women praised David more highly than they praised Saul. "And Saul eyed David from that day and forward" (1 Sam. 18:9).

[4] Melville had first written "reacting bite." Hayford and Sealts speculate about some Latin derivations possibly in Melville's mind, but that possibility is not very likely. He simply meant that the serpent of envy bit in reaction to the object of envy.

sented in Billy Budd[5]. And the insight but intensified his passion, which assuming various secret forms within him, at times assumed that of cynic disdain—disdain of innocence. To be nothing more than innocent! Yet in an aesthetic way he saw the charm of it, the courageous free-and-easy temper of it, and fain would have shared it, but he despaired of it.

°With no power to annul the elemental evil in him, though   142
readily enough he could hide it; apprehending the good, but powerless to be it; a nature like Claggart's surcharged with energy as such natures almost invariably are, what recourse is left to it but to recoil upon itself and like the scorpion for which the Creator alone is responsible, act out to the end the part allotted it.

[5] The "one person excepted" is Captain Vere.

[14]

143 °PASSION, and passion in its profoundest, is not a thing demanding a palatial stage whereon to play its part. Down among the groundlings, among the beggars and rakers of the garbage, profound passion is enacted. And the circumstances that provoke it, however trivial or mean, are no measure of its power. In the present instance the stage is a scrubbed gun-deck, and one of the external provocations a man-of-war's-man's spilled soup.

Now when the Master-at-arms noticed whence came that greasy fluid streaming before his feet, he must have taken it—to
144 some extent wilfully, °perhaps—not for the mere accident it assuredly was, but for the sly escape of a spontaneous feeling on Billy's part more or less answering to the antipathy on his own. In effect a foolish demonstration he must have thought, and very harmless, like the futile kick of a heifer, which yet were the heifer a shod stallion, would not be so harmless. Even so was it that into the gall of Claggart's envy he infused the vitriol of his
145 contempt. °But the incident confirmed to him certain tell-tale reports purveyed to his ear by *Squeak*, one of his more cunning corporals, a grizzled little man, so nicknamed by the sailors on account of his squeaky voice, and sharp visage ferreting about the dark corners of the lower decks after interlopers, satirically suggesting to them the idea of a rat in a cellar.
146   °From his chief's employing him as an implicit tool in laying little traps for the worriment of the foretopman—for it was from the Master-at-arms that the petty persecutions heretofore adverted to had proceeded—the corporal having naturally enough concluded that his master could have no love for the sailor, made it his business, faithful understrapper that he was, to foment the
147 ill blood by perverting to his chief °certain innocent frolics of the good natured foretopman, besides inventing for his mouth sundry

contumelious epithets he claimed to have overheard him let fall. The Master-at-arms never suspected the veracity of these reports, more especially as to the epithets, for he well knew how secretly unpopular may become a Master-at-arms, at least a Master-at-arms of those days zealous in his function, and how the blue-jackets shoot at him in private their raillery and wit; the nickname by which he goes among them (*Jemmy Legs*) implying under the form of merriment their cherished disrespect and dislike. °But in view of the greediness of hate for pabulum it hardly needed a purveyor to feed Claggart's passion.   148

An uncommon prudence is habitual with the subtler depravity, for it has everything to hide. And in case of an injury but suspected, its secretiveness voluntarily cuts it off from enlightenment or disillusion; and, not unreluctantly, action is taken upon surmise as upon certainty. And the retaliation is apt to be in monstrous disproportion to the supposed offence; for when in anybody was revenge in its exactions aught else but an inordinate usurer? °But how with Claggart's conscience? For though consciences are unlike as foreheads, every intelligence, not excluding the Scriptural devils who "believe and tremble,"[1] has one. But Claggart's conscience being but the lawyer to his °will, made ogres of trifles, probably arguing that the motive imputed to Billy in spilling the soup just when he did, together with the epithets alleged, these, if nothing more, made a strong case against him; nay, justified animosity into a sort of retributive righteousness. The Pharisee is the Guy Fawkes prowling in the hid chambers underlying the Claggarts.[2]   149 150

---

[1] "Thou believest that there is one God; thou dost well: the devils also believe, and tremble" (James 2:19).

[2] The Pharisees were known for their religious purism, fanaticism, legalism, and a holier-than-thou separation from all whom they considered more common than they. The association of Pharisaic pride with Claggart does not elevate him to purity but rather indicates the eager watchfulness with which he imputes baseness to all men and the bitter satisfaction with which he ferrets it out. Guy Fawkes (1570–1606) is the man whose name is remembered in connection with the Gunpowder Plot, in which a group of Roman Catholics planned to massacre the King and Parliament on November 5, 1605. A zealous convert, Fawkes mined the cellar under the House of Lords but was discovered and arrested at the eleventh hour among his thirty-six barrels of gunpowder. Melville is referring back to what he

And they can really form no conception of an unreciprocated
151 malice. °Probably, the Master-at-arms' clandestine persecution of
Billy was started to try the temper of the man; but it had not
developed any quality in him that enmity could make official use
of or even pervert into plausible self-justification; so that the
occurrence at the mess, petty if it were, was a welcome one to
that peculiar conscience assigned to be the private mentor of
Claggart. And, for the rest, not improbably it put him upon new
experiments.

---

already has explained about the surface edifice of cool and urbane respectability in Claggart's personality: below that edifice the brooding,
Pharisaic, suspicious pride is waiting to blow everything into insane
violence (see leaf 188). Melville's political and historical references all
relate to the central problem introduced by the political and historical
background of the *Bellipotent*'s "inside narrative": rebellion and order and
their relationship to the welfare of mankind. Thus, references to con-
spiracy, mutiny, repression, armed force, become enlarged in importance
in the general context of the narrative.

[15]

°NOT MANY DAYS after the last incident narrated, something   152
befell Billy Budd that more gravelled him than aught that had
previously occurred.

It was a warm night for the latitude; and the foretopman,
whose watch at the time was properly below, was dozing on the
uppermost deck whither he had ascended from his hot hammock,
one of hundreds suspended so closely wedged together over a
lower gun-deck that there was little or no swing to them. He lay
as in the shadow of a hill-side, stretched under the lee of the
booms, °a piled ridge of spare spars amidships between fore-mast   153
and main-mast and among which the ship's largest boat, the
launch, was stowed. Alongside of three other slumberers from
below, he lay near that end of the booms which approaches the
fore-mast; his station aloft on duty as a foretopman being just
over the deck-station of the forecastlemen, entitling him according to usage to make himself more or less at home in that
neighborhood.

°Presently he was stirred into semi-consciousness by somebody,   154
who must have previously sounded the sleep of the others, touching his shoulder, and then as the foretopman raised his head,
breathing into his ear in a quick whisper, "Slip into the lee fore-
chains, Billy; there is something in the wind. Don't speak. Quick,
I will meet you there"; and disappeared.

Now Billy, like sundry other essentially good-natured ones, had
some of the weaknesses inseparable from essential good nature;
and among these was a reluctance, almost an incapacity of
plumply saying *no* to an abrupt proposition not obviously absurd,
on the face of it, nor obviously unfriendly, nor iniquitous. And
being of warm blood he had not the phlegm tacitly to negative

155 any proposition by unresponsive inaction. °Like his sense of fear,
his apprehension as to aught outside of the honest and natural was
seldom very quick. Besides, upon the present occasion, the drowse
from his sleep still hung upon him.

However it was, he mechanically rose, and sleepily wondering
what could be in the wind, betook himself to the designated place,
a narrow platform, one of six, outside of the high bulwarks and
screened by the great dead-eyes and multiple columned lanyards
of the shrouds and back-stays;[1] and, in a great war-ship of that
time, of dimensions commensurate to the hull's magnitude; a tarry
balcony in short, overhanging the sea, and so secluded that one
156 mariner °of the *Bellipotent*, a non-conformist old tar of a serious
turn, made it even in daytime his private oratory.

In this retired nook the stranger soon joined Billy Budd. There
was no moon as yet; a haze obscured the star-light. He could not
distinctly see the stranger's face. Yet from something in the out-

---

[1] The chains are narrow platforms where the leadsman stands to heave
the lead when it is necessary to take soundings. The fore-chains are on
either side of the bow and project out over the sides of the ship just behind the foremast. There are also two more pairs of chains, the main-chains
on each side of the hull amidship and the mizzen-chains on each side of the
hull aft. Thus, the lee fore-chains was "a narrow platform, one of six,
outside of the high bulwarks," or walls, of the ship's sides. The fore-, main-,
and mizzen-chains function as anchor points for the shrouds and backstays
supporting the fore-, main-, and mizzenmasts respectively. The backstays
are heavy ropes stretched from the mastheads and angled slightly aft to the
chains. The backward angled backstays are supports for the masts against
the forward drive of the sails and act like the guy-wires that hold telephone
poles steady in a high wind. Similarly, the shrouds are ropes stretched from
the masthead to the chains on each side of the mast, giving lateral support
to the masts against the side to side roll of the ship. Deadeyes, thick disks
of wood with holes drilled through them and hooped about with bands of
iron or stout rope, are fastened to the chains. Lanyards, which are heavy
ropes, are reaved through the holes in the deadeye to another deadeye
above. The top deadeye is connected to the shroud or stay. Thus, lanyards
stretched between the two deadeyes, like ropes stretched between two
pulleys, look like rope columns, a rope for each hole in the deadeye. By
tightening or loosening the length of lanyard between the deadeyes, the
sailors could tighten or loosen the shrouds and stays. The lee fore-chains
into which the conspirator took Billy was a platform "screened by the
great dead-eyes and multiple columned lanyards of the shrouds and backstays."

line and carriage, Billy took him to be, and correctly, one of the afterguard.[2]

"Hist! Billy," said the man in the same quick cautionary whisper as before. "You were impressed, weren't you? Well, so was I"; and he paused, as to mark the effect. But Billy, not knowing exactly what to make of this, °said nothing. Then the other: "We are not the only impressed ones, Billy. There's a gang of us.— Couldn't you—help—at a pinch?"   157

"What do you mean?" demanded Billy, here thoroughly shaking off his drowse.

"Hist, hist!" the hurried whisper now growing husky, "see here"; and the man held up two small objects faintly twinkling in the nightlight; "see, they are yours, Billy, if you'll only—"

But Billy broke in, and in his resentful eagerness to deliver himself, his vocal infirmity somewhat intruded: "D-D-Damme, I don't know what you are d-d-driving °at, or what you mean, but you had better g-g-go where you belong!" For the moment the fellow, as confounded, did not stir; and Billy springing to his feet, said, "If you d-don't start I'll t-t-toss you back over the r-rail!" There was no mistaking this and the mysterious emissary decamped disappearing in the direction of the mainmast in the shadow of the booms.   158

"Hallo, what's the matter?" here came growling from a forecastleman awakened from his deck-doze by Billy's raised voice. And as the foretopman reappeared and was recognized by him; "Ah, *Beauty*, °is it you? Well, something must have been the matter for you st-st-stuttered."   159

"O," rejoined Billy, now mastering the impediment; "I found an afterguardsman in our part of the ship here and I bid him be off where he belongs."

---

[2] In contrast to the advanced and respected rank of able seaman, which is given Billy as a foretopman and as the proficient, Handsome Sailor, the station of afterguardsman denotes an ordinary seaman or an apprentice assigned to attending the aftersails. Thus Billy's position is physically loftier and more fore-ward than the afterguardsman's. As in the case of pale Claggart, who lurks in the dark bowels of the ship (see note 14, leaf 31, above), Melville uses the physical facts of a seaman's station as suggestive signs of the contrasts, in all ways, between the seamen who inhabit these stations.

"And is that all you did about it, foretopman?" gruffly demanded another, an irascible old fellow of brick-colored visage and hair, and who was known to his associate forecastlemen as *Red Pepper;* "Such sneaks I should like to marry to the gunner's daughter!" by that expression meaning that he would like to subject them to disciplinary castigation over a gun.

160   °However, Billy's rendering of the matter satisfactorily accounted to these inquirers for the brief commotion, since of all the sections of a ship's company, the forecastlemen, veterans for the most part and bigoted in their sea-prejudices, are the most jealous in resenting territorial encroachments, especially on the part of any of the afterguard, of whom they have but a sorry opinion, chiefly landsmen, never going aloft except to reef or furl the mainsail, and in no wise competent to handle a marlinspike[3] or turn in a *dead-eye,* say.

[3] A marlinspike is a tapered, pointed iron instrument used to separate strands of rope in the process of splicing. It requires considerable experience to join the various strands properly.

[16]

°THIS INCIDENT sorely puzzled Billy Budd. It was an entirely   161
new experience; the first time in his life that he had ever been
personally approached in underhand intriguing fashion. Prior
to this encounter he had known nothing of the afterguardsman,
the two men being stationed wide apart, one forward and aloft
during his watch, the other on deck and aft.

What could it mean? And could they really be guineas, those
two glittering objects the interloper had held up to his eyes?
°Where could the fellow get guineas? Why even spare buttons   162
are not so plentiful at sea. The more he turned the matter over,
the more he was non-plussed, and made uneasy and discomforted.
In his disgustful recoil from an overture which though he but ill
comprehended he instinctively knew must involve evil of some
sort, Billy Budd was like a young horse fresh from the pasture
suddenly inhaling a vile whiff from some chemical factory, and
by repeated snortings trying to get it out of his nostrils and lungs.
This frame of mind barred all desire of holding further °parley   163
with the fellow, even were it but for the purpose of gaining
some enlightenment as to his design in approaching him. And yet
he was not without natural curiosity to see how such a visitor in
the dark would look in broad day.

He espied him the following afternoon in his first dog-watch
below, one of the smokers on that forward part of the upper
gun-deck allotted to the pipe. He recognized him by his general
cut and build, more than by his round freckled face and glassy
eyes of pale blue, veiled with lashes all but white. °And yet Billy   164
was a bit uncertain whether indeed it were he—yonder chap about
his own age chatting and laughing in free-hearted way, leaning
against a gun; a genial young fellow enough to look at, and something of a rattle-brain, to all appearance. Rather chubby too for a

73

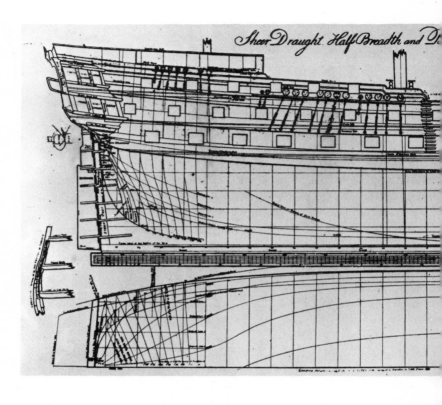

Sheer Draught. Half Breadth and D...

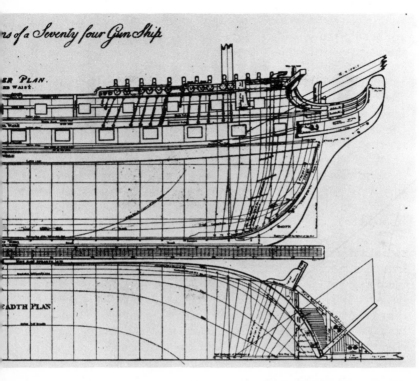

ns of a Seventy four Gun Ship

ER PLAN.
IN WAIST.

EADTH PLAN.

From E. Keble Chatterton, *Ships and Ways of Other Days*. London: Sidwick & Jackson, 1913. Reproduced by permission.

Longitudinal plans of an early nineteenth-century 74-gun ship.

sailor, even an afterguardsman. In short the last man in the world, one would think, to be overburthened with thoughts, especially those perilous thoughts that must needs belong to a conspirator in any serious project, or even to the underling of such a conspirator.

165 °Although Billy was not aware of it, the fellow, with a sidelong watchful glance had perceived Billy first, and then noting that Billy was looking at him, thereupon nodded a familiar sort of friendly recognition as to an old acquaintance, without interrupting the talk he was engaged in with the group of smokers. A day or two afterwards, chancing in the evening promenade on a gun deck, to pass Billy, he offered a flying word of good-fellowship as it were, which by its unexpectedness, and equivocalness under

166 the circumstances °so embarrassed Billy that he knew not how to respond to it, and let it go unnoticed.

Billy was now left more at a loss than before. The ineffectual speculations into which he was led were so disturbingly alien to him that he did his best to smother them. It never entered his mind that here was a matter which from its extreme questionableness, it was his duty as a loyal blue-jacket to report in the proper quarter. And, probably, had such a step been suggested to him, he

167 would have been deterred from taking it by the thought, °one of novice-magnanimity, that it would savor overmuch of the dirty work of a tell-tale. He kept the thing to himself. Yet upon one occasion, he could not forbear a little disburthening himself to the old Dansker, tempted thereto perhaps by the influence of a balmy night when the ship lay becalmed; the twain, silent for the most part, sitting together on deck, their heads propped against the bulwarks. But it was only a partial and anonymous account that Billy gave, the unfounded scruples above referred to preventing full disclosure to anybody. Upon hearing Billy's version, the sage

168 Dansker seemed to °divine more than he was told; and after a little meditation during which his wrinkles were pursed as into a point, quite effacing for the time that quizzing expression his face sometimes wore—"Didn't I say so, Baby Budd?"

"Say what?" demanded Billy.

"Why, *Jemmy Legs* is *down* on you."

"And what," rejoined Billy in amazement, "has *Jemmy Legs* to do with that cracked afterguardsman?"

"Ho, it was an afterguardsman then. A cat's-paw, a cat's-paw!" And with that exclamation, which, whether it had reference to a light puff of air just then coming over the calm sea, or a subtler relation to the afterguardsman, there is no telling, the old Merlin gave a twisting wrench with his °black teeth at his plug of to-   169
bacco, vouchsafing no reply to Billy's impetuous question, though now repeated, for it was his wont to relapse into grim silence when interrogated in skeptical sort as to any of his sententious oracles, not always very clear ones, rather partaking of that obscurity which invests most Delphic deliverances from any quarter.

Long experience had very likely brought this old man to that bitter prudence which never interferes in aught and never gives advice.

[17]

170 °YES, despite the Dansker's pithy insistence as to the Master-at-arms being at the bottom of these strange experiences of Billy on board the *Bellipotent*, the young sailor was ready to ascribe them to almost anybody but the man who, to use Billy's own expression, "always had a pleasant word for him." This is to be wondered at. Yet not so much to be wondered at. In certain matters, some sailors even in mature life remain unsophisticated enough. But a young seafarer of the disposition of our athletic foretopman, is much of a child-man. And yet a child's utter innocence is
171 but its blank ignorance, and the innocence °more or less wanes as intelligence waxes. But in Billy Budd intelligence, such as it was, had advanced, while yet his simple mindedness remained for the most part unaffected. Experience is a teacher indeed; yet did Billy's years make his experience small. Besides, he had none of that intuitive knowledge of the bad which in natures not good or incompletely so foreruns experience, and therefore may pertain, as in some instances it too clearly does pertain, even to youth.
172 °And what could Billy know of man except of man as a mere sailor? And the old-fashioned sailor, the veritable man-before-the-mast, the sailor from boyhood up, he, though indeed of the same species as a landsman, is in some respects singularly distinct from him. The sailor is frankness, the landsman is finesse. Life is not a game with the sailor, demanding the long head; no intricate game of chess where few moves are made in straightforwardness, and ends are attained by indirection; an oblique, tedious, barren game hardly worth that poor candle burnt out in playing it.
173 °Yes, as a class, sailors are in character a juvenile race. Even their deviations are marked by juvenility. And this more especially holding true with the sailors of Billy's time. Then, too, certain things which apply to all sailors, do more pointedly operate

here and there, upon the junior one. °Every sailor, too, is accus-   174
tomed to obey orders without debating them; his life afloat is
externally ruled for him; he is not brought into that promiscuous
commerce with mankind where unobstructed free agency on
equal terms—equal superficially, at least—soon teaches one that
unless upon occasion he exercise a distrust keen in proportion to
the fairness of the appearance, some foul turn may be served him.
A ruled undemonstrative distrustfulness is so habitual, not with
business-men so much, as with men who know their kind in less
shallow relations than business, namely, certain men-of-the-world,
that they °come at last to employ it all but unconsciously; and   175
some of them would very likely feel real surprise at being charged
with it as one of their general characteristics.

[18]

176 °BUT AFTER the little matter at the mess Billy Budd no more
found himself in strange trouble at times about his hammock or
his clothesbag or what not. While, as to that smile that occasionally sunned him, and the pleasant passing word, these were if not
more frequent, yet if anything more pronounced than before.
But for all that, there were certain other demonstrations now.
177 When Claggart's unobserved glance happened to °light on belted
Billy rolling along the upper gun-deck in the leisure of the second dog-watch, exchanging passing broadsides of fun with other
178 young promenaders in the crowd; that glance °would follow the
cheerful sea-Hyperion[1] with a settled meditative and melancholy
expression, his eyes strangely suffused with incipient feverish
tears. Then would Claggart look like the man of sorrows.[2] Yes,
and sometimes the melancholy expression would have in it a
touch of soft yearning, as if Claggart could even have loved Billy
but for fate and ban. But this was an evanescence, and quickly
repented of, as it were, by an immitigable look, pinching and
shrivelling the visage into the momentary semblance of a wrinkled
179 walnut. °But sometimes catching sight in advance of the foretop-

[1] Hyperion, a Titan, was the father of Helios. But from Homer on, the
father's name was applied to Helios, the sun god. Hyperion (Helios) was
characterized by outstanding bright beauty.

[2] "The man of sorrows" usually refers to Christ as presented in interpre-
tations of Isaiah 53:1-5 and as used by Melville in the famous chapter, "The
Try-Works," in *Moby-Dick:* "The truest of all men was the Man of
Sorrows, and the truest of all books is Solomon's and Ecclesiastes is the fine
hammered steel of woe." Here, in the context of the imagery Melville used
to build his characterization of Claggart, the phrase does not make Claggart
Christly. Rather it emphasizes the sad yearning that occasionally overcomes
Claggart, and the language of the entire passage is more reminiscent of
certain moods of Milton's Satan than of Christ.

man coming in his direction, he would, upon their nearing, step aside a little to let him pass, dwelling upon Billy for the moment with the glittering dental satire of a Guise.[3] But upon any abrupt unforseen encounter a red light would forth from his eye like a spark from an anvil in a dusk smithy. °That quick fierce light was   180 a strange one, darted from orbs which in repose were of a color nearest approaching a deeper violet, the softest of shades.

Though some of these caprices of the pit could not but be observed by their object, yet were they beyond the construing °of   181 such a nature. And the thews of Billy were hardly compatible with that sort of sensitive spiritual organisation which in some cases instinctively conveys to ignorant innocence an admonition of the proximity of the malign. He thought the Master-at-arms acted in a manner rather queer at times. That was all. But the occasional frank air and pleasant word went for what they purported to be, the young sailor never having heard as yet of the "too fair-spoken man."

°Had the foretopman been conscious of having done or said   182 anything to provoke the ill will of the official, it would have been different with him, and his sight might have been purged if not sharpened. As it was, innocence was his blinder.

So was it with him in yet another matter. Two minor officers —the Armorer and Captain of the Hold—with whom he had never exchanged a word, his position in the ship not bringing him into contact with them; these men now for the first began to cast upon Billy when they chanced to encounter him, that peculiar °glance which evidences that the man from whom it comes   183 has been some way tampered with and to the prejudice of him

[3] The Guise family formed a branch of the House of Lorraine from 1528 to 1675. Ultra-Catholic, the family was involved in anti-Protestant intrigues and struggles for the control of France. After the bloody St. Bartholomew's Day massacre of the Huguenots in 1572, the family strength was dissipated in defeats and unprincipled adventurism, especially in the mid-seventeenth century. Claggart's hypocritical appearance here is cast in an image that continues the nature of the historical and political references. It is interesting that so many of the references, concerned as they are with rebellion and order, truth and falsehood, should center on Catholic-Protestant tensions and plots (see note 2, leaf 90, where Claggart is associated with Titus Oates, and note 2, leaf 150, where he is associated with Guy Fawkes).

upon whom the glance lights. Never did it occur to Billy as a thing to be noted or a thing suspicious, though he well knew the fact, that the Armorer and Captain of the Hold, with the ship's-yeoman, apothecary, and others of that grade, were by naval usage, mess-mates of the Master-at-arms, men with ears convenient to his confidential tongue.

184   °But the general popularity that came from our *Handsome Sailor's* manly forwardness upon occasion, and irresistible good nature indicating no mental superiority tending to excite an invidious feeling; this good will on the part of most of his shipmates made him the less to concern himself about such mute aspects toward him as those whereto allusion has just been made, aspects he could not so fathom as to infer their whole import.

185   °As to the afterguardsman, though Billy for reasons already given necessarily saw little of him, yet when the two did happen to meet, invariably came the fellow's off-hand cheerful recognition, sometimes accompanied by a passing pleasant word or two. Whatever that equivocal young person's original design may really have been, or the design of which he might have been the deputy, certain it was from his manner upon these occasions, that he had wholly dropped it.

186   °It was as if his precocity of crookedness (and every vulgar villain is precocious) had for once deceived him, and the man he had sought to entrap as a simpleton had, through his very simplicity ignorantly baffled him.

But shrewd ones may opine that it was hardly possible for Billy to refrain from going up to the afterguardsman and bluntly demanding to know his purpose in the initial interview, so abruptly closed in the fore-chains. Shrewd ones may also think it but

187   natural in Billy to set about °sounding some of the other impressed men of the ship in order to discover what basis, if any, there was for the emissary's obscure suggestions as to plotting disaffection aboard. Yes, the shrewd may so think. But something more, or rather, something else than mere shrewdness is perhaps needful for the due understanding of such a character as Billy Budd's.

°As to Claggart, the monomania in the man—if that indeed it   188
were—as involuntarily disclosed by starts in the manifestations de-
tailed, yet in general covered over by his self-contained and rational demeanor; this, like a subterranean fire was eating its way
deeper and deeper in him. Something decisive must come of it.

[19]

189 °AFTER THE MYSTERIOUS INTERVIEW in the fore-chains, the one so abruptly ended there by Billy, nothing especially germane to the story occurred until the events now about to be narrated.

Elsewhere it has been said that in the lack of frigates (of course better sailers than line-of-battle ships) in the English squadron up
190 the Straits[1] at that period, the *Bellipotent* 74 °was occasionally employed not only as an available substitute for a scout, but at times on detached service of more important kind. This was not alone because of her sailing qualities, not common in a ship of her rate, but quite as much, probably, that the character of her commander, it was thought, specially adapted him for any duty where under unforeseen difficulties a prompt initiative might have to be taken in some matter demanding knowledge and ability in addi-
191 tion to those qualities implied in good seamanship. °It was on an expedition of the latter sort, a somewhat distant one, and when the *Bellipotent* was almost at her furthest remove from the fleet, that in the latter part of an afternoon-watch she unexpectedly came in sight of a ship of the enemy. It proved to be a frigate. The latter perceiving through the glass that the weight of men and metal would be heavily against her, invoking her light heels, crowded sail to get away. After a chase urged almost against hope
192 and lasting until about the middle of the first dog-watch, °she signally succeeded in effecting her escape.

Not long after the pursuit had been given up, and ere the excitement incident thereto had altogether waned away, the Master-at-arms, ascending from his cavernous sphere, made his appearance

---

[1] The Straits of Gibraltar. The Mediterranean Fleet was patrolling off Cádiz in the same locale in which the same Fleet, eight years later, engaged in the Battle of Trafalgar.

cap in hand by the mainmast, respectfully waiting the notice of Captain Vere, then solitary walking the weather-side of the quarter-deck, doubtless somewhat chafed at the failure of the pursuit. The spot where Claggart stood was the place allotted to men of lesser grades seeking some more particular interview either °with the officer-of-the-deck or the Captain himself. But from the   193
latter it was not often that a sailor or petty-officer of those days would seek a hearing; only some exceptional cause, would, according to established custom, have warranted that.

Presently, just as the Commander, absorbed in his reflections, was on the point of turning aft in his promenade, he became sensible of Claggart's presence, and saw the doffed cap held in deferential expectancy. °Here be it said that Captain Vere's personal   194
knowledge of this petty-officer had only begun at the time of the ship's last sailing from home, Claggart then for the first, in transfer from a ship detained for repairs, supplying on board the *Bellipotent* the place of a previous Master-at-arms disabled and ashore.

No sooner did the Commander observe who it was that now deferentially stood awaiting his notice, than a peculiar expression came over him. It was not unlike that which uncontrollably will flit across the °countenance of one at unawares encountering a   195
person who, though known to him indeed, has hardly been long enough known for thorough knowledge, but something in whose aspect nevertheless now for the first provokes a vaguely repellent distaste. But coming to a stand, and resuming much of his wonted official manner, save that a sort of impatience lurked in the intonation of the opening word, he said, "Well? what is it, Master-at-arms"?

With the air of a subordinate grieved at the necessity of being a messenger of ill tidings, and while conscientiously determined to be frank, yet equally resolved upon shunning overstatement, °Claggart at this invitation, or rather summons to disburthen,   196
spoke up. What he said, conveyed in the language of no uneducated man, was to the effect following, if not altogether in these words, namely, that during the chase and preparations for the possible encounter he had seen enough to convince him that at least one sailor aboard was a dangerous character in a ship muster-

ing some who not only had taken a guilty part in the late serious
troubles, but others also who, like the man in question, had entered His Majesty's service under another form than enlistment.

197   °At this point Captain Vere with some impatience, interrupted
him: "Be direct, man; say 'impressed men'."

198   Claggart made a gesture of subservience, and proceeded. °Quite
lately he (Claggart) had begun to suspect that on the gun-decks
some sort of movement prompted by the sailor in question was
covertly going on, but he had not thought himself warranted in
reporting the suspicion so long as it remained indistinct. But from
what he had that afternoon observed in the man referred to, the
suspicion of something clandestine going on had advanced to a
point less removed from certainty. He deeply felt, he added, the
serious responsibility assumed in making a report involving such
possible consequences to the individual mainly concerned, besides
tending to augment those natural anxieties which every naval com-

199   mander °must feel in view of extraordinary outbreaks so recent
as those which, he sorrowfully said it, it needed not to name.

Now at the first broaching of the matter Captain Vere, taken
by surprise, could not wholly dissemble his disquietude. But as
Claggart went on, the former's aspect changed into restiveness
under something in the testifier's manner in giving his testimony.
However, he refrained from interrupting him. And Claggart,

200   continuing, concluded with this: °"God forbid, your honor, that
the Bellipotent's should be the experience of the—"

"Never mind that!" here peremptorily broke in the superior,
his face altering with anger, instinctively divining the ship that
the other was about to name, one in which the Nore Mutiny had
assumed a singularly tragical character that for a time jeopardized
the life of its commander. Under the circumstances he was indig-
nant at the purposed allusion. When the commissioned officers

201   themselves °were on all occasions very heedful how they referred to the recent events in the Fleet, for a petty-officer un-
necessarily to allude to them in the presence of his Captain, this
struck him as a most immodest presumption. Besides, to his quick
sense of self-respect, it even looked under the circumstances something like an attempt to alarm him. Nor at first was he without
some surprise that one who, so far as he had hitherto come under

his notice, had shown considerable tact in his function should in this particular evince such lack of it.

°But these thoughts and kindred dubious ones flitting across 202 his mind were suddenly replaced by an intuitional surmise which, though as yet obscure in form, served practically to affect his reception of the ill tidings. Certain it is, that long versed in °everything pertaining to the complicated gun-deck life, which 203 like every other form of life, has its secret mines and dubious side, the side popularly disclaimed, Captain Vere did not permit himself to be unduly disturbed by the general tenor of his subordinate's report.

Furthermore, if in view of recent events prompt action should be taken at the first palpable sign of recurring insubordination, for all that, not judicious would it be, he thought, to keep the idea of lingering disaffection alive by undue forwardness in crediting an °informer, even if his own subordinate, and charged among 204 other things with police surveillance of the crew. °This feeling 205 would not perhaps have so prevailed with him were it not that upon a prior occasion the patriotic zeal officially evinced by Claggart had somewhat irritated him as appearing rather supersensible and strained. Furthermore, something even in the official's self-possessed and somewhat ostentatious manner in making his specifications strangely reminded him of a bandsman, a perjurous witness in a capital case before a court-martial ashore of which when a Lieutenant he, Captain Vere, had been a member.

°Now the peremptory check given to Claggart in the matter of 206 the arrested allusion was quickly followed up by this: "You say that there is at least one dangerous man aboard. Name him."

"William Budd. A foretopman, your honor—"

"William Budd," repeated Captain Vere with unfeigned astonishment; "and mean you the man that Lieutenant Ratcliffe took from the merchantman not very long ago—the young fellow who seems to be so popular with the men— Billy, the Handsome Sailor, as they call him?"

°"The same, your honor; but for all his youth and good looks, a 207 deep one. Not for nothing does he insinuate himself into the good will of his shipmates, since at the least all hands will at a pinch say a good word for him at all hazards. Did Lieutenant Ratcliffe

happen to tell your honor of that adroit fling of Budd's jumping
up in the cutter's bow under the merchantman's stern when he was
being taken off? It is even masqued by that sort of good humored
air that at heart he resents his impressment. You have but noted
his fair cheek. A man-trap may be under his ruddy-tipped daisies."

208   °Now the *Handsome Sailor*, as a signal figure among the crew,
had naturally enough attracted the Captain's attention from the
first. Though in general not very demonstrative to his officers, he
had congratulated Lieutenant Ratcliffe upon his good fortune in
lighting on such a fine specimen of the genus homo, who in the
nude might have posed for a statue of young Adam before the
Fall.

As to Billy's adieu to the ship *Rights-of-Man*, which the boarding Lieutenant had indeed reported to him but in a deferential way
more as a good story than aught else, Captain Vere, though mistakenly understanding it as a satiric sally, had but thought so
much the better of the impressed man for it; as a military sailor,
admiring the spirit that could take an arbitrary enlistment so
209   merrily and sensibly. °The foretopman's conduct, too, so far as it
had fallen under the Captain's notice, had confirmed the first
happy augury, while the new recruit's qualities as a *sailor-man*
seemed to be such that he had thought of recommending him to
the executive officer for promotion to a place that would more
frequently bring him under his own observation, namely, the captaincy of the mizzen-top, replacing there in the starboard watch
a man not so young whom partly for that reason he deemed less
210   °fitted for the post. Be it parenthesized here that since the mizzen-
top-men have not to handle such breadths of heavy canvas as the
lower sails on the main-mast and fore-mast, a young man if of the
right stuff not only seems best adapted to duty there, but in fact
is generally selected for the captaincy of that top, and the company under him are light hands and often but striplings. In sum,
Captain Vere had from the beginning deemed Billy Budd to be
what in the naval parlance of the time was called a *"King's bar-*
211   *gain,"* that is to say, for His °Britannic Majesty's navy a capital
investment at small outlay or none at all.

After a brief pause during which the reminiscences above mentioned passed vividly through his mind and he weighed the import

of Claggart's last suggestion conveyed in the phrase "man-trap under the daisies," and the more he weighed it the less reliance he
felt in the informer's good faith, suddenly he turned upon him and
in a low voice demanded: "Do you come to me, Master-at-arms,
with so foggy a tale? As to Budd, cite me an act or spoken word
of his confirmatory of what you in general charge against him.
Stay," drawing nearer to him, "heed what °you speak. Just now,   212
and in a case like this, there is a yard-arm-end for the false-wit-
ness."

   "Ah, your honor!" sighed Claggart mildly shaking his shapely
head as in sad deprecation of such unmerited severity of tone.
Then, bridling—erecting himself as in virtuous self-assertion, he
circumstantially alleged certain words and acts, which collec-
tively, if credited, led to presumptions mortally inculpating Budd.
And for some of these averments, he added, substantiating proof
was not far.

   °With gray eyes impatient and distrustful essaying to fathom   213
to the bottom Claggart's calm violet ones, Captain Vere again
heard him out; then for the moment stood ruminating. The mood
he evinced, Claggart—himself for the time liberated from the
other's scrutiny—steadily regarded with a look difficult to render
—a look curious of the operation of his tactics, a look such as
might have been that of the spokesman of the envious children of
Jacob deceptively imposing upon the troubled patriarch the blood-
dyed coat of young Joseph.[2]

   °Though something exceptional in the moral quality of Captain 214
Vere made him, in earnest encounter with a fellow-man, a veritable touch-stone of that man's essential nature, yet now as to
Claggart and what was really going on in him, his feeling partook
less of intuitional conviction than of strong suspicion clogged by
strange dubieties. The perplexity he evinced proceeded less from
aught touching the man informed against—as Claggart doubtless

---

   [2] Joseph's brothers envied and hated him because he stood highest in
the favor of Jacob, their father. To get rid of Joseph, they sold him to the
Ishmaelites, took his distinctive, many-colored coat and dipped it in the
blood of a kid they killed for the purpose. Then they brought the bloody
coat to Jacob, asking him if he could positively identify the garment.
Jacob was gulled and believed that Joseph was dead (Gen. 37:1–36).

opined—than from considerations how best to act in regard to the
215 informer. At first indeed he was naturally for °summoning that
substantiation of his allegations which Claggart said was at hand.
But such a proceeding would result in the matter at once getting
abroad, which in the present stage of it, he thought, might un-
desirably affect the ship's company. If Claggart was a false witness—that closed the affair. And therefore before trying the
accusation, he would first practically test the accuser; and he
thought this could be done in a quiet, undemonstrative way.

The measure he determined upon involved a shifting of the
216 °scene, a transfer to a place less exposed to observation than the
broad quarter-deck. For although the few gun-room officers there
at the time had, in due observance of naval etiquette, withdrawn
to leeward the moment Captain Vere had begun his promenade
on the deck's weather-side; and though during the colloquy with
Claggart they of course ventured not to diminish the distance;
and though throughout the interview Captain Vere's voice was
far from high, and Claggart's silvery and low; and the wind in
the cordage and the wash of the sea helped the more to put them
217 beyond earshot; °nevertheless, the interview's continuance already
had attracted observation from some topmen aloft and other sailors
in the waist or further forward.

Having determined upon his measures, Captain Vere forthwith took action. Abruptly turning to Claggart he asked, "Master-
at-arms, is it now Budd's watch aloft?"

"No, your honor." Whereupon, "Mr. Wilkes!" summoning the
nearest midshipman, "tell Albert to come to me." Albert was the
Captain's hammock-boy, a sort of sea-valet in whose discretion
218 and fidelity his master had much °confidence. The lad appeared.
"You know Budd the foretopman?"

"I do, Sir."

"Go find him. It is his watch off. Manage to tell him out of
219 earshot that he is wanted aft. Contrive it that he speaks °to
nobody. Keep him in talk yourself. And not till you get well aft
here, not till then let him know that the place where he is wanted
is my cabin. You understand. Go.—Master-at-arms, show yourself
on the decks below, and when you think it time for Albert to be
coming with his man, stand by quietly to follow the sailor in."

Thomas Hearne, *circ.* 1775
National Maritime Museum, London

The quarterdeck of the ship-of-the-line, *Deal Castle*. "Men of lesser
grades seeking some more particular interview with the officer-of-the-
deck or the Captain himself" waited by the mainmast, the nearer of the
two masts in the center of the picture.

[20]

NOW when the foretopman found himself closeted there, as it were, in the cabin with the Captain and Claggart, he was surprised
220 enough. But it °was a surprise unaccompanied by apprehension or distrust. To an immature nature essentially honest and humane, forewarning intimations of subtler danger from one's kind come tardily if at all. The only thing that took shape in the young sailor's mind was this: Yes, the Captain, I have always thought, looks kindly upon me. Wonder if he's going to make me his coxswain.[1] I should like that. And maybe now he is going to ask the Master-at-arms about me.
221 °"Shut the door there, sentry," said the commander; "stand without, and let nobody come in.—Now, Master-at-arms, tell this man to his face what you told of him to me"; and stood prepared to scrutinize the mutually confronting visages.

With the measured step and calm collected air of an asylum-physician approaching in the public hall some patient beginning to show indications of a coming paroxysm, Claggart deliberately advanced within short range of Billy, and mesmerically looking him in the eye, briefly recapitulated the accusation.
222 °Not at first did Billy take it in. When he did, the rose-tan of his cheek looked struck as by white leprosy. He stood like one impaled and gagged. Meanwhile the accuser's eyes removing not as yet from the blue dilated ones, underwent a phenomenal change, their wonted rich violet color blurring into a muddy purple. Those lights of human intelligence losing human expression,

---

[1] The coxswain is the sailor in charge of the captain's gig and its crew. He steers the boat when the captain is rowed to and from the ship. In effect, he is the captain's personal chauffeur and handyman, enjoying certain privileges and lighter chores.

gelidly protruded like the alien eyes of certain uncatalogued crea-
tures of the deep. The first mesmeric glance was one of serpent
fascination; the last was as the hungry lurch of the torpedo-fish.

°"Speak, man!" said Captain Vere to the transfixed one, struck   223
by his aspect even more than by Claggart's. "Speak! defend yourself." Which appeal caused but a strange dumb gesturing and
gurgling in Billy; amazement at such an accusation so suddenly
sprung on inexperienced nonage; this, and, it may be, horror of
the accuser's eyes serving to bring out his lurking defect and in
this instance for the time intensifying it into a convulsed tongue-
tie; while the intent head °and entire form straining forward in   224
an agony of ineffectual eagerness to obey the injunction to speak
and defend himself, gave an expression to the face like that of a
condemned Vestal priestess in the moment of being buried alive,
and in the first struggle against suffocation.

Though at the time Captain Vere was quite ignorant of Billy's
liability to vocal impediment, he now immediately divined it, since
vividly Billy's aspect recalled to him that of a bright young
schoolmate of his whom he had once seen struck by much the
same °startling impotence in the act of eagerly rising in the class   225
to be foremost in response to a testing question put to it by the
master. Going close up to the young sailor, and laying a soothing hand on his shoulder, he said, "There is no hurry, my boy.
Take your time, take your time." Contrary to the effect intended,
these words so fatherly in tone, doubtless touching Billy's heart
to the quick, prompted yet more violent efforts at utterance—
efforts soon ending for the time in confirming the paralysis, and
bringing to his face an expression which was as a crucifixion to
behold. The next °instant, quick as the flame from a discharged   226
cannon at night, his right arm shot out, and Claggart dropped to
the deck. Whether intentionally or but owing to the young
athlete's superior height, the blow had taken effect full upon the
forehead, so shapely and intellectual-looking a feature in the
Master-at-arms; so that the body fell over lengthwise, like a heavy
plank tilted from erectness. A gasp or two, and he lay motionless.

"Fated boy," breathed Captain Vere in tone so low as to be
almost a whisper, "what have you done! But here, help me."

227   °The twain raised the felled one from the loins up into a sitting
position. The spare form flexibly acquiesced, but inertly. It was
like handling a dead snake. They lowered it back. Regaining
erectness Captain Vere with one hand covering his face stood to
all appearance as impassive as the object at his feet. Was he absorbed in taking in all the bearings of the event and what was best
not only now at once to be done, but also in the sequel? Slowly
he uncovered his face; and the effect was as if the moon emerging
228 from eclipse should reappear with quite another °aspect than that
which had gone into hiding. The father in him, manifested
towards Billy thus far in the scene, was replaced by the military
disciplinarian. In his official tone he bade the foretopman retire to
a state-room aft (pointing it out), and there remain till thence
summoned. This order Billy in silence mechanically obeyed. Then
going to the cabin-door where it opened on the quarter-deck,
Captain Vere said to the sentry without, "Tell somebody to send
Albert here." When the lad appeared his master so contrived it
that he should not catch sight of the prone one. "Albert," he
229 said to him, °"tell the Surgeon I wish to see him. You need not
come back till called."

        When the Surgeon entered—a self-poised character of that
grave sense and experience that hardly anything could take him
aback—Captain Vere advanced to meet him, thus unconsciously
intercepting his view of Claggart, and interrupting the other's
wonted ceremonious salutation, said, "Nay, tell me how it is with
yonder man," directing his attention to the prostrate one.
230   °The Surgeon looked, and for all his self-command, somewhat
started at the abrupt revelation. On Claggart's always pallid
complexion, thick black blood was now oozing from nostril and
ear. To the gazer's professional eye it was unmistakably no living
man that he saw.

        "Is it so then?" said Captain Vere intently watching him. "I
thought it. But verify it." Whereupon the customary test confirmed the Surgeon's first glance, who now looking up in unfeigned concern, cast a look of intense inquisitiveness upon his
231 superior. °But Captain Vere, with one hand to his brow, was
standing motionless. Suddenly, catching the Surgeon's arm con-

vulsively, he exclaimed, pointing down to the body—"It is the
divine judgement on Ananias![2] Look!"

Disturbed by the excited manner he had never before observed
in the *Bellipotent*'s Captain, and as yet wholly ignorant of the
affair, the prudent Surgeon nevertheless held his peace, only again
looking an earnest interrogation as to what it was that had resulted in such a tragedy.

°But Captain Vere was now again motionless standing absorbed   232
in thought. But again starting, he vehemently exclaimed—"Struck
dead by an angel of God! Yet the angel must hang!"

At these passionate interjections, mere incoherences to the
listener as yet unapprised of the antecedents, the Surgeon was profoundly discomposed. But now as recollecting himself, Captain
Vere in less harsh tone briefly related the circumstances leading
up to the event. °"But come; we must despatch," he added. "Help   233
me to remove him (meaning the body) to yonder compartment,"
designating one opposite that where the foretopman remained im-
mured. Anew disturbed by a request that as implying a desire for
secrecy, seemed unaccountably strange to him, there was nothing
for the subordinate to do but comply.

"Go now," said Captain Vere with something of his wonted
manner—"Go now. I shall presently call a drum-head court.[3] Tell
the Lieutenants what has happened, and tell Mr. Mordant," meaning the Captain of marines, "and charge them °to keep the matter   234
to themselves."

[2] The followers of Jesus and the Apostles gave up all their worldly
goods into a common fund, selling all their land and laying the money
thus gained at the Apostles' feet. But Ananias and his wife, Sapphira, con-
spired together to hold back for themselves part of the price they had
received for their land. When Ananias laid the money at Peter's feet,
Peter told him that with his lie he was not cheating men but God. Thereupon God struck Ananias dead. Three hours later Peter similarly confronted Sapphira, and God struck her dead, too (Acts 4:23–34 and 5:1–11).

[3] So called because summary courts held for judgment on the spot, either
in the line of march or in a battle, convened around a drumhead, which
was used for a table.

[21]

FULL OF DISQUIETUDE and misgiving the Surgeon left the cabin. Was Captain Vere suddenly affected in his mind, or was it but a transient excitement, brought about by so strange and extraordinary a happening? As to the drum-head court, it struck the Surgeon as impolitic, if nothing more. The thing to do, he thought, was to place Billy Budd in confinement and in a way dictated by usage, and postpone further action in so extraordinary a case, to such time as they should rejoin the squadron, and then refer it to the Admiral. He recalled the unwonted agita-
235   tion of Captain Vere and his excited exclamations °so at variance with his normal manner. Was he unhinged?

But assuming that he is, it is not so susceptible of proof. What then can he do? No more trying situation is conceivable than that of an officer subordinate under a Captain whom he suspects to be, not mad indeed, but yet not quite unaffected in his intellect. To argue his order to him would be insolence. To resist him would be mutiny.

In obedience to Captain Vere he communicated what had happened to the Lieutenants and Captain of marines; saying nothing as to the Captain's state. They fully shared his own surprise and
236   concern. °Like him too they seemed to think that such a matter should be referred to the Admiral.

[22]

WHO IN THE RAINBOW can draw the line where the violet tint ends and the orange tint begins? Distinctly we see the difference of the colors, but where exactly does the one first blendingly enter into the other? So with sanity and insanity. In pronounced cases there is no question about them. But in some supposed cases, in various degrees supposedly less pronounced, to draw the exact line of demarkation few will undertake though for a fee some professional experts will. There is nothing namable but that some men will undertake to do it for pay.

°Whether Captain Vere, as the Surgeon professionally and   237
privately surmised, was really the sudden victim of any degree of aberration, one must determine for himself by such light as this narrative may afford.

That °the unhappy event which has been narrated could not   238
have happened at a worse juncture was but too true. For it was close on the heel of the suppressed insurrections, an aftertime very critical to naval authority, demanding from every English sea-commander two qualities not readily interfusable—prudence and rigor. Moreover there was something crucial in the case.[1]

°The year 1797, the year of this narrative, belongs to a period   229d
which, as every thinker now feels, involved a crisis for Christendom not exceeded in its undetermined momentousness at the time by any other era whereof there is record. The opening proposition made by the Spirit of that Age involved °the rectification of   229e
the Old World's hereditary wrongs. In France, to some extent, this was bloodily effected. But what then? Straightway the Revo-

[1] Leaves 229d, 229e, and 229f, which follow from this point, have never been placed here in any other edition. Hayford and Sealts delete them entirely. For a discussion of inclusion and placement of these leaves, see Appendix One, pp. 152–155.

lution regency as righter of wrongs itself became a wrongdoer, one more oppressive than the Kings. Under Napoleon it enthroned upstart kings, and initiated that prolonged agony of Continental war whose final throe was at Waterloo. During those years not the wisest could have foreseen that the outcome of all would be what to some thinkers apparently it has since turned out to be, a political advance along nearly the whole line for Europeans.

229f   °Now, as elsewhere hinted, it was something caught from the Revolutionary Spirit that at Spithead emboldened the man-of-war's men to rise against real abuses, long-standing ones, and afterwards at the Nore to make inordinate and aggressive demands, successful resistance to which was confirmed only when the ringleaders were hung for an admonitory spectacle to the anchored fleet. Yet in a way analogous to the operation of the Revolution at large, the Great Mutiny, though by Englishmen naturally deemed monstrous at the time, doubtless gave the first latent prompting to most important reforms in the British navy.

239   °In the jugglery of circumstances preceding and attending the event on board the *Bellipotent*, and in the light of that martial code whereby it was formally to be judged, innocence and guilt personified in Claggart and Budd in effect changed places. In a legal view the apparent victim of the tragedy was he who had sought to victimize a man blameless; and the indisputable deed of the latter, navally regarded, constituted the most heinous of military crimes. Yet more. The essential right and wrong involved in

240   the matter, the clearer that might be, so much the °worse for the responsibility of a loyal sea-commander inasmuch as he was not authorized to determine the matter on that primitive basis.

Small wonder then that the *Bellipotent*'s Captain, though in general a man of rapid decision, felt that circumspectness not less than promptitude was necessary. Until he could decide upon his

241   course, and in each detail; and not only so, but until the °concluding measure was upon the point of being enacted, he deemed it advisable, in view of all the circumstances to guard as much as possible against publicity. Here he may or may not have erred. Certain it is however that subsequently in the confidential talk of

more than one or two gun-rooms and cabins he was not a little
criticized by some officers, a fact imputed by his friends, and
vehemently by his cousin Jack Denton, to professional jealousy of
Starry Vere. Some imaginative ground for invidious comment
there was. The maintenance °of secrecy in the matter, the con-   242
fining all knowledge of it for a time to the place where the homicide occurred, the quarter-deck cabin; in these particulars lurked
some resemblance to the policy adopted in those tragedies of the
palace which have occurred more than once in the capital founded
by Peter the Barbarian.[2]

°The case indeed was such that fain would the *Bellipotent*'s   243
Captain have deferred taking any action whatever respecting it
further than to keep the foretopman a close prisoner till the ship
rejoined the squadron and then submitting the matter to the
judgement of his Admiral.

But a true military officer is in one particular like a true monk.
Not with more of self-abnegation will the latter keep his vows of
monastic obedience than the former his vows of allegiance to
martial duty.

°Feeling that unless quick action was taken on it, the deed of   244
the foretopman, so soon as it should be known on the gun-decks
would tend to awaken any slumbering embers of the Nore among
the crew, a sense of the urgency of the case overruled in Captain
Vere every other consideration. But though a conscientious disciplinarian he was no lover of authority for mere authority's sake.
Very far was he from embracing opportunities for monopolizing
to himself the perils of moral responsibility, none at least that
could properly be referred to an official superior °or shared with   245
him by his official equals or even subordinates. So thinking he was
glad it would not be at variance with usage to turn the matter
over to a summary court of his own officers, reserving to himself,
as the one on whom the ultimate accountability would rest, the
right of maintaining a supervision of it, or formally or informally

---

[2] St. Petersburg (now Leningrad), founded by Peter the Great, Emperor
of Russia (1672–1725). The courts of the Czars became known for their
intrigues as the rule of the Czars became a symbol of absolute despotism.

interposing at need. Accordingly a drum-head court was sum-marily convened, he electing the individuals composing it, the First Lieutenant, the Captain of marines, and the Sailing Master.[3]

246   °In associating an officer of marines with the sea-Lieutenant and the Sailing Master in a case having to do with a sailor the Com-mander perhaps deviated from general custom. He was prompted

[3] Hayford and Sealts point out that Melville was not familiar with the British naval regulations in effect in 1797 (see their discussion, n. 233, pp. 175–176 and n. 245, pp. 178–179). Although the commander of any part of the fleet detached for separate service (recall that the *Bellipotent* was on detached service at the time Billy killed Claggart—see leaves 189–191) was empowered "to hold Courts Martial during the Time of such separate Service" (statute 22 George II, Cap. 33, Sect. VIII, *A Collection of the Statutes Relating to the Admiralty, Navy, Shipping, and Navigation . . .* [London, 1810], p. 157), nevertheless there were "no inferior or divisional courts-martial in the British navy analogous to regimental or garrison courts-martial in the army" (*H&S*, p. 176). Furthermore, according to statute 22 George II, Cap. 33, Sect. VI, "regular naval courts-martial con-sisted of commanders and captains" (*H&S*, p. 178), not a first lieutenant, a captain of marines, and a sailing master (sailing masters were non-com-missioned navigators). Melville had Vere "deviate from general custom" in greater measure than he was aware. However, a court-martial in a ship on detached service could not be a regular court-martial to begin with, and it would be impossible to have the court consist of captains and commanders on a single ship, which has but one captain. Moreover, the absence of the equivalent of regimental courts-martial meant that a captain faced with the necessity for a court-martial would either have to call his own if he were on detached service, or would have to wait until the matter could be taken care of by the Admiralty. Melville can be both attacked and de-fended on the grounds of legal technicalities. The clear fact is that it was not according to usage for a drumhead court like Captain Vere's to have taken place. But obviously, what is important here is not the extent to which Melville was a sea-lawyer expert in British naval regulations of the eighteenth century; what is to the point is Melville's insistence that the court-martial was unusual yet had legal precedence and justification. He was concerned to indicate that Vere had nowhere to turn to hand on to others the moral and legal necessities with which he was confronted, that Vere was not acting like a man who made up his own justice as he went along but that he had solid precedent, that Vere was so pressed by the historical and psychological circumstances of the moment that he could not wait to hand the case over to the Admiral, and that Vere, bereft of the luxuries of spare time or equivocation, was morally and legally right to act, although he was more anguished than anyone by the necessity. Mel-ville's "misuse" of naval custom is much less important as a legal techni-cality than as an indication that he was attempting to justify the extreme action Vere felt compelled to take. The point of law here is crucial not to legal history but to the critical controversy that surrounds the evaluation of Captain Vere.

thereto by the circumstance that he took that soldier to be a
judicious person, thoughtful, and not altogether incapable of
grappling with a difficult case unprecedented in his prior experience. Yet even as to him he was not without some latent misgiving, for withal he was an extremely good-natured man, an
°enjoyer of his dinner, a sound sleeper, and inclined to obesity,   247
a man who though he would always maintain his manhood in
battle might not prove altogether reliable in a moral dilemma
involving aught of the tragic. As to the First Lieutenant and the
Sailing Master, Captain Vere could not but be aware that though
honest natures, of approved gallantry upon occasion, their intelligence was mostly confined to the matter of active seamanship
and the fighting demands of their profession. The court was held
in the same cabin where the unfortunate affair had taken place.
This cabin, the Commander's, embraced the entire area under the
poop-deck. Aft, and on either side, °was a small state-room; the   248
one room temporarily a jail and the other a dead-house, and a yet
smaller compartment leaving a space between, expanding forward
into a goodly oblong of length coinciding with the ship's beam.
A skylight of moderate dimension was overhead and at each end
of the oblong space were two sashed port-hole windows easily
convertible back into embrasures for short carronades.

All being quickly in readiness, Billy Budd was arraigned,
Captain Vere necessarily appearing as the sole witness in the case,
and as such, temporarily sinking his rank, though singularly maintaining it in a °matter apparently trivial, namely, that he testified   249
from the ship's weather-side, with that object having caused the
court to sit on the lee-side.[4] Concisely he narrated all that had led
up to the catastrophe, omitting nothing in Claggart's accusation
and deposing as to the manner in which the prisoner had received
it. At this testimony the three officers glanced with no little surprise at Billy Budd, the last man they would have suspected either

---

[4] Vere maintains the same physical position of superiority that naval
etiquette accords to the captain in command of his quarterdeck (see leaves
76 and 216). The "apparently trivial" matter is Vere's way of announcing
that he assumes responsibility and direction, "reserving to himself as the one
on whom the ultimate accountability would rest, the right of maintaining
a supervision" of the court (leaf 245; see also Vere's actions, leaves 259–
260).

of the mutinous design alleged by Claggart or the undeniable deed
250 he himself had done. °The First Lieutenant, taking judicial primacy and turning toward the prisoner, said, "Captain Vere has
spoken. Is it or is it not as Captain Vere says?" In response came
syllables not so much impeded in the utterance as might have been
anticipated. They were these: "Captain Vere tells the truth. It is
just as Captain Vere says, but it is not as the Master-at-arms said.
I have eaten the King's bread and I am true to the King."

"I believe you, my man," said the witness, his voice indicating a
suppressed emotion not otherwise betrayed.
251   °"God will bless you for that, Your Honor!" not without stam-
mering said Billy, and all but broke down. But immediately he was
recalled to self-control by another question, to which with the
same emotional difficulty of utterance he said, "No, there was no
malice between us. I never bore malice against the Master-at-arms.
I am sorry that he is dead. I did not mean to kill him. Could I
have used my tongue I would not have struck him. But he foully
lied to my face and in presence of my Captain, and I had to say
252 something, and I °could only say it with a blow, God help me!"

In the impulsive above-board manner of the frank one, the court
saw confirmed all that was implied in words that just previously
had perplexed them, coming as they did from the testifier to the
tragedy and promptly following Billy's impassioned disclaimer
of mutinous intent—Captain Vere's words, "I believe you, my
man."

Next it was asked of him whether he knew of or suspected
aught savoring of incipient trouble (meaning mutiny, though the
explicit term was avoided) going on in any section of the ship's
company.
253   °The reply lingered. This was naturally imputed by the court
to the same vocal embarrassment which had retarded or obstructed previous answers. But in main it was otherwise here; the
question immediately recalling to Billy's mind the interview with
the afterguardsman in the forechains. But an innate repugnance
to playing a part at all approaching that of an informer against
one's own ship mates—the same erring sense of uninstructed honor
which had stood in the way of his reporting the matter at the

time though as a loyal man-of-war-man it was incumbent on him, and failure so to do if charged against him and proven, would have subjected him to the heaviest of penalties; °this, with the 254 blind feeling now his, that nothing really was being hatched, prevailed with him. When the answer came it was a negative.

"One question more," said the officer of marines now first speaking and with a troubled earnestness. "You tell us that what the Master-at-arms said against you was a lie. Now why should he have so lied, so maliciously lied, since you declare there was no malice between you?"

At that question unintentionally touching on a spiritual sphere wholly °obscure to Billy's thoughts, he was non-plussed, evinc- 255 ing a confusion indeed that some observers, such as can readily be imagined, would have construed into involuntary evidence of hidden guilt. Nevertheless he strove some way to answer, but all at once relinquished the vain endeavor, at the same time turning an appealing glance towards Captain Vere as deeming him his best helper and friend. Captain Vere who had been seated for a time rose to his feet, addressing the interrogator. "The question you put to him comes naturally °enough. But how can he rightly an- 256 swer it? or anybody else? unless indeed it be he who lies within there," designating the compartment where lay the corpse. "But the prone one there will not rise to our summons. In effect, though, as it seems to me, the point you make is hardly material. Quite aside from any conceivable motive actuating the Master-at-arms, and irrespective of the provocation to the blow, a martial court must needs in the present case confine its attention to the blow's consequence, which consequence justly is to be deemed not otherwise than as the striker's deed."

°This utterance, the full significance of which it was not at all 257 likely that Billy took in, nevertheless caused him to turn a wistful interrogative look toward the speaker, a look in its dumb expressiveness not unlike that which a dog of generous breed might turn upon his master seeking in his face some elucidation of a previous gesture ambiguous to the canine intelligence. Nor was the same utterance without marked effect upon the three officers, more especially the soldier. Couched in it seemed to them a meaning

258 unanticipated, involving a °prejudgement on the speaker's part. It served to augment a mental disturbance previously evident enough.

The soldier once more spoke; in a tone of suggestive dubiety addressing at once his associates and Captain Vere: "Nobody is present—none of the ship's company, I mean, who might shed lateral light, if any is to be had, upon what remains mysterious in this matter."

"That is thoughtfully put," said Captain Vere: "I see your drift. Ay, there is a mystery; but, to use a Scriptural phrase, it is 'a
259 mystery of °iniquity,' a matter for psychologic theologians to discuss. But what has a military court to do with it? Not to add that for us any possible investigation of it is cut off by the lasting tongue-tie of—him—in yonder," again designating the mortuary state-room. "The prisoner's deed—with that alone we have to do."

To this, and particularly the closing reiteration, the marine soldier knowing not how aptly to reply, sadly abstained from saying aught. The First Lieutenant who at the outset had not un-
260 naturally assumed primacy in the court, now °overrulingly instructed by a glance from Captain Vere, a glance more effective than words, resumed that primacy. Turning to the prisoner, "Budd," he said, and scarce in equable tones, "Budd, if you have aught further to say for yourself, say it now."

Upon this the young sailor turned another quick glance towards Captain Vere; then, as taking a hint from that aspect, a hint confirming his own instinct that silence was now best, replied to the Lieutenant, "I have said all, Sir."

The marine—the same who had been the sentinel without the
261 cabin-door °at the time that the foretopman, followed by the Master-at-arms, entered it—he, standing by the sailor throughout these judicial proceedings, was now directed to take him back to the after compartment originally assigned to the prisoner and his custodian. As the twain disappeared from view, the three officers as partially liberated from some inward constraint associated with Billy's mere presence, simultaneously stirred in their seats. They exchanged looks of troubled indecision, yet feeling that decide
262 they must and without long delay. °For Captain Vere, he for the time stood unconsciously with his back towards them, apparently

in one of his absent fits, gazing out from a sashed port-hole to windward upon the monotonous blank of the twilight sea. But the court's silence continuing, broken only at moments by brief consultations in low earnest tones, this seemed to arm him and energize him. Turning, he to-and-fro paced the cabin athwart; in the returning ascent to windward, climbing the slant deck in the ship's lee roll; without knowing it symbolizing thus in his action a mind resolute to surmount difficulties even if against primitive instincts strong as the wind and the sea. °Presently he 263 came to a stand before the three. After scanning their faces he stood less as mustering his thoughts for expression, than as one inly deliberating how best to put them to well-meaning men not intellectually mature, men with whom it was necessary to demonstrate certain principles that were axioms to himself. Similar impatience as to talking is perhaps one reason that deters some minds from addressing any popular assemblies.

°When speak he did, something both in the substance of what 264 he said and his manner of saying it, showed the influence of unshared studies modifying and tempering the practical training of an active career. This, along with his phraseology now and then was suggestive of the grounds whereon rested that imputation of a certain pedantry socially alleged against him by certain naval men of wholly practical cast, captains who nevertheless would frankly concede that His Majesty's navy mustered no °more 265 efficient officers of their grade than *Starry Vere.*

What he said was to this effect: "Hitherto I have been but the witness, little more; and I should hardly think now to take another tone, that of your coadjutor, for the time, did I not perceive in you—at the crisis too—a troubled hesitancy, proceeding, I doubt not from the clash of military duty with moral scruple —scruple vitalized by compassion. For the compassion, how can I otherwise than share it? But, mindful of paramount obligations I strive against °scruples that may tend to enervate decision. Not, 266 gentlemen, that I hide from myself that the case is an exceptional one. Speculatively regarded, it well might be referred to a jury of casuists. But for us here acting not as casuists or moralists, it is a case practical, and under martial law practically to be dealt with.

"But your scruples: do they move as in a dusk? Challenge them.

Make them advance and declare themselves. Come now: do they import something like this: If, mindless of palliating circum-

267 stances, °we are bound to regard the death of the Master-at-arms as the prisoner's deed, then does that deed constitute a capital crime whereof the penalty is a mortal one? But in natural justice is nothing but the prisoner's overt act to be considered? How can we adjudge to summary and shameful death a fellow-creature innocent before God, and whom we feel to be so?—Does that state it aright? You sign sad assent. Well, I too feel that, the full force of that. It is Nature. But do these buttons that we wear

268 attest that °our allegiance is to Nature? No, to the King. Though the ocean, which is inviolate Nature primeval, though this be the element where we move and have our being as sailors, yet as the King's officers lies our duty in a sphere correspondingly natural? So little is that true, that in receiving our commissions we in the most important regards ceased to be natural free-agents. When war is declared are we the commissioned fighters previously con- sulted? We fight at command. If our judgements approve the war, that is but coincidence. So in other particulars. So now. For sup-

269 pose °condemnation to follow these present proceedings. Would it be so much we ourselves that would condemn as it would be martial law operating through us? For that law and the rigour of it, we are not responsible. Our vowed responsibility is in this:

270 That however pitilessly °that law may operate in any case, we nevertheless adhere to it and administer it.

"But the exceptional in the matter moves the hearts within you. Even so too is mine moved. But let not warm hearts betray heads that should be cool. Ashore in a criminal case will an upright judge allow himself off the bench to be waylaid by some tender kinswoman of the accused seeking to touch him with her tearful plea? Well the heart here, sometimes the feminine in man, is as that piteous woman, and hard though it be, she must here be ruled out."

271 °He paused, earnestly studying them for a moment; then resumed.

"But something in your aspect seems to urge that it is not solely the heart that moves in you, but also the conscience, the private conscience. But tell me whether or not, occupying the position we do, private conscience should not yield to that imperial one formulated in the code under which alone we officially proceed?"

Here the three men moved in their seats, less convinced than agitated by the course of an argument troubling but the more the spontaneous conflict within.

°Perceiving which, the speaker paused for a moment; then abruptly changing his tone, went on.   272

"To steady us a bit, let us recur to the facts.—In war-time at sea a man-of-war's-man strikes his superior in grade, and the blow kills. Apart from its effect the blow itself is, according to the Articles of War, a capital crime. Furthermore—"

"Ay, Sir," emotionally broke in the officer of marines, "in one sense it was. But surely Budd purposed neither mutiny nor homicide."

°"Surely not, my good man. And before a court less arbitrary and more merciful than a martial one, that plea would largely extenuate. At the Last Assizes it shall acquit. But how here? We proceed under the law of the Mutiny Act.[5] In feature no child can resemble his father more than that Act resembles in spirit the thing from which it derives—War. In His Majesty's service—in this ship indeed—there are Englishmen forced to fight for the King against their will. Against their conscience, for aught we know. °Though as their fellow-creatures some of us may appreciate their position, yet as navy officers, what reck we of it? Still   273

274

[5] As Hayford and Sealts point out, Melville is in error here. He is quite correct in having Vere claim that the Articles of War demand the death penalty for striking—or even offering to strike or drawing a weapon against—a superior officer. But the Mutiny Acts, added to annually, were pertinent to the British army. "The British *navy* in 1797 was operating under an entirely separate Act of 1749, one that consolidated and clarified prior naval laws, together with the *King's Regulations and Admiralty Instructions* of 1772" (*H&S*, p. 181). Again, what is important is not the legal technicality but the nature of the conflict: on the one hand laws—be they Mutiny Acts or Articles of War—which are harsh, despotic, and inflexible, but in turn made necessary by the kind of history Melville presents in the "Spirit of the Age"; on the other hand the "handsome sailor" impulses of natural instinct and love, made inoperative in an ugly world of pressing historical necessities. Vere's speech in effect is a summation of the career of Billy Budd, who is taken from *The Rights of Man* and put on the *Bellipotent*. Melville uses Vere's statements to make it clear that the Captain is painfully aware of the infuriating frustrations and agonizing contradictions within the terrible and inhuman complexities of history.

less recks the enemy. Our impressed men he would fain cut down in the same swath with our volunteers. As regards the enemy's naval conscripts, some of whom may even share our own abhorrence of the regicidal French Directory, it is the same on our side. War looks but to the frontage, the appearance. And the Mutiny Act, War's child, takes after the father. Budd's intent or non-intent is nothing to the purpose.

275 °"But while, put to it by those anxieties in you which I can not but respect, I only repeat myself—while thus strangely we prolong proceedings that should be summary—the enemy may be sighted and an engagement result. We must do; and one of two things must we do—condemn or let go."

"Can we not convict and yet mitigate the penalty?" asked the Sailing Master here speaking, and falteringly, for the first.

"Sailing Master, were that clearly lawful for us under the cir-
276 cumstances °consider the consequences of such clemency. The people" (meaning the ship's company) "have native sense; most of them are familiar with our naval usage and tradition; and how would they take it? Even could you explain to them—which our official position forbids—they, long molded by arbitrary discipline have not that kind of intelligent responsiveness that might qualify them to comprehend and discriminate. No, to the people the foretopman's deed however it be worded in the announcement will be plain homicide committed in a flagrant act of mutiny.
277 What °penalty for that should follow, they know. But it does not follow. *Why?* they will ruminate. You know what sailors are. Will they not revert to the recent outbreak at the Nore? Ay. They know the well-founded alarm—the panic it struck throughout England. Your clement sentence they would account pusillanimous. They would think that we flinch, that we are afraid of them—afraid of practising a lawful rigor singularly demanded at
278 this juncture lest it should provoke new troubles. °What shame to us such a conjecture on their part, and how deadly to discipline. You see then, whither prompted by duty and the law I steadfastly drive. But I beseech you, my friends, do not take me amiss. I feel as you do for this unfortunate boy. But did he know our hearts, I take him to be of that generous nature that he would feel

even for us on whom in this military necessity so heavy a compulsion is laid."

°With that, crossing the deck he resumed his place by the   279
sashed port-hole, tacitly leaving the three to come to a decision.
On the cabin's opposite side the troubled court sat silent. Loyal
lieges, plain and practical, though at bottom they dissented from
some points Captain Vere had put to them, they were without
the faculty, hardly had the inclination, to gainsay one whom they
felt to be an earnest man, one too not less their superior in mind
than in naval rank. But it is not improbable °that even such of his   280
words as were not without influence over them, less came home
to them than his closing appeal to their instinct as sea-officers in
the forethought he threw out as to the practical consequences to
discipline, considering the unconfirmed tone of the fleet at the
time, should a man-of-war's-man's violent killing at sea of a
superior in grade be allowed to pass for aught else than a capital
crime demanding prompt infliction of the penalty.

Not unlikely they were brought to something more or less akin
to that harassed frame of mind which in the year 1842 °actuated   281
the commander of the U.S. brig-of-war *Somers* to resolve, under
the so-called Articles of War, Articles modelled upon the English
Mutiny Act, to resolve upon the execution at sea of a midshipman
and two petty-officers as mutineers designing the seizure of the
brig.[6] Which resolution was carried out though in a time of peace

---

[6] The affair of the brig *Somers* has long been taken as one of the major
sources of *Billy Budd*. (See Charles R. Anderson, "The Genesis of Billy
Budd"; Newton Arvin, "A Note on the Background of *Billy Budd*"; and
H. Hayford, ed., *The Somers Mutiny Affair*.) However, Hayford and
Sealts conclude (pp. 27–30, 181–183) that although the *Somers* affair played
a part in Melville's development of the story, it was neither an initial nor
a large source. In 1842, the year of the *Somers* case, Melville's first cousin,
Guert Gansevoort, was the First Lieutenant aboard the brig. He and two
other officers were convened by the Captain, Alexander Slidell Mackenzie,
to "advise" in the sentencing of three men suspected of mutiny. Without
trial (the three accused men were not notified of the drumhead court),
Mackenzie and his officers hanged the three—Acting Midshipman Philip
Spencer, who was the son of the Secretary of War, Boatswain's Mate
Samuel Cromwell, and Seaman Elisha Small. Melville is mistaken about the
Articles of War as justification for the hanging. The case took place in
peacetime, and Mackenzie himself knew that he was not justified by the

and within not many days sail of home. An act vindicated by a
naval court of inquiry subsequently convened ashore. History,
282 and here cited without comment. °True, the circumstances on
board the *Somers* were different from those on board the *Bellipotent*. But the urgency felt, well-warranted or otherwise, was
much the same.

Says a writer whom few know, "Forty years after a battle it is
easy for a non-combatant to reason about how it ought to have
been fought. It is another thing personally and under fire to direct
the fighting while involved in the obscuring smoke of it. Much
283 so with respect to other emergencies involving °considerations
both practical and moral, and when it is imperative promptly to
act. The greater the fog the more it imperils the steamer, and
speed is put on though at the hazard of running somebody down.
Little ween the snug card-players in the cabin of the responsibilities of the sleepless man on the bridge."[7]

In brief, Billy Budd was formally convicted and sentenced to

Articles of War. He defended himself against a charge of murder by basing
his case on the necessities of the moment and his power of command. (He
and his officers were acquitted by a court of inquiry.) As Seaman Small, a
great favorite with the crew, was run up the yardarm, his parting words
were supposed to have been, "God bless the flag!" The case was a *cause
célèbre* for a time and made a particularly deep impact on the young
Melville because Cousin Guert, who had long been a particular favorite
and hero of Herman, was suddenly discredited as a villain in the eyes of
the common sailors of the fleet (see the "Introduction," pp. viii–x). As the
ranks of the three hanged men indicate, Melville was mistaken not only about
the Articles of War but about calling them "a midshipman and two petty
officers." Hayford and Sealts undertake to rewrite the passage for Melville
by changing "a midshipman and two petty officers" (leaf 281) to "a midshipman and two sailors." This edition restores the passage to what Melville
actually wrote and relegates correction of Melville's error to this footnote,
for, once again, the real point at issue here is not Melville's accuracy as a
historian or lawyer, but his use of his materials: presumably the hanging of
two petty officers would be even more serious or unusual than the hanging
of common seamen, and Melville obviously uses the incident as "history
. . . cited without comment" in order to provide an analogous incident
which tends to justify or at least explain Vere's actions. In every instance
Melville seeks to exculpate Vere.

[7] The "writer whom few know" is Herman Melville. Melville's dodge,
which allows him to speak directly to the reader, is one more clear sign
that Melville's sympathies lie with Captain Vere.

be hung at the yard-arm in the early morning-watch, it being now night. Otherwise, as is customary in such cases, the sentence would forthwith have been carried out. In war-time on the field °or in the fleet, a mortal punishment decreed by a drum-head 284 court—on the field sometimes decreed by but a nod from the general—follows without delay on the heel of conviction without appeal.

E. Hull, 1829
National Maritime Museum, London

A sergeant of marines.

[23]

285 °IT WAS Captain Vere himself who of his own motion communicated the finding of the court to the prisoner; for that purpose going to the compartment where he was in custody and
bidding the marine there to withdraw for the time.

Beyond the communication of the sentence what took place at
this interview was never known. But in view of the character of
the twain briefly closeted in that state-room, each radically shar-
286 ing in the rarer qualities of °our nature—so rare indeed as to be
all but incredible to average minds however much cultivated—
some conjectures may be ventured.

It would have been in consonance with the spirit of Captain
Vere should he on this occasion have concealed nothing from the
condemned one—should he indeed have frankly disclosed to him
the part he himself had played in bringing about the decision, at
the same time revealing his actuating motives. On Billy's side it is
287 not improbable that such a confession °would have been received
in much the same spirit that prompted it. Not without a sort of
joy indeed he might have appreciated the brave opinion of him
implied in his Captain's making such a confidant of him. Nor, as to
the sentence itself could he have been insensible that it was im-
parted to him as to one not afraid to die. Even more may have
been. Captain Vere in the end may have developed the passion
sometimes latent under an exterior stoical or indifferent. He was
old enough to have been Billy's father. The austere devotee of
288 military duty, letting himself melt °back into what remains
primeval in our formalized humanity, may in the end have caught
Billy to his heart even as Abraham may have caught young Isaac
on the brink of resolutely offering him up in obedience to the

exacting behest.[1] But there is no telling the sacrament, seldom if in any case revealed to the gadding world, wherever under circumstances at all akin to those here attempted to be set forth, two of great Nature's nobler order embrace. There is privacy at the time, inviolable to the survivor, and holy oblivion, the °sequel to 289 each diviner magnanimity, providentially covers all at last.

The first to encounter Captain Vere in act of leaving the compartment was the senior Lieutenant. The face he beheld, for the moment one expressive of the agony of the strong, was to that officer, though a man of fifty, a startling revelation. That the condemned one suffered less than he who mainly had effected the condemnation was apparently indicated by the former's exclamation in the scene soon perforce to be touched upon.

---

[1] In order to test Abraham's pious devotion, God ordered him to sacrifice his beloved son, Isaac, as a burnt offering to the Lord. Abraham obeyed, and was reaching for the knife with which to kill Isaac, whom he had bound upon the woodpile on the altar, when an angel stayed his hand. God blessed Abraham and Isaac was saved (Gen. 22:1–18).

[24]

290 °OF A SERIES of incidents within a brief term rapidly following each other, the adequate narration may take up a term less brief, especially if explanation or comment here and there seem requisite to the better understanding of such incidents. Between the entrance into the cabin of him who never left it alive, and him who when he did leave it left it as one condemned to die; between

291 °this and the closeted interview just given, less than an hour and a half had elapsed. It was an interval long enough however to awaken speculations among no few of the ship's company as to what it was that could be detaining in the cabin the Master-at-arms and the sailor; for a rumor that both of them had been seen to enter it and neither of them had been seen to emerge, this rumor had got abroad upon the gun-decks and in the tops; the people of a great warship being in one respect like villagers taking microscopic note of every outward movement or non-move-

292 ment going on. When therefore in weather °not at all tempestuous all hands were called in the second dog-watch, a summons under such circumstances not usual in those hours, the crew were not wholly unprepared for some announcement extraordinary, one having connection too with the continued absence of the two men from their wonted haunts.

There was a moderate sea at the time; and the moon, newly risen and near to being at its full, silvered the white spar-deck wherever not blotted by the clear-cut shadows horizontally thrown of fixtures and moving men. On either side of the quarter-

293 deck, the marine °guard under arms was drawn up; and Captain Vere standing in his place surrounded by all the ward-room officers, addressed his men. In so doing his manner showed neither more nor less than that properly pertaining to his supreme position aboard his own ship. In clear terms and concise he told them

what had taken place in the cabin; that the Master-at-arms was dead; that he who had killed him had been already tried by a summary court and condemned to death; and that the execution would take place in the early morning watch. °The word *mutiny*   294
was not named in what he said. He refrained too from making the occasion an opportunity for any preachment as to the maintenance of discipline, thinking perhaps that under existing circumstances in the navy the consequence of violating discipline should be made to speak for itself.

Their captain's announcement was listened to by the throng of standing sailors in a dumbness like that of a seated congregation of believers in hell listening to the clergyman's announcement of his Calvinistic text.

°At the close, however, a confused murmur went up. It began   295
to wax. All but instantly, then, at a sign, it was pierced and suppressed by shrill whistles of the Boatswain and his mates. The word was given to about ship.[1]

To be prepared for burial Claggart's body was delivered to certain petty-officers of his mess. And here, not to clog the sequel with lateral matters, it may be added that at a suitable hour, the Master-at-arms was committed to the sea with every funeral honor properly belonging to his naval grade.

°In this proceeding as in every public one growing out of the   296
tragedy, strict adherence to usage was observed. Nor in any point could it have been at all deviated from, either with respect to Claggart or Billy Budd, without begetting undesirable speculations in the ship's company, sailors, and more particularly men-of-war's-men, being of all men the greatest sticklers for usage. For similar cause, all communication between Captain Vere and the condemned one ended with the closeted interview already given, the latter being now surrendered to the °ordinary routine   297
preliminary to the end. His transfer under guard from the Captain's quarters was effected without unusual precautions—at least no visible ones. If possible, not to let the men so much as surmise that their officers anticipate aught amiss from them is the tacit rule

[1] See the statement for leaf 295 in Appendix Two, p. 179.

in a military ship. And the more that some sort of trouble should really be apprehended the more do the officers keep that apprehension to themselves; though not the less unostentatious vigilance may be augmented. °In the present instance the sentry placed over the prisoner had strict orders to let no one have communication with him but the Chaplain. And certain unobtrusive measures were taken absolutely to insure this point.

[25]

°IN A SEVENTY-FOUR of the old order the deck known as the 299
upper gun-deck was the one covered over by the spar-deck which
last, though not without its armament, was for the most part exposed to the weather. In general, it was at all hours free from hammocks; those of the crew swinging on the lower gun-deck, and
berth-deck, the latter being not only a dormitory but also the place
for the stowing of the sailors' bags, and on both sides lined with the
large chests or movable pantries of the many messes of the men.

°On the starboard side of the *Bellipotent*'s upper gun-deck, 300
behold Billy Budd under sentry, lying prone in irons, in one of
the bays formed by the regular spacing of the guns comprising
the batteries on either side. All these pieces were of the heavier
calibre of that period. Mounted on lumbering wooden carriages
they were hampered with cumbersome harness of breeching and
strong side-tackles for running them out. Guns and carriages, together with the long rammers and shorter lintstocks lodged in
loops overhead[1]—all these, as customary, were painted black; and
the heavy hempen breechings, tarred to the same tint, wore the
like °livery of the undertakers. In contrast with the funereal hue 301

---

[1] The cannons were held in place by heavy ropes called breechings,
which ran through the heavy iron loop (cascabel) behind the breech of
muzzle-loaders and were fastened to the side of the ship. When in use, the
guns were run back so they could be loaded, and then were run forward
so that their muzzles projected beyond the portholes. The rammers were
long poles used to drive home the charge down the muzzle, and the lintstocks were long iron forks used to hold the match that touched off the
charge. When not in use, the muzzles of the guns were covered by tom-
pions (wooden plugs) or by metal or canvas caps. For the setting of a scene
which allows him to talk about the irony of a chaplain aboard a man-of-
war, Melville chains the white-clothed and innocent "Baby" amid the dark
instruments of war.

of these surroundings the prone sailor's exterior apparel, white
jumper and white duck trousers, each more or less soiled, dimly
glimmered in the obscure light of the bay like a patch of dis-
colored snow in early April lingering at some upland cave's black
mouth. In effect he is already in his shroud or the garments that
shall serve him in lieu of one. Over him, but scarce illuminating
him, two battle-lanterns swing from two massive beams of the
deck above. Fed with the oil supplied by the war-contractors
(whose gains, honest or otherwise, are in every land an antici-
302   pated portion of the harvest of death), with °flickering splashes
of dirty yellow light they pollute the pale moon-shine all but
ineffectually struggling in obstructed flecks through the open
ports from which the tompioned cannon protrude. Other lanterns
at intervals serve but to bring out somewhat the obscurer bays
which, like small confessionals or side-chapels in a cathedral,
branch from the long dim-vistaed broad aisle between the two
batteries of that covered tier.

Such was the deck where now lay the Handsome Sailor.
Through the rose-tan of his complexion, no pallor could have
shown. It would have taken days of sequestration from the winds
303   and the sun to have brought about the effacement of that. °But
the skeleton in the cheekbone at the point of its angle was just
beginning delicately to be defined under the warm-tinted skin. In
fervid hearts self-contained, some brief experiences devour our
human tissue as secret fire in a ship's hold consumes cotton in the
bale.

But now lying between the two guns, as nipped in the vice of
fate, Billy's agony, mainly proceeding from a generous young
heart's virgin experience of the diabolical incarnate and effective
in some men—the tension of that agony was over now. It survived not the something healing in the closeted interview with
304   Captain Vere. °Without movement, he lay as in a trance. That
adolescent expression previously noted as his, taking on something
akin to the look of a slumbering child in the cradle when the
warm hearth-glow of the still chamber at night plays on the dim-
ples that at whiles mysteriously form in the cheek, silently coming
and going there. For now and then in the gyved one's trance a
305   serene happy light born of some wandering reminiscence °or

dream would diffuse itself over his face, and then wane away only anew to return.

The Chaplain coming to see him and finding him thus, and perceiving no sign that he was conscious of his presence, attentively regarded him for a space, then slipping aside, withdrew for the time, peradventure feeling that even he the minister of Christ, though receiving his stipend from Mars, had no consolation to proffer which could result in a peace transcending that which he beheld. But in the small hours he came again. And the prisoner, now awake to his surroundings, noticed his approach, °and civilly,   306 all but cheerfully, welcomed him. But it was to little purpose that in the interview following the good man sought to bring Billy Budd to some godly understanding that he must die, and at dawn. True, Billy himself freely referred to his death as a thing close at hand; but it was something in the way that children will refer to death in general, who yet among their other sports will play a funeral with hearse and mourners.

°Not that like children Billy was incapable of conceiving what   307 death really is. No, but he was wholly without irrational fear of it, a fear more prevalent in highly civilized communities than those so-called barbarous ones which in all respects stand nearer to unadulterate Nature. And, as elsewhere said, a barbarian Billy radically was; as much so, for all the costume, as his countrymen the British captives, living trophies, made to march in the Roman triumph of Germanicus.[2] Quite as much so as those later barbar- ians, young men probably, and picked specimens among the °ear-   308 lier British converts to Christianity, at least nominally such, and taken to Rome (as today converts from lesser isles of the sea may be taken to London) of whom the Pope of that time,[3] admiring

---

[2] Germanicus Caesar (15 B.C.–19 A.D.), a Roman general, became popular for his successes against the Germans under Arminius. Tiberias, jealous of Germanicus, recalled him to Rome in 17 A.D. and staged a triumph for Germanicus' return, during which British captives were displayed.

[3] Melville is in error here. Gregory the Great (540?–604) left in his *Dialogues* a strong description of life in the monastery of which he was abbot. While abbot, he saw the Anglo-Saxon slave boys whose appearance fired him with zeal to convert the inhabitants of Britain. But the incident took place six years *before* he became Pope. The "Pope of that time" was Pelagius.

the strangeness of their personal beauty so unlike the Italian
stamp, their clear ruddy complexion and curled flaxen locks, exclaimed, "Angles" (meaning *English,* the modern derivative)
"Angles do you call them? And is it because they look so like
angels?" Had it been later in time one would think that the Pope
had in mind Fra Angelico's[4] seraphs some of whom, plucking
309 apples in gardens of the Hesperides[5] °have the faint rose-bud
complexion of the more beautiful English girls.

If in vain the good Chaplain sought to impress the young barbarian with ideas of death akin to those conveyed in the skull,
dial, and cross-bones on old tombstones; equally futile to all appearance were his efforts to bring home to him the thought of
salvation and a Savior. Billy listened, but less out of awe or rever-
ence perhaps than from a certain natural politeness; doubtless at
bottom regarding all that in much the same way that most
mariners of his class take any discourse abstract or out of the com-
310 mon tone of the work-a-day world. °And this sailor-way of taking clerical discourse is not wholly unlike the way in which the
primer of Christianity full of transcendent miracles was received
long ago on tropic isles by any superior *savage* so called—a Tahi-
tian say of Captain Cook's time or shortly after that time.[6] Out of

[4] During his trip to Europe in 1857 Melville had seen the works of Fra
Angelico (Giovanni da Fiesole, 1387–1455) in Florence. His real name was
Guido di Pietro, but he took the name of Fra Giovanni when he entered
the Dominican order. The name of "Angelico" was given him posthumously
in celebration of the quality of his life and the angelic nature of his paint-
ings. Melville chose a nicely appropriate painter with whom to associate
the Angles he identified with Billy Budd.

[5] In classical mythology the gardens of the golden apples in North
Africa, guarded by a sleepless dragon and by the virgin sisters known as
the Hesperides.

[6] "Captain Cook's time or shortly after that time" was the last quarter
of the eighteenth century. James Cook (1728–1779) came to Tahiti on a
scientific expedition in 1769 and explored the neighboring islands as well as
the coasts of New Zealand and Australia. He sailed to the South Seas again
in 1774 and from 1776 to 1779. He was killed in a fight with natives of
Hawaii (which he discovered) in 1779. In Melville's view, the South Seas
natives at the time Cook discovered them were innocent and generally pure
and good. In short, they are representative of the naturally upright barbarian morally superior to "citified man." See also the statement for leaf
311 ("an irruption of heretic thought hard to suppress") in Appendix Two,
pp. 180–181.

natural courtesy he received, but did not appropriate. It was like a gift placed in the palm of an out-reached hand upon which the fingers do not close.

But the *Bellipotent*'s Chaplain was a discreet man possessing the good sense of a good heart. So he insisted not in his vocation here. At the instance of Captain Vere, °a Lieutenant had apprised him   311 of pretty much everything as to Billy; and since he felt that innocence was even a better thing than religion wherewith to go to Judgement, he reluctantly withdrew; but in his emotion not without first performing an act strange enough in an Englishman, and under the circumstances yet more so in any regular priest. Stooping over, he kissed on the fair cheek his fellow-man, a felon in martial law, one whom though on the confines of death he felt he could never convert to a dogma; nor for all that did he fear for his future, (an irruption of heretic thought hard to suppress).[7]

Marvel not that having been made acquainted with the young sailor's essential innocence °the worthy man lifted not a finger to   312 avert the doom of such a martyr to martial discipline. So to do would not only have been as idle as invoking the desert, but would also have been an audacious transgression of the bounds of his function, one as exactly prescribed to him by military law as that of the Boatswain or any other naval officer. Bluntly put, a chaplain is the minister of the Prince of Peace serving in the host of the God of War—Mars. As such, he is as incongruous as a musket would be on the altar at Christmas. Why then is he there? Because he indirectly subserves the purpose attested by the cannon; because too he lends the sanction of the religion of the meek to that which practically is the abrogation of everything but brute Force.

[7] See the statement for leaf 311 in Appendix Two, pp. 180–181.

The lower gun deck of the *Victory*. This deck is much like the upper gun deck of the *Bellipotent*, where Billy lay "prone in irons in one of the bays formed by the regular spacing of the guns. . . ."

[26]

°THE NIGHT, so luminous on the spar-deck, but otherwise on   313
the cavernous ones below, levels so like the tiered galleries in a coal-
mine—the luminous night passed away. But, like the prophet in
the chariot disappearing in heaven and dropping his mantle to
Elisha,[1] the withdrawing night transferred its pale robe to the
breaking day. A meek shy light appeared in the East, where
stretched a diaphanous fleece of white furrowed vapor. °That   314
light slowly waxed. Suddenly *eight bells* was struck aft, responded
to by one louder metallic stroke from forward. It was four o'clock
in the morning. Instantly the silver whistles were heard summoning all hands to witness punishment. Up through the great hatch-
ways rimmed with racks of heavy shot, the watch below came
pouring, overspreading with the watch already on deck the space
between the main-mast and fore-mast including that occupied by
the capacious launch and the black booms tiered on either side of
it, boat and booms making a summit of observation for the pow-
der-boys and younger tars. °A different group comprising one   315
watch of topmen leaned over the rail of that sea-balcony,[2] no
small one in a seventy-four, looking down on the crowd below.
Man or boy, none spake but in whisper, and few spake at all.
Captain Vere—as before, the central figure among the assembled
commissioned officers—stood nigh the break of the poop-deck
facing forward. Just below him on the quarter-deck the marines
in full equipment were drawn up much as at the scene of the
promulgated sentence.

[1] The prophet Elijah "went up by a whirlwind into heaven," riding in a
chariot of fire drawn by horses of fire. Elisha took the mantle that fell from
Elijah and put it on, "and when the sons of the prophets . . . saw him,
they said, The spirit of Elijah doth rest on Elisha" (2 Kings 2:9–15).

[2] The foretop.

316   °At sea in the old time, the execution by halter of a military sailor was generally from the fore-yard. In the present instance, for special reasons the main-yard was assigned. Under an arm of that yard the prisoner was presently brought up, the Chaplain attending him. It was noted at the time and remarked upon afterwards, that in this final scene the good man evinced little or nothing of the perfunctory. Brief speech indeed he had with the

317   condemned one, °but the genuine Gospel was less on his tongue than in his aspect and manner towards him. The final preparations personal to the latter being speedily brought to an end by two boatswain's-mates, the consummation impended. Billy stood facing aft. At the penultimate moment, his words, his only ones, words wholly unobstructed in the utterance were these—"God bless Captain Vere!" Syllables so unanticipated coming from one with the ignominious hemp about his neck—a conventional felon's benediction directed aft towards the quarters of honor; syllables

318   too delivered in the clear melody of a singing-bird °on the point of launching from the twig—had a phenomenal effect, not unenhanced by the rare personal beauty of the young sailor spiritualized now through late experiences so poignantly profound.

       Without volition as it were, as if indeed the ship's populace were but the vehicles of some vocal current electric, with one voice from alow and aloft came a resonant sympathetic echo—"God bless Captain Vere!" And yet at that instant Billy alone must have been in their hearts, even as he was in their eyes.

       At the pronounced words and the spontaneous echo that

319   voluminously rebounded them, °Captain Vere, either through stoic self-control or a sort of momentary paralysis induced by emotional shock, stood erectly rigid as a musket in the ship-armorer's rack.

       The hull deliberately recovering from the periodic roll to leeward was just regaining an even keel, when the last signal, a preconcerted dumb one, was given. At the same moment it chanced that the vapory fleece hanging low in the East, was shot through with a soft glory as of the fleece of the Lamb of God

320   seen in mystical vision, °and simultaneously therewith, watched

by the wedged mass of upturned faces, Billy ascended; and, ascending, took the full rose of the dawn.[3]

In the pinioned figure, arrived at the yard-end, to the wonder of all no motion was apparent, none save that created by the slow roll of the hull, in moderate weather so majestic in a great ship ponderously cannoned.

[3] Melville suggests both the Ascension of Christ in the early dawn as given in the Gospels (Matt. 28:1-7, Mark 16:2-6, Luke 24:1-6, and John 20:1-16), and also the Vision of the Lamb of God according to St. John the Divine (Rev. 5:6-14). The most complete study of Biblical allusion in Melville's works is by Nathalia Wright, *Melville's Use of the Bible* (Durham, N.C., 1949).

[27]

°*A digression*

WHEN SOME DAYS afterward in reference to the singularity just mentioned, the Purser, a rather ruddy rotund person more accurate as an accountant than profound as a philosopher, said at mess to the Surgeon, "What testimony to the force lodged in will-power," the latter—saturnine spare and tall, one in whom a discreet causticity went along with a manner less genial than polite, replied, "Your pardon, Mr. Purser. In a hanging scientifically conducted—and under special orders I myself directed how Budd's was to be effected—any movement following the completed suspension and originating in the body suspended, such movement indicates °mechanical spasm in the muscular system. Hence the absence of that is no more attributable to will-power as you call it than to horse-power—begging your pardon."

"But this muscular spasm you speak of, is not that in a degree more or less invariable in these cases?"

"Assuredly so, Mr. Purser."

"How then, my good sir, do you account for its absence in this instance?"

"Mr. Purser, it is clear that your sense of the singularity in this matter equals not mine. You account for it by what you call will-power, a term not yet included in the lexicon of science. For me I do not, °with my present knowledge, pretend to account for it at all. Even should we assume the hypothesis that at the first touch of the halyards the action of Budd's heart, intensified by extraordinary emotion at its climax, abruptly stopped—much like a watch when in carelessly winding it up you strain at the finish, thus snapping the chain—even under that hypothesis, how account for the phenomenon that followed?"

"You admit then that the absence of spasmodic movement was phenomenal."

"It was phenomenal, Mr. Purser, in the sense that it was an appearance °the cause of which is not immediately to be assigned." 324

"But tell me, my dear sir," pertinaciously continued the other, "was the man's death effected by the halter, or was it a species of euthanasia?"[1]

"*Euthanasia*, Mr. Purser, is something like your *will-power:* I doubt its authenticity as a scientific term—begging your pardon again. It is at once imaginative and metaphysical—in short, Greek. But," abruptly changing his tone, "there is a case in the sick-bay that I do not care to leave to my assistants. Beg your pardon, but excuse me." And rising from the mess he formally withdrew.

[1] Hayford and Sealts remark that according to Sealts' list of Melville's readings, in 1891 Melville read Schopenhauer's *Counsels and Maxims*, wherein euthanasia is described as "an easy death, not ushered in by disease, and free from all pain and struggle." Schopenhauer considered that "death in this form is not an evil but the highest consummation of life" (*H&S*, p. 193). See also Walter Sutton, "Melville and the Great God Budd." It is questionable whether Melville read Schopenhauer before composing leaf 324, but whether he did or not, what remains essential here is not so much the source of Melville's use of the term "euthanasia" as his intention to show that men like the Purser and the Surgeon are either bumblingly or coldly incapable of imaginatively comprehending the special nature and therefore special death of Billy Budd. Melville had prepared the reader for the expectation that those around Billy would not really understand his nature by insisting that with but a couple of exceptions (presumably Claggart and Vere) no man aboard the *Bellipotent* was equipped to apprehend the nature of Billy.

[28]

325 °THE SILENCE at the moment of execution and for a moment
or two continuing thereafter, a silence but emphasized by the
regular wash of the sea against the hull or the flutter of a sail
caused by the helmsman's eyes being tempted astray, this emphasized silence was gradually disturbed by a sound not easily to be
verbally rendered. Whoever has heard the freshet-wave of a tor-
326 rent suddenly °swelled by pouring showers in tropical mountains,
showers not shared by the plain; whoever has heard the first muffled murmur of its sloping advance through precipitous woods,
may form some conception of the sound now heard. The seeming
remoteness of its source was because of its murmurous indistinct-
ness since it came from close by, even from the men massed on the
ship's open deck. Being inarticulate, it was dubious in significance
further than it seemed to indicate some capricious revulsion of
327 thought or feeling such as mobs °ashore are liable to, in the
present instance possibly implying a sullen revocation on the men's
part of their involuntary echoing of Billy's benediction. But ere
the murmur had time to wax into clamor it was met by a strategic
command, the more telling that it came with abrupt unexpectedness:

"Pipe down the starboard watch, Boatswain, and see that they
go."

Shrill as the shriek of the sea-hawk the silver whistles of the
Boatswain and his mates pierced that ominous low sound, dis-
328 sipating it; and °yielding to the mechanism of discipline, the
throng was thinned by one half. For the remainder most of them
were set to temporary employments connected with trimming the
yards and so forth, business readily to be got up to serve occasion
by any officer-of-the-deck.

Now each proceeding that follows a mortal sentence pronounced at sea by a drum-head court is characterised by promptitude not perceptibly merging into hurry, though bordering that.
The hammock, the one which had been Billy's bed when alive,
having already been ballasted with shot and otherwise prepared
°to serve for his canvas coffin, the last offices of the sea-under-   329
takers, the Sail-Maker's mates, were now speedily completed.
When everything was in readiness a second call for all hands,
made necessary by the strategic movement before mentioned, was
sounded, and now to witness burial.

The details of this closing formality it needs not to give. But
when the tilted plank let slide its freight into the sea, a second
strange human murmur was heard, blended now with another inarticulate sound proceeding from certain larger sea-fowl, whose
attention having been °attracted by the peculiar commotion in   330
the water resulting from the heavy sloped dive of the shotted
hammock into the sea, flew screaming to the spot. So near the hull
did they come, that the stridor or bony creak of their gaunt
double-jointed pinions was audible. As the ship under light airs
passed on, leaving the burial-spot astern, they still kept circling
it low down with the moving shadow of their outstretched wings
and the croaked requiem of their cries.

Upon sailors as superstitious as those of the age preceding ours,
men-of-war's-men too who had just °beheld the prodigy of repose   331
in the form suspended in air and now foundering in the deeps;
to such mariners the action of the sea-fowl, though dictated by
mere animal greed for prey, was big with no prosaic significance.
An uncertain movement began among them, in which some en-
croachment was made. It was tolerated but for a moment. For
suddenly the drum beat to quarters, which familiar sound happening at least twice every day, had upon the present occasion a signal peremptoriness in it. True martial discipline long continued
superinduces in average man a sort of impulse of docility whose
operation at the official word of command much resembles in its
promptitude the effect of an instinct.

°The drum-beat dissolved the multitude, distributing most of   332
them along the batteries of the two covered gun-decks. There, as

wont, the guns' crews stood by their respective cannon erect and silent. In due course the First Officer, sword under arm and standing in his place on the quarter-deck, formally received the successive reports of the sworded Lieutenants commanding the sections of batteries below; the last of which reports being made, the summed report he delivered with the customary salute to the Commander. All this occupied time, which in the present case, 333 was the object of beating to quarters at an °hour prior to the customary one. That such variance from usage was authorized by an officer like Captain Vere, a martinet as some deemed him, was evidence of the necessity for unusual action implied in what he deemed to be temporarily the mood of his men. "With mankind," he would say, "forms, measured forms are everything; and that is the import couched in the story of Orpheus[1] with his lyre spellbinding the wild denizens of the wood." And this he once applied to the disruption of forms going on across the Channel and the consequences thereof.

At this unwonted muster at quarters, all proceeded as at the regular hour. The band on the quarter-deck played a sacred air. 334 After which the Chaplain went through °the customary morning service. That done, the drum beat the retreat, and toned by music and religious rites subserving the discipline and purpose of war, the men in their wonted orderly manner dispersed to the places allotted them when not at the guns.

And now it was full day. The fleece of low-hanging vapor had vanished, licked up by the sun that late had so glorified it. And the circumambient air in the clearness of its serenity was like smooth white marble in the polished block not yet removed from the marble-dealer's yard.

---

[1] In Greek mythology Orpheus was a Thracian poet who was taught by the Muses to use Apollo's lyre. His music was so compelling and perfect that it moved animals, trees, rocks, and the gods of the underworld.

[29]

°THE SYMMETRY of form attainable in pure fiction can not so readily be achieved in a narration essentially having less to do with fable than with fact. Truth uncompromisingly told will always have its ragged edges; hence the conclusion of such a narration is apt to be less finished than an architectural finial.

How it fared with the Handsome Sailor during the year of the Great Mutiny has been faithfully given. But though properly the story ends with his life, something in way of sequel °will not be amiss. Three brief chapters will suffice.

In the general re-christening under the Directory of the craft originally forming the navy of the French monarchy, the *St. Louis* line-of-battle ship was named the *Athée*.[1] Such a name, like some other substituted ones in the Revolutionary fleet, while proclaiming the infidel audacity of the ruling power was yet, though not

[1] Melville had written above the blank space he had left for the name of the ship the word "Athéiste," and his wife had written in the blank space the words "the Atheiste." *H&S* rewrites the word in its correct French form, *Athée*, and this edition agrees with *H&S* in undertaking this minor bit of proofreading for Melville. Although Melville had "irruptions of heretical" impulses about organized Christianity and often equated it with hypocrisy, smugness, privilege, foolishness, repressiveness, and metaphysical blindness, he equated atheism with the destruction of the "forms, measured forms" that make an organized social community possible. In the critical argument about Melville's use of Captain Vere, it is instructive to note that Melville immediately followed the "forms, measured forms" speech with "And this he once applied to the disruptions of forms going on across the Channel and the consequences thereof." Significantly, in an earlier draft the *Athéiste* was to have been named the *Directory*. It is also instructive that Melville subtly related Claggart to foreign origins across the Channel and related Billy to pure Anglo-Saxon descent, heritages ironically reversed by the misinformed and misinforming official version (leaves 341–343) in which understanding of "forms" had become debased into ideological cant.

132

HERMAN MELVILLE

so intended to be, the aptest name, if one consider it, ever given to a war-ship; far more so indeed than the *Devastation,* the *Erebus* (the *Hell*) and similar names bestowed upon fighting-ships.

337   °On the return-passage to the English fleet from the detached cruise during which occurred the events already recorded, the *Bellipotent* fell in with the *Athée.* An engagement ensued; during which Captain Vere, in the act of putting his ship alongside the enemy with a view of throwing his boarders across her bulwarks, was hit by a musket-ball from a port-hole of the enemy's main cabin. More than disabled he dropped to the deck and was carried below to the same cock-pit where some of his men already lay. The senior Lieutenant took command. Under him the enemy was

338   °finally captured and though much crippled was by rare good fortune successfully taken into Gibraltar, an English port not very distant from the scene of the fight. There, Captain Vere with the rest of the wounded was put ashore. He lingered for some days, but the end came. Unhappily he was cut off too early for the Nile and Trafalgar.[2] The spirit that spite its philosophic austerity may yet have indulged in the most secret of all passions, ambition, never attained to the fulness of fame.

339   Not long before death, °while lying under the influence of that magical drug which soothing the physical frame mysteriously operates on the subtler element in man, he was heard to murmur words inexplicable to his attendant—"Billy Budd, Billy Budd." That these were not the accents of remorse, would seem clear from what the attendant said to the *Bellipotent*'s senior officer of marines who, as the most reluctant to condemn of the members of the drum-head court, too well knew, though here he kept the knowledge to himself, who Billy Budd was.

[2] Vere died in 1797. The Battle of the Nile was fought on August 1, 1798, and Trafalgar was fought on October 21, 1805.

[30]

°SOME FEW WEEKS after the execution, among other matters   340
under the head of *News from the Mediterranean*, there appeared
in a naval chronicle of the time, an authorized weekly publication,
an account of the affair. It was doubtless for the most part written
in good faith, though the medium, partly rumor, through which
the facts must have reached the writer, served to deflect and in
part falsify them. The account was as follows:—

"On the tenth of the last month a deplorable occurrence took
°place on board H.M.S. *Bellipotent*. John Claggart, the ship's   341
Master-at-arms, discovering that some sort of plot was incipient
among an inferior section of the ship's company, and that the
ring-leader was one William Budd; he, Claggart, in the act of
arraigning the man before the Captain was vindictively stabbed
to the heart by the suddenly drawn sheath-knife of Budd.

"The deed and the implement employed, sufficiently suggest
that though mustered into the service under an English name, the
assassin was no Englishman, but one of those aliens adopting English cognomens whom °the present extraordinary necessities of   342
the Service have caused to be admitted into it in considerable
numbers.

"The enormity of the crime and the extreme depravity of the
criminal appear the greater in view of the character of the victim,
a middle-aged man respectable and discreet, belonging to that
minor official grade, the petty-officers, upon whom, as none know
better than the commissioned gentlemen, the efficiency of His
Majesty's navy so largely depends. His function was a responsible
one; at once onerous & thankless and his fidelity in it the °greater   343
because of his strong patriotic impulse. In this instance as in so
many other instances in these days, the character of this unfortunate man signally refutes, if refutation were needed, that peevish

saying attributed to the late Dr. Johnson,[1] that patriotism is the last refuge of a scoundrel.

"The criminal paid the penalty of his crime. The promptitude of the punishment has proved salutary. Nothing amiss is now apprehended aboard H.M.S. *Bellipotent*."

344   The above, appearing in a publication now °long ago superannuated and forgotten, is all that hitherto has stood in human record to attest what manner of men respectively were John Claggart and Billy Budd.[2]

[1] Samuel Johnson (1709–1784), a great man of English letters, died only thirteen years before the events of this narrative and might still be quoted as a shaper of contemporary attitudes by the author of "News from the Mediterranean."

[2] Hayford and Sealts point out an inconsistency in Melville's rendering of the official account: "Note that the 'chronicle' makes no reference to Vere by name, nor to the engagement during which he received his mortal wound, though this significant episode is said to have taken place on 'the return passage to the English fleet from the detached cruise during which occurred the events already recorded' (leaf 337)—i.e., the deaths of Claggart and Budd reported here. The explanation, confirmed by analysis of the manuscript, is that the substance of the present chapter actually antedates Melville's whole elaboration of the character evidently at first identified not by name but only as 'the commander' or 'the captain,' as here. Again, in its statement that the treatment of Billy afforded by the 'chronicle' is 'all that hitherto has stood in human record' (leaf 344) the chapter contradicts the assertion below that 'Billy in the Darbies' was 'printed at Portsmouth as a ballad' (leaf 347). These inconsistencies, growing out of changes in Melville's plans concerning the development of the story and the ordering of its closing chapters, are evidence that *Billy Budd* was literally 'unfinished'—Mrs. Melville's term . . . —at the time of his death" (*H&S*, p. 200).

[31]

°EVERYTHING is for a term venerated in navies. Any tangible   345
object associated with some striking incident of the service is
converted into a monument. The spar from which the foretopman was suspended, was for some few years kept trace of by the
blue-jackets. Their knowledge followed it from ship to dock-
yard and again from dock-yard to ship, still pursuing it even when
at last reduced to a mere dock-yard boom. To them a chip of it
was as a piece of the Cross. Ignorant though they were of the
secret facts of the tragedy, and not thinking but that the penalty
was somehow unavoidably inflicted from the naval point of view,
°for all that they instinctively felt that Billy was a sort of man   346
as incapable of mutiny as of wilful murder. They recalled the
fresh young image of the Handsome Sailor, that face never de-
formed by a sneer or subtler vile freak of the heart within. This
impression of him was doubtless deepened by the fact that he was
gone, and in a measure mysteriously gone. On the gun-decks of
the *Bellipotent,* the general estimate of his nature and its unconscious simplicity eventually found rude utterance from another
foretopman, one of his own watch, gifted, as some sailors are, with
an artless *poetic* temperament; the tarry hands made some lines
which after circulating °among the shipboard crew for a while,   347
finally got rudely printed at Portsmouth as a ballad. The title
given to it was the sailor's.

Billy in the Darbies[1]

°Good of the Chaplain to enter Lone Bay   348
    And down on his marrow-bones here and pray

[1] Darbies are chains. As Hayford and Sealts point out, *Billy Budd* began
as a ballad, which went through various revisions. At one point Melville

135

For the likes just o' me, Billy Budd.—But look:
Through the port comes the moon-shine astray!
It tips the guard's cutlas and silvers this nook;
But 'twill die in the dawning of Billy's last day.
A jewel-block they'll make of me tomorrow,
Pendant pearl from the yard-arm-end
Like the ear-drop I gave to Bristol Molly—

349   °O, 'tis me, not the sentence they'll suspend.
Ay, Ay, all is up; and I must up too
Early in the morning, aloft from alow.
On an empty stomach, now, never it would do.
They'll give me a nibble—bit o' biscuit ere I go.
Sure, a messmate will reach me the last parting cup;
But, turning heads away from the hoist and the belay,[2]
Heavens knows who will have the running of me up!

---

wrote a prose introduction to the ballad, and that eventually blossomed into the full narrative. In the prose sketch, "Billy is nicknamed 'the Jewel,' an expression that survives in Captain Graveling's reference to him . . . as 'my best man . . . , the jewel of 'em.' So originally Melville had Billy punning on his nickname in the seventh line of the ballad: 'A jewel-block they'll make of me tomorrow'—jewel-blocks, which hang from the ends of the yards where studding-sails are hoisted, carry those sails to the extreme ends of the yards. . . . The words 'all is up; and I must up too' (involving another play on words) have further affiliations with the prose sketch. The third surviving draft leaf of the ballad . . . follows this line with, 'Early in the morning the deed they will do/Our little game's up they must needs obey.' 'Our little game' presumably refers to the 'incipient mutiny' for which Billy, as ringleader, was to be hanged, according to the sketch. The word-plays and the 'little game,' as well as the further play on words in the line 'O, 'tis me, not the sentence they'll suspend,' stem from Melville's earlier conception of Billy when he was evidently not so simple and innocent" (H&S, pp. 201–202). The same might be said about Billy's concern with food and grog, which does not accord with the supernatural nature of Billy's hanging. Melville's placement of the ballad at the end (at the conclusion of leaf 351 he wrote, "End of Book/April 19th/1891) suggests his intention to maintain the sense of something immortal about Billy—the narrative voice in the ballad is that of Billy speaking either in a dream of his death or after his death from the depths of the sea. The title of the ballad suggests the former, but the last two lines suggest the latter.

[2] The men assigned to hang him will turn their heads away as they run him up and belay (make fast) the line.

No pipe to those halyards.[3]—But aren't it all sham?
A blur's in my eyes; it is dreaming that I am.
A hatchet to my hawser? all adrift to go?
°The drum roll to grog, and Billy never know?   350
But Donald he has promised to stand by the plank;
So I'll shake a friendly hand ere I sink.
But—no! It is dead then I'll be, come to think.—
I remember Taff the Welshman when he sank.
And his cheek it was like the budding pink.
But me they'll lash in hammock, drop me deep.
°Fathoms down, fathoms down, how I'll dream fast asleep.   351
I feel it stealing now. Sentry, are you there?
Just ease these darbies at the wrist,
And roll me over fair,
I am sleepy, and the oozy weeds about me twist.

[3] Melville's meaning here is cloudy. Presumably he is using the word
"pipe" not in a particularly nautical sense, but in the current slang, akin to
"pipe dream": that is, the halyard from which he'll hang is very real and not
his mere dream of it.

Appendices

Appendix One

Editorial Principles

LIZZIE MELVILLE sat staring at the papers on Herman's huge mahogany desk. There were folders and more papers on the broad wooden table that occupied the alcove in his study. She sighed. The last few years had been full of a mellow autumnal peace for Herman, a peace ripened by financial security for the first time in their married lives; but those years had also been full of death and illness. She shuffled the papers in her hand: Billy Budd. *The manuscript was acutely familiar to her, but it was in a state of chaos. Even though Herman had been able to prepare his own fair copies of manuscripts ever since he had taken the penmanship lessons ten years ago to correct his own naturally atrocious hand, nonetheless she had helped him with proofreading, numbering, and rearrangement. The many pages, blue crayoned, brown crayoned, red, green, orange—pages inked and pencilled, numbered and renumbered, revised again and again—made her memory sly and evasive. What was it Herman had said about the title?*

She was almost seventy years old and had had her own continuing bout with illness, and her recollections were not as clear as they should have been for the task at hand. And she was tired. There had been the death of their son Stanwyx just a month after Herman had retired; there had been Herman's raging erysipelas, and she had nursed him through his feverish attacks. Then at last New Year's time, Herman had had that sudden fit of dizziness and lasting weakness—what was it he had said about the title of this last story of his? She had helped him as much as she could while he stayed upstairs writing, rearranging, reminiscing to him-

141

self, and preparing a volume of poems, Timoleon, *through the ragged end of winter and the bleak weather of early spring. By mid-April he had finished his revisions of* Billy Budd *and was adding some last changes preparatory to a "final" (how many times had she heard* that *during the last three years?) fair copy fit for the printer. But as the blessed, welcome warm weather came on, Herman languished with a heart ailment. By the end of September he was dead.* Billy Budd *lay as it had been, unfinished, bits of it in folders. Alone at the desk she felt wearily the uselessness of her task, but her sense of duty kept her there. As the papers in her hands blurred under her heavy gaze, she recalled conversations with Herman about his work. Yes, that title. What did she think about his first title, that he had partly erased:* Billy Budd, Foretopman? What befell him in the year of the Great Mutiny &c. *She retraced the words* Billy Budd, Foretopman *where they had been lined out and erased. She clipped the leaf to a paper that she placed on top of the pile of papers. But there was that other, later title that Herman had pencilled at the top of the very first page of the story:* Billy Budd, Sailor. (An inside narrative). *She stared quietly at the pages and gave up. Had he ever really said anything about the title? She didn't remember. She knew that it was too soon after Herman's death for her to try to arrange his papers.*

This scene probably never took place. Possibly nothing even remotely like it ever took place. It is pure fiction and has nothing to do with the cold facts of scholarship. Yet, the imagined scene— in which the cold facts are accurate—of Elizabeth Shaw Melville working with her late husband's papers has everything to do with the scholarship surrounding *Billy Budd*.

No one will ever know what facts and implications are denied the editor of *Billy Budd* because the scene took place and he didn't know it. Suppose it did. Suppose this, suppose that. Any editor of *Billy Budd* knows that the basis of much editorial choice must remain on supposititious ground. "But the *might-have-been* is but boggy ground to build on," warns Melville in this unfinished story. Editors of this tale have all become enmired in speculation—all editors—and all editors of uncompleted manuscripts necessarily have to negotiate one little patch of quicksand or other whether or not they take the trouble to really learn the terrain (some do not). But some paths through the bog are firmer than others, and the most solid ground for *Billy Budd* has been marked by two scholars, Harrison Hayford and Merton M. Sealts, Jr., who have blazed a coherent trail through the swampy state of the manuscript. All subsequent editions will owe and should acknowledge a deep and lasting debt to them, and all editions using their transcription of the manuscript ("The Genetic Text") as a point of departure will be more or less valuable according to the ways in which they agree or disagree with Hayford's and Sealts' conclusions in their version of "The Reading Text."

There are many principles upon which to base editorial choices. The Hayford and Sealts edition is based primarily upon correctness. The syntax is correct, the spelling is correct, the punctuation is correct, the diction is correct, and all inclusions indisputably belong. The principle of correctness and purity is certainly justifiable, but there are other, perhaps in this case better, principles upon which to proceed. If all the inclusions in the *H&S* "Reading Text" unquestionably belong, it is not equally true that all deletions from *H&S* unquestionably are wise or even correct ones. Although Melville's syntax and diction and punctuation are not always grammatically correct, they are, after all, the basic ingredients of his own particular style and flavor. Whenever the matter of inclusion is problematical, I have included where *H&S* has deleted. As long as Melville's own words and sentence structure do not occasion incoherence or confusion, I have preferred the actual Melville to the proofreader's cleanliness. In short, with a manuscript that offers as many loose ends as *Billy Budd* does, one may aim at a "correct" text, as do Hayford and Sealts, or at a "real" text, as I do. My own general principle has been simple: make a correct text, but in any problematical instance, when there is a conflict between editorial propriety and what I call the "flavor" of Melville's prose, give the reader as much of the actual Melville as possible. But I am not saying by any means that Melville's prose is to be reproduced in all its inconsistencies or in any of its obvious misspellings and slips of the pen—this is, after all,

a reading edition. In fact, I follow *H&S* in most of its corrections
and editorial housekeeping. But this edition offers itself as an alternative to the reading text in *H&S*, an alternative scrupulously
based upon the genetic text, but one that in some cases makes
consistency and grammatical correctness secondary to what Melville actually wrote, and in some cases of problematical deletion
has made inclusion rather than deletion the preferred choice.

Composition and History of Billy Budd

In their analysis of the manuscript, Hayford and Sealts define
three major phases of development comprising several stages,
substages, and sub-substages. Phase I, composed of those leaves
of the manuscript that Hayford and Sealts call stage A, was probably written shortly after Melville retired from the customhouse
(or was one of the poems he first turned his attention to after he
retired) and is the aforementioned ballad, "Billy in the Darbies,"
with its brief prose headnote. At this point it was no more than
another of the kind of poems that went into the *John Marr* volume. Stage A, complete, probably was five or six leaves long.

Phase II was an expansion and dramatization of the story implicit in phase I. (It is an interesting fact, by the way, that contrary to what some critics, most notably Charles Olson and R. P.
Blackmur, have found in Melville's prose, he did not work toward
essay statement but away from it. His revisions are attempts to
enlarge his ideas by means of dramatic situation.) In 1886 and
1887 Melville introduced and dramatically developed the character of John Claggart, master-at-arms aboard the *Indomitable*, as
the ship was called at this stage. In exploring the mysterious character of Claggart, Melville changed the character of Billy in order
to enrich the implications of the opposition of Billy and Claggart.
He made Billy younger, made him absolutely guiltless of mutiny,
and created the innocent, natural, animal Adam-Christ who has
become so familiar to readers of Melville criticism. Phase II underwent considerable revision. Hayford and Sealts identify three
stages in the development of phase II, each stage composed of

many substages and sub-substages of rearrangement and revision.[1] Phase II was substantially completed by November of 1888 and was 150 leaves long.

Phase III was begun sometime after November 1888, and is almost totally given over to the introduction and development of Captain Vere. As the quantity of leaves and revisions indicates, the development of Vere concerned Melville more than any other aspect of the story. In phase II Vere had merely been the nameless captain before whom Billy struck Claggart when the master-at-arms falsely accused him of mutiny. But musing on the questions of guilt, innocence, and responsibility, Melville found the focus that consumed him most. To phase III Hayford and Sealts attribute five stages and an indeterminate number of substages in the pencil revisions of two of those stages.[2] By April 19, 1891, when Melville wrote "End of Book" on the last leaf, what had begun as five or six leaves and had then grown to 150 leaves was now 351 leaves long, not counting discarded leaves, extra clips and patches, and some leaves separated from the manuscript proper. The manuscript was a collection of leaves cut up into clips and patches that were added to other leaves (some of the clips and patches were later removed or lost) and which had been revised and numbered in their various stages by several color-code and numbering systems Melville had used and that incorporated the scribblings of the several substages. Most probably some of the late pencil revisions were made after Melville had written "End of Book" and was about to prepare the variously re-ordered leaves into one coherent manuscript for the printer.

[1] Stage B, composed of substages Ba, Bb (in turn comprising sub-substages Bba, Bbb), Bc (in turn comprising sub-substages Bca and Bcb); stage C, composed of substage Ca (in turn comprising sub-substages Caa, Cab), Cb (in turn comprising sub-substages Cba, Cbb), and Cc (including sub-substage Cca); and stage D, composed of substages Da (in turn comprising sub-substages Daa and Dab) and Db.

[2] Stage X (pencil revisions supposedly incorporated into stages F and G—no fixed number of substages can be attributed to this stage); stage E, composed of substages Ea (including sub-substage Eab), Eb, Ec, Ed, Ed/F, and E/G; stage F, composed of substages Fa and Fb; stage G, composed of substages Ga and Gb; and stage p (late pencil revisions of no determinate number of substages).

In fact, some of the various stages of the manuscript had been fair copies prepared for the printer, but each time, as Melville had made just a "few" quick changes before sending off the manuscript, he had been drawn in once more by the fascination of the possibilities in his story and those few changes became involved series of revisions yet once more. But, presumably, the manuscript as it stood after April 19 was the "final" final version and needed only a few corrections and minor changes before being redone once more as a final fair copy. Melville was in the process of those "final" changes when he died. The manuscript was left unfinished. The leaves were not even all in one place, but several were in separate folders. It was, in short, a mess. Mrs. Melville made an attempt to sort her late husband's papers, but she left them in no reliable order and added to the confusion by occasionally writing her own notations on some of the pages and making her own re-ordering of leaves.

Thirty years after Melville's death, his granddaughter, Eleanor Melville Metcalf, allowed Raymond Weaver to look at Melville's manuscripts, and that moment resulted in the public discovery of the existence of *Billy Budd*. In 1924 Weaver edited the manuscript and published his edition, which was filled with errors. Weaver was an intelligent editor but he did not assume that the importance of the work was very great and consequently he did not take very great pains. Occasionally he rewrote Melville's sentences. He presented a coherent and usable version of the story as one of the inclusions in volume thirteen of *The Works of Herman Melville* (1922–1924), published by Constable in London, and for many years the standard edition of Melville, though incomplete. Weaver re-edited his own text four years later for the publishing house of Horace Liveright (*The Shorter Novels of Herman Melville*). He checked his earlier edition against the manuscript, correcting many errors, but also making some new ones; basically both editions offer the same version of the text and this version, "the Weaver text," became the standard for two decades.

In 1948 F. Barron Freeman collated Weaver's texts with the manuscript. He worked out a new edition, one in which he attempted to present a more literal version of what was in the manuscript, and one which succeeded in supplanting the Weaver text. Weaver had aimed at a reader's edition, not at a scholar's edition, which would have to be a faithful reproduction of what Melville had actually written, word for word. Weaver had made some obvious corrections and changes, acting as "final" proofreader for Melville, but in the process he missed many instructions that a long and thorough examination of the manuscript would have given him. Freeman, attempting to supply an accurate transcription of the manuscript rather than a reader's text, made several compromises in order to arrive at a text that was at all readable. Furthermore, he followed Weaver's version in the ordering of the parts of the story, and although he corrected many of Weaver's errors, he made others of his own. His text, *Melville's Billy Budd* (Harvard University Press, 1948) became the received report on the state of the manuscript. In 1951 and 1952, Miss Elizabeth Treeman of the Harvard University Press worked on the manuscript at Harvard's Houghton Library, where Mrs. Metcalf had deposited Melville's papers. She checked Freeman's edition against the manuscript and in 1952 issued a set of corrections for Freeman's book, but some confusions were perpetuated in a few new errors Miss Treeman supplied. The Treeman corrigenda became the basis of a new version of the Freeman text in *The American Tradition in Literature*, edited in 1956 by Bradley, Beatty, and Long for the publishing house of W. W. Norton. There have been several editions based on the Freeman text, among them the text offered by Jay Leyda in *The Portable Melville* of the Viking Press (1952), and my edition *(Typee and Billy Budd)* for E. P. Dutton in 1958, differing from the Bradley, Beatty and Long, but also based upon the Freeman-Treeman text and checked against my own readings of the manuscript. Like Leyda, I made some corrections (and some errors), but did not undertake a totally new analysis of the manuscript. In effect, then, until 1962 there had been two basic texts, two basic readings of the manuscript, the Weaver and the Freeman, with the several variations they were put through by different editors.

Then, in 1962, Hayford and Sealts published the results of the many years of work they had put into a completely new reading of the manuscript. For the first time the leaves of *Billy Budd* were given a thorough, total, and painstaking analysis, were placed in a new and probably correct order, and were transcribed with minute and absolute care in the *H&S* "Genetic Text." The errors in the readings of all previous editors were corrected and the corrections supplied by previous editors were incorporated. The genetic text together with a reading text based upon it were published as *Billy Budd, Sailor* by the University of Chicago Press. The book contains a lengthy and informative introduction, the reading text, copious notes and commentary upon the reading text, an analysis of the manuscript, a discussion of foliations and an accompanying table, and the genetic text. All scholars, editors, and students of Melville will be permanently grateful to Hayford and Sealts for the genetic text, for in effect it gives every reader the original manuscript in his own library. However, the genetic text is unusable as a reading version—a sampling of one leaf chosen at random will quickly show why. The following is the *H&S* transcription of manuscript leaf 30 at stage Ba of Melville's composition (*H&S*, pp. 290–291):

30: [Ba ?7[7], Bc ?8[1]]; Da 22; Ea 27.
[Ba *foliation mostly trimmed off after* E.]

Ba

To be sure Billy's action was a terrible breach of naval decorum. [*p* <decorum. ⫸ discipline. {<discipline. ≫decorum.}] But in that [>decorum {*p* <decorum *add* discipline} { ⫷ discipline ≫decorum}] he had never been instructed; in consideration of which the lieutenant would have passed it over had it not been [*Ba⁺p* <passed it over> (*below, circled*) thought nothing more of it {*Bb* ⫷ thought . . . it> (*before* have) hardly> (*after* have) been so energetic <had it not been ⫸ in reproof}] but for the concluding farewell to the ship. This he [>rather] took as meant to convey a sly [*p Bc* <sly>covert] sally on Billy→<Billy→the captive's [*p Bc* <captive's> new recruit's] part [*p add comma*] against [*p*< against ⫸ a sly sally→<sally→slur as to {*Bc* ⫷ a

sly slur as to *add* a sly slur at}] impressment in general, and that of himself in especial. [*Bb add* And yet,]

The genetic text assembles the evidence. The reading text is the result of editorial judgment based on that evidence.

This Edition and H&S

Because all editions of *Billy Budd* from now on will be based upon the genetic text, the problems of editorial choice must be worked out through an understanding of the manuscript—Weaver and Freeman will no longer serve the purpose—and the principles upon which use of the manuscript is founded. Hayford and Sealts based their several choices upon various appropriate principles (see *H&S*, pp. 213–220), but they based their most important substantive choices upon a principle that I have called "correctness," which insists upon grammatical propriety and upon consistency and upon exclusion of any material that is only problematically part of the "final" manuscript. They have omitted sections that have been long familiar to readers of all previous texts and they present in their own reading text only that material which they feel is indisputably defensible. In their own words, they "have excluded all verbal elements not intended by Melville himself, at the time of the latest copy stage, to be an intrinsic part of the novel" (*H&S*, p. 213). Because, as I have said earlier, I take issue in this edition with some of the choices made by Hayford and Sealts in their reading text, the reader should understand the basis of those differences.

Hayford and Sealts talk about Melville's own intentions at "the latest copy stage." The stages assigned in the genetic text to the composition of *Billy Budd* are based upon Melville's numbering systems and evidences of inks, pencil, and handwriting as well as paper. Stage A, as already explained, was only a few leaves of the ballad and a brief prose headnote. But as the story grew under his hand, Melville kept rearranging and renumbering the leaves in his constantly revised manuscript. Some leaves were numbered in green crayon at the middle of the top of the page, and this sequence is the *H&S* stage B. The sequence numbered in pencil at the left corner of the tops of the pages became stage C. Leaves numbered in green crayon at the upper left became stage D. Leaves numbered in red crayon at the upper right became stage E. Leaves numbered in pencil in the middle of the left margin became stage F. And leaves numbered in pencil in the middle of the right margin became stage G. But the *H&S* chronology also includes stages X and p (see note 2 to this Appendix, above). Stage X is supposed to have been an extensive composition draft in pencil and was supposed to have been incorporated into stages F and G. Stage p is supposed to be all the revisions in pencil made at "the latest copy stage." But Hayford and Sealts do not know (no one can) whether all the late pencillings were made after Melville's last revisions in ink (and, if after, whether long after or shortly after) or prior to his last ink revisions or both before and after.[3] In short, no one can be absolutely certain about the time during the development of the manuscript that all pencillings were made. It is possible, for instance, that some pencillings might have been made as early as stage B. There is no way to be absolutely certain that some of the pencillings attributed to stage X were not made at stage p or *vice versa*. Furthermore, in identifying substages and sub-substages (one is reminded of Ishmael's sub-sub librarian and is tempted to say with Ishmael, "Give it up, Sub-Subs!"), Hayford and Sealts assign classifications according to the evidence of the ink and the handwriting. But there is no absolute evidence that in all cases similar inkings and similar handwriting characteristics belong to the same chronological classifications. A man's handwriting after a long and tiring day's work is not the same as it was at the beginning of the day's work, but it is the same day's work. Different inks and different pens might have been used on the same day, similar inks and pens on different days.[4] Revisions in stage C attributed to stage F

[3] For Hayford's and Sealts' uncertainties and best guesses, see *H&S*, pp. 238–240.

[4] For Hayford's and Sealts' reliance on inks and pens, see *H&S*, p. 237. For their reliance on handwriting, see *H&S*, p. 224.

could conceivably belong in reality and contrary to probability to stages C, D, E, or G.

Although Hayford and Sealts occasionally call attention to uncertainties, in effect they dismiss them. They have to—in making a decision, one does, after all, have to choose one thing or another—and they made choices according to the greatest probability. However, there are possibilities, as I suggest, that allow leeway in the conclusions one draws from the evidence insofar as those conclusions appear as a reading text. My major disagreement with the *H&S* reading text is that the editors acted in their conclusions—especially in the deletion of portions of the manuscript—as though there were no leeway. Clearly, it was wise for Hayford and Sealts to make the choice of *greatest probability,* but in providing a reading text in a case like this, an editor should accommodate rather than exclude questionable material precisely because the true choice might be the lesser probability as long as all doubts are not settled with absolute conclusiveness. In the case of *Billy Budd* there are too many uncertainties and possibilities, and because the editor acts, in effect, as censor over what the reader shall see and what he shall not see, it seems to me that in instances even only slightly problematical the principle of inclusion should replace the principle of exclusion.

The *might-have-been* is but boggy ground to build on indeed, but the point that must be met is that in a manuscript left in the state *Billy Budd* was in by the time Hayford and Sealts got to it, the *might-have-been* cannot be dismissed in instances of any doubt whatever. Unfortunately the *H&S* reading text is offered as though the evidence itself were firmly reliable and consistently conclusive at all points and as though the conclusions drawn by the editors from the manuscript were fixed, final, and closed to question.

But because the supposititious is not entirely laid to rest and the manuscript, by its very nature, will always remain open to a few questions of *might-have-been*, a puristic principle upon which to base a reading text is an editorial luxury paid for by the reader. In this present edition I have chosen to restore certain passages deleted in *H&S* and to replace them in the junctures where they most probably belong, if belong they do, while pointing in footnotes or in the list of "Textual Changes" to the problematical nature of their inclusion. I follow no whimsical urge in adopting this principle, and there is formidable precedent in scholarship for such policy. The editors of Shakespeare, in the endless problems of deletion and inclusion created by choices between quarto and folio, have decided in the Globe edition at least that the wisest course is to combine the two so that the reader may be given as much Shakespeare as possible. I specify agreements and disagreements with *H&S* and with the manuscript in Appendix Two, the list of "Textual Changes," where the variations will be handy for those who are interested and where they will be out of the way for those who couldn't care less. But here it is necessary for me to discuss three major matters of inclusion which are singled out in pages 18–20 of the *H&S* edition.

Following leaf 238 in this edition are three leaves—229d, 229e, and 229f—which in all editions prior to *H&S* had been published as the "Preface" to *Billy Budd*. Mrs. Melville had written on the first of them, "Preface for Billy Budd?" No editors prior to Hayford and Sealts recognized that the writing was Mrs. Melville's and all previous editors had attributed the notation to Melville himself. Hayford and Sealts minimize Mrs. Melville's authority and point out that whatever authority she might have had is destroyed by the question mark at the end of the notation. That, together with the fact that these leaves had been separated from their original place, led Hayford and Sealts to assume that the three leaves had been discarded. Perhaps they had. There is no absolute proof that they were discarded although it is likely that they were. There are some considerations to be faced, however, which are not raised in *H&S*.

First of all, the isolation of leaves is not by itself a basis for exclusion. What became chapters 4 and 7 were in separate folders, removed from the body of the manuscript as other leaves had been. Yet they are included as part of the *H&S* text as they had been included in other editions (see *H&S*, pp. 8, 12). Secondly, one cannot judge Mrs. Melville's relation to the manuscript only on the basis of what remains in writing. No one knows what Melville said to her as she helped him or as he lay dying. Perhaps —again perhaps—he said nothing to her. But one cannot dismiss Mrs. Melville as though her only authority were in what researchers can find in the holdings of the Houghton Library. After all, Herman and Elizabeth *talked* to each other, lived with each other daily, and one can assume that in the final months of his life the husband discussed his work with his wife. Most assuredly, one cannot base an edition upon such surmises. But that is just the point: one cannot absolutely dismiss Mrs. Melville any more than one can absolutely trust her. It is clear that she was only guessing that the leaves were a preface. It is not at all clear that she was wrong or even only guessing in her assumption that the leaves *belonged somewhere* in the manuscript. The matter remains problematical, with just that touch of shadowy ambiguity that would appeal to Melville's ghost. Third, superseded leaves in the manuscript are clearly superseded: either they are cancelled with a sweep of pencil or crayon, or they are left unfinished as placeless fragments of a superseded leaf (like leaf 229c—see p. 154), or they obviously and totally, or almost totally, have been incorporated in other leaves. But leaves 229d, e, and f *have not been so superseded*. And there is yet one more consideration. *Billy Budd* has long been an established work in the Melville canon. Readers, critics, teachers, students are familiar with the leaves that used to be the "Preface." That portion has become a part of *Billy Budd* whether Melville intended them to be or not. That alone certainly is no argument for inclusion; indeed, such an argument would be specious and dangerous if it were established that Melville did *not* want those leaves included. But because there is as much argument for including the leaves as for deleting them, once more it seems that the most wise and generous choice for the reader's benefit is to let the material stand.

Hayford and Sealts assert that all criticism based on the "Preface" must now be held invalid because those leaves—in effect— don't really exist. But that is an unfortunate conclusion. The matter included in those leaves is echoed in so many ways in the story, is so very much a part of the tissue and pulse of the tale, that the leaves "exist" in any case. Critical conclusions "based" on those leaves—for good or for ill—are no more or less "correct" than those same conclusions would be given the rest of *Billy Budd* without the "Preface" materials. The very fact that the matter in the three disputed leaves is so integral to the total is one more factor in favor of showing them to the reader.

Moreover, the problem of placing those leaves within the tale offers some further argument for inclusion. In the genetic text, Hayford and Sealts place the three leaves after three other superseded leaves (229a, 229b, and 229c), which are a version of the scene between Vere and the Surgeon after Billy has felled Claggart. It is clear that leaf 230 follows from leaf 229, and that leaves 229a, b, c, d, e, and f, therefore, are in the way (which is part of Hayford's and Sealts' reason for deleting the disputed three leaves). At one stage of composition they probably belonged there, but their place was superseded. Melville cancelled leaf 229a with pencil and incorporated its material in the Vere-Surgeon scene as it remained in its "final" revised form. The same is true of leaf 229b except that Melville cancelled this one with blue crayon. Leaf 229c, however, poses a problem. Melville never cancelled it entirely: in fact, he drew a blue-crayoned box around the last eight lines of the leaf. They read as follows: "unforeseeable fatalities; the prudent method adopted by Captain Vere to obviate publicity and trouble having resulted in an event that necessitated the former, and, under existing circumstances in the navy indefinitly [sic] magnified the latter." The circumstances existing in the navy are then amplified in the following three leaves, which are the disputed leaves in question. Thus the three disputed leaves are left, not superseded beyond doubt, but preceded by superseded leaves and left with no place to go.

In an earlier edition of *Billy Budd* based on *H&S* (volume II of the Viking Portable Library's *American Literature Survey*, 1968) I had placed the three leaves after leaf 243, for a careful consideration of the substantive matter indicates that that was a logical place for the leaves to go. However, another scrutiny of the genetic text now suggests to me that at one time Melville had begun to prepare a place for them other than as a separate chapter (the first of the three leaves, 229d, began with Melville's mark for a chapter-beginning, which was probably what prompted Mrs. Melville to think of them as a separate chapter, perhaps a "Preface"), and that the place he prepared was closer to their probable original position than leaf 243. There is a superseded leaf, 238a (Melville crossed it out with brown crayon), that was partly incorporated into leaf 238 and that refers to the time in which the killing of Claggart occurred. The leaf reads as follows: "Both directly and indirectly the era lent emphasis to the difficulties professional and moral falling on Captain Vere by reason of the tragic event just recounted; difficulties not adequately to be estimated by every sea-officer of our time, and still less by most landsmen. Look at it." Melville's invitation to consider the era— "Look at it"—was crossed out. Originally it seems clearly intended to have introduced the portrait of the era beginning on leaf 229d, the first of the three disputed leaves: "The year 1797, the year of this narrative, belongs to a period which as every thinker now feels, involved a crisis for Christendom not exceeded in its undetermined momentousness at the time by any other era whereof there is record." Melville cancelled "Look at it," not liking that particular wording of the invitation, and then crossed out the entire invitation. The fact that he did so can be used to argue that he intended to delete leaves 229d, e, and f if, indeed, those leaves were to follow 238a. Or, the same fact can be used to argue that Melville felt that leaf 238 was a clear enough introduction to the three leaves without the need for 238a. In fact, the three leaves follow perfectly from 238. No one should bet his life on either argument. The substantive evidence, however, is enough to suggest that if the three disputed leaves are to be included, the most likely place for their inclusion is after leaf 238, and they are so placed for the first time in this edition.

The second major "error" that Hayford and Sealts attribute to both Weaver and Freeman is the inclusion of leaves 135a and 135b, "Lawyers, Experts, Clergy." Once again the "error" arose because Weaver and Freeman thought the notation pencilled on leaf 135a was by Melville. It read, "For Billy Budd/Find proper place for insertion." But it was in Mrs. Melville's hand, and for

this reason *H&S* dismiss the notation. For reasons just outlined
I believe that it is injudicious for an editor either to dismiss or to
be ruled by the notation: once more we are in a shadowy area
when we consider Mrs. Melville's authority. Furthermore, leaves
135a and 135b are not certainly superseded. They belong to that
class of leaves, like 229d, e, and f, which are neither clearly incorporated in other leaves nor cancelled by Melville. In fact, at
one point, Melville had cut the end off leaf 135a but had then
written the notation "Restore," and had rejoined the two cut seg-
ments by mounting them on a blank piece of paper. In short, one
cannot conclude absolutely that these leaves are to be thrown out
of a reading text. One *may* so conclude, but we are back in the
might-have-been. For additional discussion of inclusion and placement of leaves 135a and 135b as well as explanation of the difference in chapter numbering between this edition and *H&S*, see the
statement for leaf 135a in Appendix Two, pp. 169–170.

The third major "error" that Hayford and Sealts repudiate in
earlier texts is the title

Billy Budd
Foretopman
What befell him
in the year of the
Great Mutiny
&c

Melville pencilled a different title,

Billy Budd
Sailor
(An inside narrative)

in the upper left corner of leaf 2 of the manuscript next to the
notations "Friday Nov. 16, 1888./Began." and "Revise—began/
March 2d 1889." Again, Hayford and Sealts present this title as
an unquestionable certainty. They are probably right in their
choice. The evidence points to acceptance of the "inside narrative" title, but the "Great Mutiny" title cannot be simply
banished from the text.

Melville had left a pencilled slip which was mounted on a separate piece of paper either by himself or his wife, and which was placed at the head of the manuscript almost certainly by Mrs. Melville. What was written on the slip was the "Great Mutiny" title. The words "Billy Budd" and "Foretopman" had been cancelled (presumably by Melville) and then the letters were traced over again in Mrs. Melville's hand. It is impossible to explain with perfect certainty why both titles remained in the manuscript. The greatest probability is that Melville abandoned the "Great Mutiny" title in favor of the "inside narrative" title, and that Mrs. Melville restored the "Great Mutiny" title.

In arguing against the "Great Mutiny" title, Hayford and Sealts point out that twice in the narrative Melville approximates the phrase "what befell him" (leaves 111 and 335). They argue that because Melville directly tells the reader that he now embarks on three brief chapters that go beyond "what befell" Billy (leaf 335), that Melville could not have felt that the words "what befell him" were appropriate in the title. What Melville could or could not have felt brings us back to supposing, and if we are to do so, the arguments advanced in *H&S* become neither conclusive nor convincing. For one thing, it should be noted that though Melville cancelled the words "Billy Budd/Foretopman," he *never* cancelled the words "What befell him/in the year of the/Great Mutiny /&c." The ampersand, moreover, accommodates whatever goes beyond what befell Billy.[5] The ampersand could also refer to words Melville intended to add to the title. Or it could indicate that Melville treated the title casually because he did not intend to use it in that form. But finally, whether the ampersand were there or not, there is really nothing in the story to prevent Mel-

---

[5] Hayford and Sealts make a major point of noting an ampersand on a folder holding some of the *Billy Budd* materials. Freeman had thought the leaves of Melville's "Daniel Orme" had originally been *Billy Budd* material, for it was in a folder that Freeman announced was marked, "Daniel Orme/omitted of Billy Budd." However, Hayford and Sealts point out, the folder was marked "Daniel Orme/&/Omitted of Billy Budd," and they repudiate Freeman's conclusions because he "ignored the large ampersand" (*H&S*, p. 17). In marshalling arguments about the disputed title, one must pay attention to the title's ampersand as well.

ville's using the phrase "What befell him" in the title. The chapters after Billy's death are of epilogue nature to begin with. Moreover, the entire narrative is concerned with what befell Billy; Melville does deliberately and heavily invoke the ambience of the Great Mutiny; and the final chapters that go "beyond" what befell Billy are so totally concerned with reflecting back on what befell him that there is neither substantive, aesthetic, nor structural reason to conclude that the words "What befell him in the year of the Great Mutiny" are in any way inappropriate to the narrative or that Melville would have felt they were. Rejection of the title on the critical grounds advanced in *H&S* is unacceptable. The strongest grounds for rejection are the evidence of the manuscript (no part of the "inside narrative" title is cancelled) and the questionable nature of Mrs. Melville's authority.

My disagreement with the editorial choices made in *H&S* concerning the title is closely related to the strong doubts that must persist concerning the *H&S* omission of the disputed leaves, 229d, e, and f. The relationship between the disputed leaves and the "Great Mutiny" title is substantively clear. And then, there is always the possibility that Melville saved the "Great Mutiny" title because he intended to combine the uncancelled parts of it with the "inside narrative" title. In fact, a couple of previous editions (see the bibliography, p. lvii)—W. T. Stafford's *Melville's* Billy Budd *and the Critics* (1961) and my *Typee and Billy Budd* (1958)—have indeed made just such a combination. It is *probably* incorrect, but by no means indefensible. The combination appeared as

Billy Budd
Sailor
(An inside narrative)
What befell him
in the year of the
Great Mutiny
&c.

It is probably the *best* of the three choices if one is to pick a nineteenth-century title, but most probably the *true* title, at least at the unfinished last stage of the manuscript's development, is the one given in *H&S* and followed in this edition. The "Great Mutiny" title is consigned, in this edition, to this appendix for it should be given some *lebensraum* in all editions.

In addition to the three major differences between this edition and *H&S* (only two of them are visible in this text, for I follow *H&S* in the printed title), there are other, smaller differences that are worth noting here. For example, where Melville had written chapter headings, Hayford and Sealts delete those titles because Melville did not title most of his chapters and his doing so in four cases (leaves 58, 135a, 136, and 321) was inconsistent. Inconsistent and lumpy it certainly was, but why should we demand that Melville be consistent and smooth for the sake of our sense of symmetry? As Hayford and Sealts themselves note (*H&S*, p. 39), Melville advances his own warning in *Billy Budd:* "The symmetry of form attainable in pure fiction can not so readily be achieved in a narration essentially having less to do with fable than with fact. Truth uncompromisingly told will always have its ragged edges; hence the conclusion of such a narration is apt to be less finished than an architectural finial" (leaf 335). Neatness is pleasant, but there is no reason supplied in the manuscript to believe that Melville desired or intended the symmetry of titles on all chapters or on none. Furthermore, since Hayford and Sealts honor an upper corner notation on the second leaf of the manuscript as the true title of the entire narrative, there is no reason why they should not honor similar notations on other leaves for individual chapters. And, as I have indicated repeatedly, presenting as much as possible of what Melville actually wrote will take precedence over neatness in this edition. Therefore this text restores the original titles deleted from *H&S* and presents the actual Melville in whatever his raggedness may be.

There are yet smaller differences. Modernizing accidentals is a good editorial choice when the old-fashioned qualities of the writing get in a reader's way. But the nineteenth-century, old-fashioned quality of Melville's writing does not intrude between the contemporary reader and his comprehension of the matter: to change that quality is to lose something in translation. For one thing, Melville tended to capitalize the titles of all officers in his story, especially when referring to specific officers. Also, he tended to hyphenate compound words thus: Master-at-arms. The modern form would be master at arms. *H&S* changes Melville's primary choice consistently to modern forms. But the manuscript indicates that Melville's first choice was capitalizing and hyphenating when he was not writing at impatient speed. This edition silently restores Melville's old fashion and makes it consistent, except in a few cases where hyphenation is so idiosyncratic that it is intrusive and fidelity is not worth the intrusion. Also unlike *H&S* this edition leaves Melville's italicized words in italics in all cases. Similarly, *H&S* consistently corrects Melville's grammar. In some cases I have chosen to allow the original Melville to stand. Those cases are ones in which the errors get in no one's way and yet transmit strongly what I have called the original "flavor" of Melville's sentences. These instances are noted in the appended list of "Textual Changes." Taken together, the capitals, hyphens, italics, and errors, though each minor alone, provide a truer feel of Melville's prose than does an antiseptically cleaned and modernized version.

With these exceptions, I have observed the proofreader's necessity for consistency in accidentals although, as I have just indicated, I take no such liberties with substantive material except in two cases—the excision of a junior lieutenant from the drumhead court and the substitution of the phrase "man-trap under the daisies" for "pitfal [sic] under the clover," which appears in the manuscript on leaf 211. (For an explanation of these changes, which agree with *H&S*, see the notes for leaves 211 and 275 in Appendix Two.) All other changes follow in the list provided in Appendix Two.

Appendix Two

Textual Changes

SOME CHANGES in substance are really no more than changes in accidence. Thus, when an editor changes the form of a word, supposedly he is making a substantive change. However, when one transforms "encoutering" in the manuscript ("the countenance of one at unawares encoutering a person who" [leaf 195]) to "encountering," the emendation amounts to no more than the most minor change in accidental matter. All occasions of similar nature in spelling and punctuation are not recorded in this list. There would be no question in a reader's mind about any of them, and in such matters this text generally follows—but not in all cases—that of *H&S*. Any scholar who might be interested in a complete list of changes made by Hayford and Sealts may consult the list they deposited in the Houghton Library of Harvard University, as announced in their edition.

The following list includes all instances listed in the *H&S* "Textual Notes" on pages 213–220 of that volume. In some cases this edition departs from the *H&S* version; in some cases it departs from the manuscript; in all instances of departure, the variation is explained immediately in the list itself unless the need for the change is so obvious that explanation is unnecessary. I have tried to confine discussion of textual changes to this list and to keep such discussion out of the footnotes, where it might distract readers. I have reserved the footnotes for identifications, explanations, and considerations of thematic importance, and I have tried to keep all footnotes to a minimum. However, where the discussion of textual changes involves a thematic point I wish to make, I have placed such discussion in the footnotes with cross references between those footnotes and this list, which should be considered an auxiliary to the footnotes.

The "Textual Changes" include all instances in which words have been added or deleted even though many of those changes really are equivalent to no more than a proofreader's minor correction of accidentals. In most cases these substantive changes are self-explanatory enough to require no comment. Where comment is needed it is supplied.

In most cases, marginalia in the manuscript have not been incorporated into the text. The major exceptions occur on leaf 2, which supplied the title; on leaf 295 ("The word was given to about ship,"); and on leaf 311 ("an irruption of heretic thought hard to suppress"); for which see the statements for the appropriate leaves in this list. Usually marginalia are treated as in note 5, leaf 54, p. 23.

Unlike *H&S*, this edition does not correct all of Melville's inaccuracies of fact in the text itself. Where it seemed that any rewriting of Melville could in the slightest way result in a change in emphasis and, therefore, in thematic intention, the correction has been confined to footnotes or to this list. For discussion of the inclusion of chapter 12, of chapter titles, and of leaves 229d, 229e, and 229f, see Appendix One pp. 152–156, 159, and this Appendix, pp. 169–170. Sometimes when words have been added, the additions are restorations of Melville's original wording before his incomplete revisions made the sentence incoherent. Sometimes the changes are the result of carrying through what seems to be his latest intention in those cases where the sense is clear, either in a particular sentence or throughout the manuscript, as in the change from *Indomitable* to *Bellipotent* (see the statement for leaf 11 in this list). Sometimes the changes are the restoration of cancelled words which were crossed out by Melville inadvertently in the heat of emendation or which were supposed to be restored. Sometimes a new word is added where it is obviously needed but was left out in Melville's rush of composition. I have supplied commentary wherever it seemed to be necessary in order to make the nature of the change clear.

Because *H&S* has supplanted editions following Weaver and

Freeman, I have listed changes in *H&S* with changes in this edition. By comparing these variants with the manuscript wording, which is also listed, a scholar may settle for himself the nature of the differences between this edition and *H&S*. Notations for the manuscript reading follow *H&S*. The wording is reproduced exactly as spelled and punctuated in the genetic text. Italicized words in brackets in the "Manuscript" column are the editor's and pertain to the manuscript words with which they are bracketed. Words following a slantline were insertions in the manuscript.

Leaf	This Edition	Manuscript	H&S
4	Scotch Highland	Scotch/Highland	Highland

There is no way to be sure that Melville did not intend to use both words, which do not necessarily compose a tautology; therefore, this edition offers the original and the addition.

5	less frequently	less frequent	less frequently
8	foot in the Flemish . . . as	foot the Flemish . . . as in	foot in the Flemish . . . as
10	to be called	to be [called *cancelled*]	to be called
11	*Bellipotent*	*Indomitable*	*Bellipotent*

Although the name *Indomitable* appears in the manuscript far more often than the name *Bellipotent*, the revisions indicate that it was Melville's latest intention to change the name of the ship to the *Bellipotent*. In an earlier edition (New York, 1958), I had suggested that *Bellipotent* had been an early choice which Melville later cancelled in favor of *Indomitable*, but *H&S* has convinced me that it was quite the other way round. All editions prior to *H&S* used the name *Indomitable*.

15	*Bellipotent*'s	*Indomitable*'s	*Bellipotent*'s
17	he dismally	dismally	he dismally
17	same time settling	same settling	same time settling
24	Lieutenant who had	[lieutenant *cancelled*/ officer *cancelled*] who had	lieutenant who had

For differences in capitalization, hyphenation, and italics between this edition and *H&S* and between this edition and the
manuscript, see Appendix One, pp. 159–160.

Leaf	This Edition	Manuscript	H&S
24	now was waxing	now waxing	now was waxing
24	*Bellipotent*	*Indomitable*	*Bellipotent*
31	*Bellipotent*	*Indomitable*	*Bellipotent*
35	*Bellipotent*	*Indomitable*	*Bellipotent*
45	of these	of of these	of these
46	hath thee, Fabian	has Thee, Fabian	hath thee, Fabian
49	*Bellipotent*	*Indomitable*	*Bellipotent*
51	the fire-brigade	[the *cancelled* / her *cancelled*] fire-brigade	the fire brigade
53	patriotic devotion of the British tar	[patriotic *inserted*] devotion of the British tar, that is, to his country [that is, to his country *is uncancelled after the insertion of* patriotic]	patriotic devotion of the British tar
53	William James	G. P. R. James	William James

In all editions prior to *H&S* the reference appeared as "G. P. R.
James," which is what Melville actually wrote. G. P. R. James
was not a naval historian but a novelist of historical romances.
Melville knew him personally, and it is understandable that he
should have mistakenly and automatically written "G.P.R." instead of "William." William James was the historian Melville
quoted (somewhat inaccurately), taking his reference from *The
Naval History of Great Britain* (6 vols., London, 1860), II, 26,
where James wrote, "The subject is a melancholy one, and one
which we would fain pass over; but historical impartiality forbids any such fastidiousness" (quoted from *H&S*, n. 53, p. 146).
This edition follows *H&S* in correcting Melville's error, in this
instance, within the text itself.

| 56 | corps and a | corps a | corps and a |

Leaf	This Edition	Manuscript	H&S
57	display and heroic	display, heroic	display and heroic
58	our world began	the world began	

Melville quoted from "Ode on the Death of the Duke of Wellington," by Tennyson. He incorrectly left the quotation as "the world" instead of "our world." Mrs. Melville had written on the leaf, "Tennyson?" evidently in a memo to check the quote. In most previous editions, consequently, the chapter title has appeared incorrectly with "the world" and with Tennyson's name (often including the question mark!) following the quote. Hayford and Sealts delete the title altogether on the grounds of consistency, reasoning which this edition rejects for this instance. See Appendix One, p. 159.

Leaf	This Edition	Manuscript	H&S
69	ships of all grades	ship of all grades	ships of all grade
70	Vice Admiral Sir Horatio	Vice Admiral Sir Horatio	Rear Admiral Sir Horatio

See note 2, leaf 70, p. 31. The error remains in this edition as originally written by Melville. It is not of the same nature as a correction in the quote from Tennyson or the attribution of a quote from William James: it is hard to know what value attached to Nelson's rank for Melville, for that rank existed in his mind rather than in fact. He makes a point of Nelson's rank more than once and when he mentions the sailors hanged in the *Somers* affair he makes a mistake in rank again in such a way as to indicate that he might have attached significance to the ranks he assigned. Probably little would be changed by correcting Nelson's rank in the text itself, but in all such cases, where there might be the least possibility of significance, this edition allows Melville's actual words to stand and relegates the correction to a footnote.

Leaf	This Edition	Manuscript	H&S
72	mere presence and heroic personality	mere presence & heroic [personality *cancelled* /presence *cancelled*]	mere presence and heroic personality
76	cabin to the open	retreat/cabin [*without cancelling* retreat] to the open	cabin to the open
77	and which shown in any	and which shown in any	which shown in any

Grammatically, *H&S* is technically correct in deleting the "and." However, Melville's ungrammatical "and" here does not at all confuse the sense of the sentence and it indicates Melville's sense of series, which he employed often in his involved sentences. The "and" is a stylistic signal indicating Melville's consciousness of multiple or continuing modifying phrases and words, and even though technically incorrect it helps a reader gain insight into Melville's own sense of the swing and cadence of his sentences. In all such cases this edition allows the original to stand and does not follow the *H&S* corrections of Melville's style. This editorial choice follows the principle that when the flavor of Melville's prose is in conflict with grammatical purity, it is preferable to preserve the original as long as confusion is not the result.

Leaf	This Edition	Manuscript	H&S
79	to fall upon	to fall to upon	to fall upon
80	*Bellipotent*'s	Indomitable's	*Bellipotent*'s
81	*Bellipotent*	*Indomitable*	*Bellipotent*
87	with the same easy air that he would cite	[with the same easy *cancelled*] air that he would cite	as he would be to cite

See note 1 for leaf 87, pp. 37–38.

Leaf	This Edition	Manuscript	H&S
88	Captain Vere's staff	Captain's Vere staff	Captain Vere's staff
88	to landsmen seem	to [some *cancelled*]/ [most *cancelled*] landsman seem	to landsmen seem
89	sword or cutlas	sword and/or cutlas	sword or cutlas
97	lend color	lends color	lend color
100	*Bellipotent*'s	*Indomitable's*	*Bellipotent*'s
102	an ingratiating	ingratiating	an ingratiating
104	in such society	in that/such society	in such society
105	by a little fellow	by by a little fellow	by a little fellow

Leaf	This Edition	Manuscript	H&S
105	a novice, an after-guardsman	a novice an after-guardsman	a novice after-guardsman

Melville had originally written, "It had been incurred by an after-guardsman . . . ," and had then added after "incurred by" the following: "by a little fellow, young, and much a novice." He then cancelled "and much." The editor's choice is either to cancel "an" before "after-guardsman" (which is done in H&S) or to let it stand as part of a series and add a comma before "an." This edition chooses the latter because Melville's revision indicates that it is by a series of terms that he wishes to define "after-guardsman," which originally had been completely unmodified.

| 106 | through remissness | though remissness | through remissness |
| 109 | but Sir Horatio | but Sir Horatio | still captain |

Melville's error about Nelson's rank is of the sort discussed in the statement for leaf 70 in this list. For "Sir Horatio" see note 1 for leaf 109, p. 50.

| 109 | and which dismantled | and which dismantled | which dismantled |

This edition does not follow the H&S change but restores the original according to editorial policy outlined in the statements for leaves 77 and 121 in this list.

| 109 | Haden's | Hayden's | Haden's |

See note 2 for leaf 109, pp. 50–51.

109	*Bellipotent*'s	*Indomitable*'s	*Bellipotent*'s
112	the name by which	the [name *cancelled*/ knickname prefix *cancelled*] by which	the name by which
113	Dansker, do tell me	Dansker, [do tell *cancelled*] me	Dansker, do tell me
114	*"Jemmy Legs!"*	*"Jimmy Legs!"*	*"Jemmy Legs!"*
114	has *Jemmy Legs*."	has *Jimmy Legs*."	has *Jemmy Legs*."

Melville had emended "Jimmy" to "Jemmy," but had not completed the intended change in all instances. See note 4 for leaf 114, p. 52.

Leaf	*This Edition*	*Manuscript*	*H&S*
119	down to	down to to	down to
120	Jemmy Legs	Jimmy Legs	Jemmy Legs
121	bitter smile, and	bitter smile, and	bitter smile,

The *H&S* deletion of Melville's "and," though grammatically pure, is confusing because momentarily it seems to make the phrase "usurping the face from the heart" modify "bitter smile" rather than "some expression less guarded." Of course, that "expression less guarded" and "some distorting expression" are one—no "and" need connect the phrases, which are modified by "usurping the face from the heart." However, the "and" confuses nothing and, once more, shows that Melville tended to build sentences by series, whether he had real series or not. Because the sense is perfectly clear in the manuscript (clearer, in fact, than the correction) and because retention of what Melville actually wrote preserves the peculiar quality of his sentences, this edition restores the original.

| 131 | within | within in | within |
| 132 | that excludes them. It is never mercenary or avaricious | that excludes them. [from anything *added in Mrs. Melville's hand*] Never mercenary or avaricious and so forth. [and so forth. *pencilled out by Mrs. Melville*] | that excludes them. It is never mercenary or avaricious |

Because Mrs. Melville's addition is incoherent and because Melville never completed the sentence outlined in "Never mercenary or avaricious and so forth," this edition agrees with the *H&S* emendation as the simplest and most sensible.

| 133 | atrocity | [atrocity *cancelled*] malignity/[atrocity *restored without cancelling* malignity] | atrocity |

Leaf	This Edition	Manuscript	H&S
134	as much as to say	as much to say	as much as to say
134	is never declared	never declared	is never declared
134	outward proceeding are	outward proceeding is/ are	outward proceeding are
134	Claggart	Claggart Claggart	Claggart
135a	Lawyers, Experts, Clergy	An Episode New Chapter Lawyers, Experts, Clergy	

See Appendix One, pp. 155–156. On the right of the leaf Melville had written "An Episode." He wrote the words "New Chapter," circled, over the mark that he employed to indicate divisions between chapters in the manuscript. In the middle of the leaf, above the chapter mark, he had written, "Lawyers, Experts, Clergy." But there is no "episode" involved in what I have designated as chapter 12 (leaves 135a and 135b). The only possible "episode" is that of the narrator's conversation with the "honest scholar"; but to utilize that episode for this brief chapter would mean that Melville intended to move the title of "Lawyers, Experts, Clergy" back to the beginning of leaf 122, incorporate chapter 12 into chapter 11, and ignore the notation, "New Chapter," on leaf 135a. There is no evidence that Melville intended to do so, for there is no notation to this effect on either leaf 122 or 135a. On the other hand, no episode beyond leaf 135 may be moved back to be incorporated here because the instructions are clear in the manuscript. Referring to the color code numbering system, Elizabeth Melville had pencilled on the top of leaf 135 the note that "146 *red* follows." Leaf 146 red is leaf 136 in the *H&S* foliation of the manuscript, followed in this edition. Leaf 136 is clearly marked as the beginning of a new chapter (chapter 13 in this text, chapter 12 in *H&S*). Therefore, no "episode" may be incorporated into leaves 135a, 135b, and 135 from leaf 136 on. Because the words, "An Episode," remain puzzling and because they were not written in the same place on the leaf with "Lawyers, Experts, Clergy," and also because "Lawyers, Experts, Clergy" clearly are applicable as the words "An Episode" are not, I have removed the words "An Episode" from the title and placed them here.

The puzzle of "An Episode" indicates the unfinished nature of these passages and highlights Hayford's and Sealts' argument for deleting the leaves, which, however, are not cancelled. The placement of this problematical chapter 12 will remain a puzzle. Most likely Melville intended either to incorporate the paragraph into another chapter or to delete it entirely. Assuming the first possibility, Elizabeth Melville had pencilled at the top of leaf 135a, "For Billy Budd/ Find proper place for insertion." Assuming the second possibility, Hayford and Sealts delete the paragraph entirely. In omitting leaves 135a and 135b from their version, they incorporate leaf 135 into chapter 11, as do I, and begin chapter 12 with leaf 136. Therefore, from leaf 134 on, the chapter numbers in this edition are different from those in *H&S*: *H&S* chapter 12 is 13 here, *H&S* 13 is 14 here, and so on. Because "An Episode" must remain one of the mysteries in the uncompleted manuscript of *Billy Budd* there is some justification for deletion by Hayford and Sealts. However, the other leaves that *H&S* claims are superseded are clearly incorporated into other leaves or are cancelled in whole or in part by one umistakable sign or another. This is not the case of leaves 135a and 135b. (See the discussion in Appendix One, pp. 155–156.) There is at least as much justification for Mrs. Melville's attempt to find a place for the paragraph as for Hayford's and Sealts' decision to delete it. It is most probable that if Melville had indeed intended the paragraph to stand it would not be likely to remain as a separate chapter, as given here—although this conclusion too must remain forever uncertain. On the principle that when there is any doubt about deletions the reader should be given rather than denied the material, I have retained "Lawyers, Experts, Clergy" as a one-paragraph chapter, numbered 12, for the foliation in the genetic text indicates that if the paragraph is to remain at all, this is most likely the place it belongs. Substantively the paragraph is so typically Melvillean, so obviously applicable to chapter 11, which precedes it and to chapter 13, which follows it, to the entire tone of Claggart's relationship with Billy, and to Vere's dilemma (especially to leaf 236, chapter 22, and to leaves 254, 255, 258, and 259), that the dubiousness concerning deletion would make omission a rather rigid act of editorial purism. The passage should be allowed to stand in all editions.

Leaf	This Edition	Manuscript	H&S
140	these went along with	these [went *cancelled*] [along with *cancelled and restored*]	these went along with
141	capable of	capable of of	capable of
143	a palatial	a a palatial	a palatial
145	a grizzled	a a grizzled	a grizzled
150	Pharisee is	Pharisee [is *cancelled*/ being *cancelled*]	Pharisee is
150	underlying the Claggarts	underlying the Claggart	underlying some natures like Claggart's

Originally Melville had written, "underlying some natures like Claggart's." Then he cancelled "some natures like" and added "the" before "Claggart's." Then he altered "Claggart's" to "Claggart" so that the phrase read, "underlying the Claggart." Presumably he cancelled "some natures like" because what he was saying applied to Claggart as a type—to *all* natures like Claggart's. Melville's revisions worked toward a comprehensive category rather than a modified category. However, "the Claggart," Melville's grammatical oversight in revision, cannot be used as common English for a category typed by name, but "the Claggarts" can. This edition alters "Claggart" to "Claggarts" in restoring Melville's latest revision and, presumably, his last intention.

151	was started	were started	was started
151	even pervert into plausible	[even *inserted*] pervert into even plausible	even pervert into plausible
151	the private mentor of	the [private mentor *cancelled*] of	the private mentor of

Melville never filled in the gap left by the cancellation of "private mentor." Restoration of the original words, though cancelled, is the only sensible editorial choice.

| 152 | than aught | that aught | than aught |
| 153 | and among which | and among which | among which |

This edition restores Melville's wording according to editorial policy outlined in the statements for leaves 77 and 121 above in this list.

Leaf	This Edition	Manuscript	H&S
153	approaches the fore-mast	approaches from the foremast	approaches the foremast
154	there"; and disappeared	there"; and disappeared	there," and disappearing

Although *H&S* is grammatically correct, Melville's own wording is perfectly clear.

154	to negative	to to negative	to negative
155	commensurate to the hull's	commensurate [to the ample *cancelled*] hull's	commensurate to the hull's

Originally Melville had written "corresponding to the ample hull," and had cancelled "corresponding to the ample" and had added an apostrophe and an "s" to "hull." He forgot to restore "to the" in his new phrasing.

156	*Bellipotent*	*Indomitable*	*Bellipotent*
156	took him to be, and correctly, one of	took him to be, and correctly, for one of	took him, and correctly, for one of

Less of Melville's sentence is changed by dropping "for" than by dropping "to be." Because there is really no chance that readers will think that "and correctly" modifies "to be," this edition departs from the *H&S* emendation.

157	husky, "see here";	husky, th see here;"	husky. "See here,"

The "th" presents no problem (Melville had begun to write "with the," had only formed the first two letters of "the" when he cancelled "with," neglecting to cancel "th"). There is no need to change Melville's sentence structure as *H&S* does. All that is needed is the obviously forgotten quotation mark before the word "see," and the transposition of the semicolon and quotation mark after "here." This edition corrects the punctuation and restores Melville's sentence structure.

Leaf	This Edition	Manuscript	H&S
159	hair, and who	hair, and who	hair who

This edition restores the original according to the editorial policy outlined in the statements for leaves 77 and 121 in this list.

Leaf	This Edition	Manuscript	H&S
160	turn in a *dead-eye*	turning in a *dead-eye*	turn in a deadeye
161	ever been person-ally	even been personally	ever been person-ally
162	discomforted	discomforted	discomfited

Although "discomfort" is the more archaic of the two, it is perfectly clear and is, moreover, currently acceptable English. This edition restores Melville's choice of words.

Leaf	This Edition	Manuscript	H&S
162	trying to get it out	tries to get it out	trying to get it out
166	were so disturb-ingly	was so disturbingly	were so disturb-ingly
168	exclamation, which, whether	exclamation, which, whether	exclamation, whether

Grammatically *H&S* is correct. However, the original is perfectly clear. Restoration of Melville's words indicates that Melville's mind tended toward compound formations and that in some awareness of this he tried to keep his modifiers clear either by series or by relative pronouns. The restoration is to be preferred because it allows a fuller sense of the syntactic mind behind the frequently complicated sentence structure than does the unnecessary correction.

Leaf	This Edition	Manuscript	H&S
170	*Bellipotent*	*Indomitable*	*Bellipotent*
170	blank ignorance	[blank *cancelled*] utter/ blank [*restored without cancellation of* utter] ig-norance	blank ignorance
173	juvenility. And this	juvenility. And this	juvenility, this

Perhaps Melville would have changed his sentence fragment into a complete sentence. But occasionally Melville employed sentence fragments and perhaps this one was intentional. Rewriting this fragment amounts to rewriting Melville's style. This edition restores Melville's sentence structure as it was found in the manuscript.

Leaf	*This Edition*	*Manuscript*	*H&S*
173	upon the junior one	upon [the *cancelled*] junior one	upon the junior one
176	While, as to	While, as to	As to

This edition restores Melville's own wording.

179	would forth	would forth	would flash forth

It is not unlike Melville to use ellipsis in this way; here "forth" does the work of a verb. It is a fairly typical Melvillean archaism. It is as probable that this was Melville's stylistic intention as that it was an oversight, and this edition restores what Melville had written.

181	an admonition	a admonition	an admonition
181	the young sailor	for [the *cancelled*] young sailor	the young sailor
184	that came from our	that our	that came from our

There are alternatives to this phrasing (see the "Note about the Text" in my edition of *Typee and Billy Budd*, New York, 1958, pp. 271–272). This present edition agrees with the *H&S* wording not because it is necessarily closest to what Melville would have written had he lived to revise the incoherent sentence he left—no one can know what he would have written —but because of the desirability of establishing a standard text.

187	Yes, the shrewd may so think	Yes, [any *cancelled*] shrewd [one would *cancelled*] [/may so] so think	Yes, shrewd ones may so think

Melville's original sentence, "Yes, any shrewd one would so think," was an intentional repetition of the phrasing in leaf 186 ("Shrewd ones may opine . . . , Shrewd ones may also think . . . "). The cancellations, however, indicate Melville's intention not to simply repeat the phrasing a third time. He left the word "one" (the repeated phrasing) cancelled. This edition therefore adds "the" before "shrewd" rather than "ones" after "shrewd," for the latest revision indicates such an intention. The unintentional extra "so" ("may so so think") is deleted, of course, in all editions.

Leaf	This Edition	Manuscript	H&S
194	Captain Vere's	Captain Vere	Captain Vere's
196	under another form	inder another form	under another form
198	Quite lately	Whereof Quite lately	Quite lately
199	the testifier's	the testifier's [a witness *written above* the testifier's *by Elizabeth Melville*]	the testifier's
201	events in the Fleet	events the Fleet	events in the fleet
205	perjurous	perjured/perjurous	perjurous
207	at all hazards	all hazards	at all hazards
210	have not to	having not to	have not to
211	man-trap under the daisies	pitfal under the clover	mantrap under the daisies

When Melville first used the image in Claggart's accusation of Billy (leaf 207), he used "clover" rather than "daisy" there, too: " . . . there is a pitfall under his ruddy clover." At one point in the development of the manuscript, then, the images on leaves 207 and 211 agreed. However, in a later revision, Melville cancelled the "ruddy clover" on leaf 207 and revised heavily. He changed "ruddy clover" to "cheek" and then to "ruddy cheek" and then to "fair cheek" and then to "red clover" and, finally, to "ruddy-tipped daisies," which he allowed to stand. However, he either forgot or never had the chance to change "pitfal under the clover" on leaf 211. Because the labored and later revision on leaf 207 indicates clearly what Melville's last preference was, the phrase is changed to "man-trap under the daisies" in order that the original agreement that Melville had intended in the two leaves be preserved.

Leaf	*This Edition*	*Manuscript*	*H&S*
211	low voice demanded	low voice	low voice demanded
217	Captain's	Captain	captain's

For a statement about disagreement in capitalization between *H&S* and this edition, see Appendix One, pp. 159–160.

222	accuser's	accuser'	accuser's
222	gelidly protruded	gelidly protruding	were gelidly protruding

Melville's common practice following a participial phrase was to use the simple past for the verb attached to the noun modified by the participial phrase (see the preceding sentence: "eyes removing . . . underwent"). Rather than change "gelidly protruding" to a continuous past in a similar construction, this edition follows Melville's more common practice and changes the word to a simple past.

223	horror of the accuser's eyes	horror [of *cancelled*/ at *cancelled*] the accuser eyes	horror of the accuser's eyes
229	character	man / character	character
229	take him aback	surprise,/take him aback	take him aback
229	and interrupting	and and interrupting	and, interrupting
229d 229e		See Appendix One, pp. 152–155	
229f			
231	the Surgeon's arm	the the Surgeon's arm	the surgeon's arm
231	*Bellipotent*'s	"Indomitable's"	*Bellipotent*'s
232	But again	But again	Again

The *H&S* edition does not prefer to allow Melville to begin two consecutive sentences with "But." This edition restores Melville's own wording.

235	What then can he do?	What then can he do?	What then can the surgeon do?

Melville had written, "what could he," then wrote "the" over the word "he" and addded "Surgeon," so that the sentence read, "what could the Surgeon do?" Melville then cancelled "what could the Surgeon" and inserted "What can" instead of the cancelled phrase. He wrote the word "then" over the word "can" and added "can he," so that the completed and revised sentence reads, "What then can he do?" To revise this to "What then can the surgeon do," as in *H&S* is to combine the revision ("then") with the original and cancelled words, without offering either the revision or the cancelled original in their true forms. Moreover, because Melville allowed his last revision to stand, this edition restores the revision, which is perfectly clear in meaning. Evidently, Hayford and Sealts were concerned about the antecedent of "he" as the subject of the sentence, thinking that readers might suppose it was Vere rather than the surgeon, and so rewrote the sentence for Melville.

Leaf	This Edition	Manuscript	H&S
238	That the unhappy	The unhappy	That the unhappy
239	*Bellipotent*	Indomitable	*Bellipotent*
240	*Bellipotent*'s	Indomitable's	*Bellipotent*'s
243	*Bellipotent*'s	*Indomitable's*	*Bellipotent*'s
246	sea-Lieutenant and the Sailing Master	sea-lieutenants	sea lieutenant and the sailing master

See the statement for leaf 275 in this list.

Leaf	This Edition	Manuscript	H&S
247	obesity, a man who	obesity, man who	obesity—a man who
251	immediately he was	immediatly was	immediately he was
262	time stood	time [stood *cancelled*]/ (sitting) unconsciously	time stood— unconsciously

When Melville changed "stood" to "(sitting)," he neglected to change the rest of the sentence and the rest of Vere's actions to fit "(sitting)." The parentheses indicate an incomplete revision at best, merely a note for intended change. Therefore the original "stood" is restored.

Leaf	*This Edition*	*Manuscript*	*H&S*
266	case is	case is is	case is
270	in any case	in any	in any instances

Originally Melville had written, "law may operate in certain instances." He substituted "the present case" for "certain instances," then cancelled "the present case" and added "any," evidently intending "in any case" instead of "in the present case," but leaving the incomplete revision, "law may operate in any." Because it seems very probable that Melville meant to cancel only "the present" instead of "the present case," this edition restores the later word, "case," rather than the earlier word, "instances."

Leaf			
273	Majesty's	Magesty	Majesty's
275	Sailing Master	junior Lieutenant	sailing master

See the entry for leaf 275, immediately below.

Leaf			
275	Sailing Master,	Lieutenant,	Gentlemen,

Originally, in leaf 245, Melville had composed the three-man court of "the First Lieutenant," a lieutenant of minor grade, and "the Sailing Master." He then cancelled "a lieutenant of minor grade" and added "the captain of marines" instead. But he either neglected or never had a chance to normalize his revision throughout all his references to the drumhead court. It is clear he did not intend to add a fourth member, for he refers repeatedly to a three-man court. Without cancelling the junior lieutenant throughout, Melville wrote "sea-lieutenants" rather than "sea-lieutenant" at the beginning of leaf 245. Similarly, on leaf 275 Melville had the now nonexistent junior lieutenant "speaking, and falteringly, for the first." Since the only member of the court at that point in the proceedings who would be speaking for the first time would be the sailing master, "junior lieutenant" has been changed to "Sailing Master." So too, in Vere's reply, "Lieutenant" has been changed to "Sailing Master" in this edition. Hayford and Sealts changed "Lieutenant" to "Gentlemen" in Vere's reply, but since in the original Melville had Vere respond directly to the individual instead of to all the members of the court, and the only change is in the title of the individual, this edition departs from *H&S* and follows Melville's intention.

Leaf	This Edition	Manuscript	H&S
280	man-of-war's-man's	man-of-war's-man	man-of-war's man's
281	two petty-officers	two petty-officers	two sailors

See note 6 for leaf 281, pp. 109–110. This edition treats this error of Melville in the same way it evaluates the errors on leaves 70 and 109 ("but Sir Horatio"), discussed in this list above.

282	*Bellipotent*	*Indomitable*	*Bellipotent*
287	Captain's	Captain	captain's
287	an exterior	a exterior	an exterior
295	mates. The word was given to about ship.	Mates piping down one watch	mates. The word was given to about ship.

The sentence has been printed as it appears in the manuscript in all editions prior to *H&S*. But Melville had pencilled on leaf 295 in the left margin, "Another order to be given here in place of this one." Piping down one watch would leave that watch free to continue the expression of discontent that was signalled when the "confused murmer" of the men "began to wax." At the top of the leaf Melville added the note (and drew a fist pointing to it), "the word was given to about ship." That order would occupy all hands, for every man had to be at his station when the ship's tack was changed in the process of going about. Although "piping down the watch" was never cancelled, Melville's latest intention and his wording were clear, and this edition follows *H&S* on this point.

296	ended with the	closed/ended with the	ended with the
300	*Bellipotent's*	*Indomitable's*	*Bellipotent's*
306	close at hand	near/close at hand	close at hand
308	and taken to Rome	and taken to Rome	taken to Rome

This edition restores the "and" according to the editorial policy outlined in the statements for leaves 77 and 121 in this list.

Leaf	This Edition	Manuscript	H&S
310	primer	primer [pioneer *added in* *Elizabeth Melville's* *hand*]	primer

Mrs. Melville wrote "pioneer" (which appears in editions prior to *H&S*) probably as her interpretation of the word in her husband's handwriting—which was almost illegible despite his penmanship lessons.

310	*Bellipotent*'s	*"Indomitable's"*	*Bellipotent*'s
311	one whom	one who	one whom
311	an irruption of heretic thought hard to suppress	[an irruption of heretic thought hard to suppress *bracketed at foot of leaf*]	

Generally, this edition follows *H&S* in omitting marginalia. This instance, however, seems to be as clearly exceptional as that on leaf 295 (see this list). Therefore, the phrase is restored here though deleted in *H&S*. Freeman, in his edition of *Billy Budd* (Cambridge, 1948), simply added the phrase in parentheses to the last words on the leaf, "Marvel not that having been made acquainted with the young sailor's essential innocense" [sic]; but, as Hayford and Sealts point out there is nothing heretical about believing in Billy's essential innocence—even the members of the drumhead court that condemned him were all convinced of his essential innocence. Hayford and Sealts speculate that the "irruption of heretic thought" was Melville's reference to some of his own ideas which he included and later discarded on some now nonexistent leaves which at one time followed leaf 311. (Melville had pencilled and circled a notation on the top of leaf 312 [at one point numbered page 77 by Melville] reading, "76 omitted.") However, if such were the case, the probability is strong that the "irruption" phrase would have been written on one of the omitted leaves, though one can never be sure of this. Moreover, as Melville's second book, *Omoo*, made perfectly clear, Melville had long held the heretical thought that the natural innocence of the islanders made them superior to the orthodox and "civilized" Christians who came to "save" them and who, in Melville's view, destroyed them. (Melville's book was bitterly attacked by Christian missionary newspapers and magazines.) Melville believed that though the upright barbarians were ignorant of the dogmas of institutionalized Christianity, they had a much better chance at heaven than the men of the cloth who instructed them. In the context of the leaf, the entire Chaplain-Billy confrontation, and the corpus of Melville's work, the "heresy" refers to the idea of salvation without adherence to orthodox Christianity or its beliefs and to the superiority of the noble savage. Whether the phrase refers to what is going on in the chaplain's mind or in Melville's mind is as problematical as the placement of the phrase, but it is central to the considerations expressed in the scene, and the reader should have a chance to see it. It was never cancelled. The main problem is its placement, and the total context of leaf, scene, and corpus indicate that the place given the phrase in this edition is the most likely place for inclusion.

Leaf	This Edition	Manuscript	H&S
312	as a musket would be on the altar at Christmas	as that musket of Beecher &c	as a musket would be on the altar at Christmas

Until my edition of *Typee and Billy Budd*, all editions following Freeman had published this sentence thus: "As such, he is as incongruous as that musket of Blücher etc. at Christmas." It was, indeed, a mysterious sentence. Blücher was an ally of Wellington, but the reference led to a dead end for all editors. Hayford and Sealts correctly re-identified the word "Blücher" as "Beecher." Melville "presumably had in mind an incident of 1865 when the Rev. Henry Ward Beecher, in the words of Paxton Hibben, 'pledged Plymouth Church to contribute twenty-five rifles' to a group of colonists in order to 'promote the just and peaceful settlement of the Kansas issue. . . . Frivolous people called Sharp's rifles "Beecher's Bibles" and the irreligious dubbed Plymouth Church "the Church of the Holy Rifles." ' See Hibben's *Henry Ward Beecher: An American Portrait* (New York, 1942), p. 134 (*H&S*, p. 187). Originally Melville had written, "As such, he is as incongruous as a musket would be on the altar at Christmas." Then he cancelled "a" before "musket" and replaced "a" with "that." He drew a caret after "musket" and wrote above the caret, "of Beecher &c" and cancelled the words "would be on the altar," leaving an incomplete revision and a note for what would have been a caustic Melvillean irony. No one can say, of course, what Melville would have written about Beecher's rifles in place of that "&c." Therefore this edition follows my 1958 edition and *H&S* and restores the original sentence.

Leaf	This Edition	Manuscript	H&S
314	*eight bells*	*one* / eight *bells*	*eight bells*
316	Under an arm	Under an [weather or lee] arm	Under an arm

Melville evidently intended to choose either "weather" or "lee" to modify "arm," but never made his choice. There is no evidence that allows an editor to make it for him. The fact that the morning of the hanging the ship had a leeward roll doesn't decide anything. This edition follows *H&S* in reproducing the original unannotated phrase.

317	a conventional	a a conventional	a conventional
318	even as he was in their eyes	even as he in their eyes	even as in their eyes

Originally Melville had written, "even as he alone was in their eyes." He cancelled "alone was" and changed the wording to "even as he monopolized [in *uncancelled*] their eyes." Then he cancelled "monopolized," which spoiled the Biblical cadence, and left "even as he in their eyes," an incomplete revision. Clearly, the choice made in *H&S* is justifiable, but it is too abrupt and loses the rhythm and therefore the poetic emphasis of the original. Melville was concerned with the last part of the sentence, which is where he concentrated his revisions. Restoring "was" rather than deleting "he" restores the accent on the latter part of the sentence. Restoring the original cadence—a balance between the first and the last of the sentence by means of parallelism and repetition—preserves the rhythm that Melville was working with.

319	a soft	a a soft	a soft
320	slow roll of the hull	ship's motion	slow roll of the hull

Editions prior to *H&S* printed this as "none save that created by the ship's motion." Melville originally had written "none save that created by the slow roll of the hull, in moderate weather so majestic in a great ship ponderously cannoned." He changed "slow roll of the hull" to "ship's motion" when he took the rest of the sentence ("in moderate . . . cannoned") and moved it back to leaf 319, where it was to follow the words "the periodic roll to leeward." However, Melville cancelled that revision and moved everything back into original place without cancelling the "ship's motion" part of the revision, which he presumably intended to do. This edition, following *H&S*, restores the original reading.

Leaf	*This Edition*	*Manuscript*	*H&S*
325	was gradually	was gradually was	was gradually
329	offices	office	offices
329	and now to witness	and now to witness	now to witness

This edition restores the "and" deleted from *H&S*. Examples of similar restorations are found in the statements for leaves 77 and 121, in this list, but the most compelling reason in this instance is that there is no useful purpose served by the deletion in the first place. The "and" lends emphasis to "now," which in turn serves to highlight the dreadful reason for which the call for all hands was sounded *this time*.

329	sea-fowl, whose attention	sea-fowl whose attention	seafowl who, their attention

Ungrammatical as it is, Melville's own wording is clearly understandable and offers a good example of the syntactical boxes his involuted sentences sometimes got him into. This edition restores Melville's own language.

331	a sort of impulse of docility	a sort of impulse docility	a sort of impulse

Originally Melville had written "an instinct" and then added "of docility." Subsequent revisions ended in the incoherent phrase which Melville didn't live to clarify. Hayford and Sealts reject "an impulse of docility" as "a basically incongruous phrase" (*H&S*, p. 194). But one can call it incongruous only in a most rigid use of the English language, and even then it is not necessarily incongruous. Perhaps Melville wanted either "impulse" or "docility" as is claimed in *H&S*, but the phrasing of the original and the revisions indicate that "impulse of docility" is just as likely if not more so. In this case, this edition restores the reading of editions prior to *H&S*.

Leaf	This Edition	Manuscript	H&S
332	as wont	as wont	as wonted

Melville's words are clearly an elliptical way to say, "as was their wont." "As wont" creates no confusion and creates a stylistically different kind of prose from "as wonted." The *H&S* correction seems prissy in this instance, as in some others, and this edition restores the original.

335	than an architectural	that an architectural	than an architectural
336	*Athée*	Athéiste [Atheiste *added in Mrs. Melville's hand*]	*Athée*

See note 1 for leaf 336, p. 131.

337	*Athée*	Athéiste [Atheiste *underlined, added in Mrs. Melville's hand*]	*Athée*
341	*Bellipotent*	Indomitable	*Bellipotent*
342	a responsible	an responsible	a responsible
343	*Bellipotent*	Indomitable	*Bellipotent*
346	*Bellipotent*	Indomitable"	*Bellipotent*
346	another foretopman	another foretopmen	another foretopman
350	me they'll lash	me they'll lash me	me they'll lash
351	these darbies	this darbies	these darbies
351		End of Book April 19th 1891	

The Library of Liberal Arts

SCHILLER, J., Wilhelm Tell

SCHLEGEL, J., On Imitation and Other Essays

SCHNEIDER, H., Sources of Contemporary Philosophical Realism in America

SCHOPENHAUER, A., On the Basis of Morality
Freedom of the Will

SELBY-BIGGE, L., British Moralists

SENECA, Medea
Oedipus
Thyestes

SHAFTESBURY, A., Characteristics

SHELLEY, P., A Defence of Poetry

SMITH, A., The Wealth of Nations (Selections)

Song of Roland, Terry, trans.

SOPHOCLES, Electra

SPIEGELBERG, H., The Socratic Enigma

SPINOZA, B., Earlier Philosophical Writings
On the Improvement of the Understanding

TERENCE, The Brothers
The Eunuch
The Mother-in-Law
Phormio
The Self-Tormentor
The Woman of Andros

Three Greek Romances, Hadas, trans.

TOLSTOY, L., What is Art?

VERGIL, Aeneid

VICO, G. B., On the Study Methods Our Time

VOLTAIRE, Philosophical Letters

WHITEHEAD, A., Interpretation of Science

WOLFF, C., Preliminary Discourse on Philosophy in General

XENOPHON, Recollections of Socrates *and* Socrates' Defense Before the Jury